A PLEASURE
AND A CALLING

Also by Phil Hogan

Hitting the Groove
The Freedom Thing
All This Will Be Yours

A PLEASURE
AND A CALLING

PHIL HOGAN

Typeset in Marveluse to Research Data, Bungay Group.
Printed and bound by CPI Group (UK) Ltd, Croydon, CR0 4YY

Penguin Random House is committed to a sustainable future for
our business, our readers and our planet. This book is made from
Forest Stewardship Council® certified paper

BLACK SWAN

TRANSWORLD PUBLISHERS
61–63 Uxbridge Road, London W5 5SA
www.transworldbooks.co.uk

Transworld is part of the Penguin Random House group of companies whose
addresses can be found at global.penguinrandomhouse.com

Penguin
Random House
UK

First published in Great Britain in 2014 by Doubleday
an imprint of Transworld Publishers
Black Swan edition published 2015

A CIP catalogue record for this book
is available from the British Library.

ISBN 9780552779395

A PLEASURE
AND A CALLING

1

IF YOU WERE TO put a gun to my head and ask me to explain myself, I suppose I might begin by saying that we are all creatures of habit. But then, you might wonder, what creature of habit is a slave to the habits of others? All I can say is that the habitual is what I love most and am made for; that the best I can do is hang on, have faith, and hope what has lately blown through our unremarkable but well-ordered town will be forgotten and all will be calm again. Right now I feel lucky to hear myself breathe. The air is dangerously thin. It seems to rush in my ears. And yet the scene is peaceful here in the half-lit, slumbering pre-dawn: a white coverlet glowing in the room, a discarded necklace of beads, a shelf of books, one face down, splayed on the bedside-table, as though it – like the whole town at this hushed time – is dead to the world. I cannot make out the title but the sight of this book with its familiar cover image (the shape of a man in raised gilt) returns me to that day, not too long ago, when the wind changed and the sky blackened and ordinary life – startled by the sudden thunderclap of the unusual – reared, kicked over the lantern and turned the barn into a raging inferno whose leaping, thrilling flames could be seen from a hundred miles away.

It was a day that started as quietly as this one. Another dawn – a dawn suffused with love, I am not afraid to say – though if I pause to mention the girl at the heart of things (or at least her habits) it is only to illustrate the contrast of events, how beauty and ugliness can live so surprisingly cheek by jowl, the one unseen by the other. How one moment you can be lying in the warm, ticking dark, awaiting the return of your special one (and here she was, arriving back from her early run, the rattle of her key in the lock, the sound of water thudding into a fragrant tub), and the next contemplating horror, drama and scandal.

This is the route my memory instantly takes to capture that day, though the truth is I didn't hear the news until she had ped-alled off into the crisp, bright morning, and I had walked to my office. The rest of our leafy, prosperous community will recall it in their own way. The point is that this was the day the Cooksons of Eastfield Lane returned from their annual spring break in the Seychelles to find a week-old dead body ruining the visual flow of their well-stocked garden with its established fruit trees, land-scaped lawns and hand-cut limestone patio.

Every estate agent has a client like the Cooksons, so don't judge me too harshly when I say I had to suppress a smile when my third in command, Zoe, her eyes wide with excitement and alarm, broke the news. We'd had the Cooksons' house – a handsome character property at the very edge of town, surrounded by fields and woods and yet only a ten-minute walk from the tennis and cricket club – on our books for eighteen months or more. In a falling market, my senior consultant Katya, an extremely efficient Lithuanian, had sold the place twice – to buyers desperate to own it but who had pulled out in acrimony and tears to take their depreciating financial packages elsewhere, reduced to an emotional frazzle by the Cooksons' failure over weeks and months to find a new ideal home for themselves, by their refusal to consider going into temporary rented accommodation to rescue these deals, and not least by their general destructive haggling over trifles. I'd lost count of the properties the Cooksons themselves had walked away from at the eleventh hour – upscale dwellings that ticked every box on an evolving wish list that had taken the three of us out to look at converted windmills and maltings, a superior Georgian townhouse on the square, a riverside apartment with long views and finished in oak and granite, a wool merchant's cottage with sizeable vegetable garden out towards Wodestringham. The paths of the couple's individual whims – hers, at any moment, for a circle of yews, his for an authentic chef's kitchen with wine cellar – rarely crossed. If one light went on, another went off. You saw them bickering quietly in their car. Once I heard Mrs Cookson refer to me as 'that fucking creep, Heming', which seemed a little severe, though in the circumstances – I was lurking in a recess on the landing directly below them as they stood disagreeing about the aesthetic merits of porthole-style windows – I suppose she was right.

'Do you think the Cooksons actually want to move house?' Katya said frequently. They probably do now, I thought.

But who could tell? They'd been in the place sixteen years. Their children had flown. He was a dentist, she owned four pharmacies. Now in their mid-forties, and better off than ever, they seemed to me stranded between possible bad choices: not just between grandstanding and downsizing, but between staying in this marriage for the rest of their lives or breaking free of it. In their terse exchanges about décor or room size you saw a larger sense of purpose draining away. They were looking for something, but a new home together wasn't it. Rather, they seemed engaged in a passive war of attrition, with house-hunting as their chosen weapon.

I didn't like the Cooksons one bit, but they did fascinate me. The last time I had seen them – or, in fact, failed to see them – was some months before their trip to the sun. I'd arranged to show them a new architect-built concrete jewel of a place with a gym and pool. I arrived a little early, checked the rooms, the automatic blinds and lighting. I ran through the blurb Katya had put together. Then I waited, pacing the rooms, pacing the drive. After twenty minutes I called Mr Cookson. He was playing golf. 'Are you sure it was today?' he said. I told him that, yes, today was the day, and paused to allow him to apologize. He didn't. 'To tell you the truth, I think my wife may have lost interest,' he said.

Normally I wouldn't have minded too much being stood up. In other circumstances I would have used the time to snoop around the house while the vendors were out. But here there were no vendors, or at least none with real lives to look into. Just the usual developers in the habit of dressing their high-spec rooms in modish finery – a leather-and-chrome Corbusier *chaise*, a shagpile rug, deluxe drapery and linens. Nothing to suggest living, breathing occupancy or personal taste; no stamp of a human form shaping its nest.

I locked up and walked. The wind was cold but it was dry. When time and weather permit, I walk. From our office – and Heming's is bang in the middle of the town map, on the north side of the old square – there's nowhere you can't get to on foot within half an hour. And what better way to sharpen the focus of everyday blur into readable information? My habit is to take arbitrary diversions. I move like a window-shopper. My antennae are alert to unusual sales clusters, incursions from rival agents. I take the trouble to read the fluttering notices pinned to fences and telegraph poles warning of private building projects or public works. I note what scaffolding is going up, contractors' vehicles, the contents of skips. The smell of fresh paint puts a spring in my step. I can spot the red dot of a newly installed alarm from a good distance. Occasionally I make use of my opera glasses (an indispensable tool of the equipped agent). But, as I make my rounds, I ask myself: who fits where? In seventeen years in the business, I have sold properties on every street in town, very often more than once. I might forget a face but, I have to tell you, I never forget a house.

So, as I approached town, cutting down Boselle Avenue – broad and well-to-do, its pavements blown with leaves and horse-chestnut flowers at this time of year – it was only natural that my eye would register a figure, some fifty yards ahead, emerging from number 4, one of a pair of thirties suburban villas set back from the road. I had handled both these houses in years past. Number 4 had been extended by way of an office-study-cum-box room over the garage. I knew the house. But I didn't recall the man. Or did I? He was walking a little dog, or, rather, yanking it along. Even at a distance, I sensed his impatience. He was a tall man, which made the poor dog – a terrier of some kind with white tufted hair – look even smaller than it was. He was wearing walking boots and hooded rainwear and his thinning hair was long and swept back. The dog was trying to sniff at gates and fences, and it yapped in protest as he tugged it away. He had the air of a man easily annoyed by life's fleeting trifles. As if compelled by the stiff wind, I found myself following him and the dog, across the main road, down the hill at the crossroads, then just past the archway and courtyard that my own modest flat overlooked, in a low-rise, honey-bricked development. And it was here, ahead of the entrance to the green, sparkling Common on the right, that he stopped to let the dog defecate in the middle of the path.

The *middle* of the path. He barely gave me a glance as I approached. The dog crouched, watchful in mid-strain, then shook its bearded jowls and yawned. I expected the man to produce a bag to scoop up the mess, but he simply waited for the dog to finish, then pulled on the leash and started to walk on.

'Hello?' I heard myself call out to him. 'Excuse me . . .'

The man – perhaps he *was* familiar – turned with a vexed look that seemed to call for the counter-balance of a civic smile and a jocular observation. 'Sorry,' I said, 'but I think your dog dropped something?'

We both looked at the turd I was pointing at, a neat steaming coil that struck me as unusually large for a small dog.

And then he stared at me. 'Well, what do you want to do about it?'

'What do *I* want to do? I rather thought *you* might want to do something about it.' I smiled again.

'Well, I do not, so piss off. And just mind your own business, you bourgeois knob.' He stared at me, lips apart, for a second more, then yanked the leash, and turned on to the path for the Common and park. I stood and watched, the dog once more protesting as they crossed the grass and headed down the steps and along the riverside path. He didn't look back.

Bourgeois knob? I've always thought of myself rather as a concerned citizen – a model citizen. There was a thin piece of card to be found in a nearby refuse bin. I eased it beneath the pyramid of cooling sludge and transferred it into a discarded fast-food carton. This I carried back up the hill to the courtyard where my car was parked outside my flat. OK, I reasoned, this maniac had humiliated me, but so what? You could either burn with fury or you could do the right thing.

I put the carton in the passenger-side footwell of my car, then nipped up to my flat to consult the files I keep there. It didn't take long. I'm very organized. It turned out we had sold the house to a Judith Bridgens in 2007. Perhaps she had resold to this rude oaf. I called the landline number I had on record. There was no answer. I drove up there and parked some way along Boselle Avenue, then strolled back down to number 4 with an armful of sales literature covering the carton. In the garden behind the high, overgrown privet, only a passer-by glancing over the gate would be likely to see me, and even then only for a second or two. I rang the bell and called the landline again. I heard the phone ringing inside. No one answered. I produced the key now from my waistcoat pocket, unlocked the door, waited, and then stepped over the threshold. Oh yes. I always enjoy the first moment of an empty house before the spell of its silence and stillness is broken by my own breathing and movement. I found my way to the kitchen and contemplated the clean oatmeal tiled floor. Would it do the job? Not quite. Perhaps the sitting room . . . I pushed open the door on to an airy space with tasteful dining area. French windows overlooked a patio and an uncut lawn and flower borders bedraggled by the weather and neglect. The owner was no gardener. He did, however, have an eye for attractive modern soft furnishings, not least a handsome, chunky, white – you might even say bourgeois – hearth-rug.

There we are, I thought.

I slid the turd, still improbably intact – like a novelty plastic one – into the rug's luxurious centre, pausing for a moment to appreciate its caramel perfection, its pleasingly vile aroma – freed now to explore this forbidden interior – rising to my nostrils. The dog would almost certainly sniff it out the moment it returned with its owner. 'Woof, woof, master! Look at this!'

I made my retreat. Not least because of the disappointments of the morning, I would have liked to embark on a full tour of the house while I was there. Mostly, I would have loved to remain, in hiding, and see the shock and bafflement on the man's face when he returned. But I did have a business to run. I exited carefully, leaving a leaflet stuck in the letterbox. The wind had dropped, and with some satisfaction I retraced my steps up Boselle, posting leaflets also at the houses on the way back to the car, then drove back to my flat where I popped the key safely away. Sweet success.

But, I hear you ask, with some scepticism (and with that gun to my head) . . . of all the many splendid houses you've sold in your seventeen years in the business, you just happened to have the key to *that* particular one? To which I would answer, of course not – I have the keys to them all.

2

I AM SIX YEARS OLD, and the things I know to be true are dissolving. The rooms have become quiet. The talking is elsewhere – my mother and father, my aunt. At night my mother kisses me, but says little. The book of rhymes she reads to me lies unfinished. My father comes home from his office. He and my mother eat dinner while I count the coins in my moneybox or watch TV in my pyjamas. Look at me, cross-legged, my ears sticking out, a glass of milk before me. Riley purrs and closes his eyes when I stroke him between the ears. These are many days rolled into one, but sometimes the memory is singular and sharp: the rough of the dark curtain on my cheek as I stand hidden, the smell of my mother's cigarette. I discover where they speak in low voices. They are wherever they think I am not. I lie squeezed beneath the sofa with a piece of bread, or behind the wicker chair in the garden room. I watch my mother touch her stomach where her baby lives. Here I am an invisible boy. When my mother is lying down, my father will not allow me in the dark room. Riley comes and goes. Sometimes I follow when my mother is asleep and creep beneath the bed.

Another time, Aunt Lillian is speaking in a low voice to my father. Her hand is on his, making my breathing stop.

Uncle Richard takes me out to the football, with its uproar and smell of fried onions. On the way home, he stops the car and the lady takes us upstairs to her house. It's strange to go upstairs to a house. The room is small. 'This is William,' Uncle Richard says to the lady, ruffling my hair. I am left alone in the room. The television is on, but when I have eaten my biscuit I go into the kitchen. It's smaller than the kitchen at our house and there are damp clothes hanging to dry. In the drawer I find a blue-and-white spoon. It is made of what cups are made of. One day, the lady will say 'Who has taken my spoon?' and the answer will be, Mister Nobody.

Later still, I am a missing child. I hear them call my name – my father, my aunt, my cousin. Soon, even our new neighbours are out looking for me. But I am snuggled down in the marshmallow-coloured velvet ottoman that stands at the foot of the bed my father now shares with Aunt Lillian. From my place among the blankets, I can hear voices in the street. In my mouth is a sweet I have taken from the jar. The house is silent. A long time goes by, though there is still light in the summer sky. Perhaps I have been asleep. When my father returns with the constable and Mr Damato, the Italian man from across the road, I am sitting on the front step reading my book. 'Where have you been?' my father demands. I blink in a way my father sometimes calls impertinent. 'Nowhere.' I refuse to satisfy them with more. He shakes me by the shoulder and the constable looks stern. Aunt Lillian comes rushing out, as if they have found me dead. Some days later, the newspaper has a picture of my unsmiling face. It says, 'Joyful William Heming, eight, safe at home after his mystery disappearance.' My cousin Isobel is thirteen. She is rubbing my nose in the newspaper because of all the trouble I have caused. 'You are nothing but trouble,' she hisses.

One afternoon when Isobel is fifteen and I am ten, she finds me standing in her wardrobe and screams the house down. All I am doing is being as quiet as a mouse. What is her problem? But now I am in worse trouble. 'I wasn't spying on her,' I tell Aunt Lillian, when she accuses me of spying on her (even with my eye to the crack, I could hardly see her face as she sang along to the pop tunes and painted her toenails), but she just glares at me with her mouth open. 'Look, he has my comb!' cries Isobel, and snatches it out of my hand. My father is furious and he cannot help but deliver me two or three sharp smacks about the head. He puts me in my own wardrobe and locks the door. 'We'll see how you like that,' he says. In fact, I don't mind at all.

In the dark I take out my moneybox key and dig a line in the wood, and then another above it. This will be my mark and no one else's, hidden here for ever. The space between the lines is as wide as my finger, which is perfect. I imagine crawling into the space and lying very still.

Isobel will not find me again. But her things are often mysteriously moved around or missing – her cotton-wool sticks and perfumed things. One time she sees me watching her kissing a boy from the lane, his arms around the back of her neck. She is furious. Now, every time she kisses a boy – there is more than one – she thinks I am there. She is always looking out for me, but I am hidden. If I wanted, I could just step out from the shadows in the park, like a spectre.

Across the street from my bedroom window I see Mrs Damato, busy with dinner. The kitchen looks bright and steamed up. How I'd love to be down there, behind the door in her pantry, hedged among the jars and strong-smelling packages and the sausages hanging like stiff arms from the ceiling. I crept in, though she knows nothing of this, during the long holiday, when the weather was hot and the kitchen door had been left open for the breeze. Mrs Damato was vacuuming upstairs. Her little boy, Anthony, was playing in his playpen in the sitting room. Little Anthony saw me and scrambled to his feet when I came in. I waved to him, like an angel just landed. He was still standing at the bars of his cage when I came out. There were cakes still warm on a wire rack, so I took one and gave him half. The drone of the vacuum cleaner stopped abruptly and we both looked at the ceiling. We could hear Mrs Damato up there, warbling on in her high Italian voice.

These are the days I remember. After the troubles with cousin Isobel, my father sent me to a school far from Norfolk. It was an opportunity, he said. My mother had left money when she died, and he said that I had to try hard for her. Even then I knew a line when I heard one. In fact I had more brains than I needed to succeed, but never quite the heart. Instead, I worked at my camouflage. I took care to avoid the extremes of triumph and failure, kept my head down in class, endured enough knocks in play to escape the casual torments of the large-thighed sporty boys, who ruled the house under the neglectful myopic gaze of our house-parent, Mrs Luckham. I shunned cliques, laughed when the others laughed, shrank from the scrutiny of masters. Neither in nor out, I cultivated a middling, willing sociability, waiting my turn, playing my part. But when, once or twice a term, I feigned mild illness or injury, it was not (as with other boys) with a view to skipping afternoon games or PE, but to secure a half-hour of freedom in which to walk the creaky, waxed corridors of Winter House or Bentham or Wood, drawn by the odour of unattended, unlocked dorms – familiar as my own in basic décor, layout and dimensions but redolent with the aura of their legitimate, absent residents. Now that was what I called an opportunity.

I hadn't much of significance to say to my fellow pupils, and vice versa, but I came to know them, or a good sum of them, through their comic books and collectables and playthings, and the letters and cards from mothers and siblings and generous godparents whose gifts of money and sweets were accompanied by witty, affectionate greetings and exhortations to prosper and enjoy life. I winkled out their secrets – their family nicknames, who among them had had an appendix or tonsils out, who was going skiing that winter, which family had a Jack Russell (picture enclosed) called Dobb, who had a new baby sister, who needed to be reminded to use their asthma inhaler. Occasionally there would be an unimaginative diary to pore over; the same tattered November issue of *Penthouse* turned up in several locations during the spring term of Year 10. I filled a spiral notebook with my findings and conjectures (Tomerton was gay, I surmised; Faulkes's stammer was the product of torture as a child), spilling into two notebooks, which became three, four, five and more as my enterprise gathered weight. I kept their lives, all of them – the weaklings, the bullies, the dolts, the young Mozarts and Einsteins – locked in my chest.

Was it too wild to think of it as a hobby? An obsessive sport? Even accounting for the allure of *Penthouse*, it was as exhilarating a thing as a boy could experience to be given a few moments alone in a cave of forbidden treasures. A sharp eye might have noticed me leaving the table before pudding, or slipping out of the library during free study. I wasn't complacent. My impulses were supported by risk assessment. I planned. I made exit strategies. I could trot out a well-rehearsed line to explain – to a cleaner or half-interested passing master – why I was where I oughtn't to be. But, of course, danger was part of the appeal. What is life without the unexpected crash of something to remind us of how the rug can be pulled from under you in an instant? At assembly Mr Williams read out a mesmerizing report in the *Yorkshire Post* of a local young man who had plunged to his death from a mountain in the Lake District. The whole town, he said, was in mourning for a lost son. My fellow pupils fell into an uncomfortable, shuffling silence, but I thought immediately of my own heedless self, walking my own ledge, beset by bracing winds above the abyss of sudden discovery – a kindred, fearless presence in the shadow of the glorious, remembered lost son. We did it – the lost son and I – because it was there, and because we both knew it felt like nothing else on earth.

In the lower sixth, and very nearly grown-up, some of us had our own room and a lockable study, though it was the work of a moment to lift a key – sometimes a small bunch on a novelty ring, with their promise of a secret something squirrelled away in a tin or wooden box – from the pocket of a blazer hanging in a changing room or on the back of a chair, or lying on the playing fields at lunch break, its contents half spilt on the grass. Hurrying to the victim's quarters, I could then safely give myself up to ten minutes' judicious foraging or just spend the time absorbing the rays of an alien atmosphere. There was often something to eat. Only on two occasions was I interrupted by the occupant returning unexpectedly – the rattle of the door handle, a muttered '*Shit . . .*' as the boy searched again for his key, then the echo of his footsteps as he retreated to the school office to face the wrath of Mrs Blake, the senior housekeeper. These were moments to test the nerve, though Mrs Blake was slow to acknowledge a careless adolescent's sense of urgency, and by the time she had followed him grimly back to his room with a master key, his own was safely in her lost-property basket, miraculously restored by an unknown hand. I carved my mark everywhere you couldn't see, everywhere I shouldn't be.

Quick though my heart beat in these moments, my mind beat quicker. But I still had a lesson to learn.

My fascination with a boy called Marrineau was hardly unique. Captain of all sports, aloof in his physical prowess and cool air of threat, everyone admired him. Our paths never crossed. I was just one of the many lower creatures who knew to keep a respectful distance from him and the entourage of bullies and jeerers – like him, rugger men and cricketers and rowers – that tumbled in his wake. On Saturday mornings we cheered as he led his team to triumphs on the sports field. I saw him in Joy's coffee bar in town with girls. There was talk that he owned a motorcycle that he kept in a secret lock-up outside the school. Whatever he had, everyone wanted it. He was untouchable.

But in the lower sixth, Marrineau and I shared a history set and a teacher, the diminutive Mr Stamp, who in the first class of spring term paired us up as 'study buddies'. That didn't happen. Marrineau only ever spoke to me twice: once, after that class, to warn me to stay out of his face; and again, a week or so later, when he pushed me up against the wall of the gym changing room with my tie and collar in his fist and said in a low voice full of meaning that if I kept following him I was dead.

Which was a pity, because this simply made me even more resolved to breach the Marrineau defences and enter his golden sanctum, a room and study beneath the south-facing gable of Hooke House. Unfortunately there seemed no way in. I knew Marrineau's timetable as intimately as my own and I pored over sporting lists and fixtures and practice schedules. There was little overlap in our movements, few chances even to bump along in his slipstream without running into his personal guard, whom Marrineau would unleash whenever he saw me hovering. Two of them sent me sprawling in the science block one afternoon, prompting laughter from the outer chorus line of sycophants. Everyone was starting to sniff blood. I retreated again to the periphery. I was in danger of exposing myself, of losing my hard-won powers of invisibility. And yet the more impossible it was to get close to Marrineau – the more hostile his demeanour – the more he became my Holy Grail.

And then I saw a way. All boys were encouraged to develop extracurricular interests. I myself had joined the film society (I grew to like westerns: nothing moved me more at this time than a languid stranger with a gun coming to the aid of respectable townsfolk beset by whooping, lawless rowdies). Also the chess club. Chess allowed sport-resistant boys to embrace the school's competitive ethos without getting hurt, but for me it was also a way to be seen to be sociable without giving anything away. As usual, I tried not to win too often, though needless to say I was three moves ahead of the class. One afternoon I spied Marrineau, square-shouldered and erect and proprietorial, moving along the main corridor like a swiftly rowed boat. I ducked into a niche to watch him. He was carrying something, though it seemed he was trying to conceal it. It was a portable chess set – not an expensive one but a plastic set in a chequered tin of the kind sold in town. I had no idea he played chess. Was he ashamed of being thought uncool? It was inconceivable that he would join the chess club, so who did he play against? Maybe he was new to the game – had caught the bug from a cleverer younger brother over the holidays and dare not yet reveal himself to the club players.

Then I knew what I had to do, and found myself running, my heart giddy with excitement. I caught up with him just as he reached one of the side doors to his block. 'Marrineau . . .'

He turned and stared at me.

'I saw you with your chess set. I thought we might have a game.'

The stare remained. 'Are you kidding me?'

'Or, if you're just getting the hang of it – I'm not saying you are, but I could teach you some openings, if you like. I'm in the chess club. People say I'm pretty good. What do you say?'

Marrineau didn't say anything. He pushed me away firmly and closed the door in my face. Had I embarrassed him? It was a good sign that he hadn't said no, I thought. There was still hope.

As things turned out, a less obvious opportunity arose in the history class we took together. Marrineau was no great scholar, contributing little and usually to be found gazing out over the quad while Mr Stamp talked about Oliver Cromwell's unfair war on the Irish. But on the day in question Marrineau was reading something beneath his desk – a letter written on pale-yellow stationery, though the envelope was white and had the look of a greetings card. Was it his birthday? He was so engrossed with the letter, and I with watching him from the row behind, that neither of us saw the diminutive Mr Stamp (or heard the sudden quiet that heralded his approach) until he tapped Marrineau's desk with the rolled-up map he used to point at illustrations and troop movements on the whiteboard. Now he was using it to point at the letter, and held out his hand for it. Marrineau handed it over.

Mr Stamp glanced through the contents and smiled sadly. 'Love letters will not help you in your English Civil War paper,' he said.

Marrineau, his eyes fixed on the letter, could not speak.

'Well?' Mr Stamp waited for an answer, though technically he had not asked a question. 'Mr Marrineau?'

'No, sir,' said Marrineau.

'No, sir,' Mr Stamp repeated. 'Seven days.' He made a show of folding the letter into the envelope and slipping it into the pocket of his shabby jacket, its cuffs rimmed with leather.

Something dawned in Marrineau's grey eyes that was more despair than defeat. What was in the letter that was so important? A love letter, Mr Stamp had said. A girl from the town, for sure. Was he afraid Mr Stamp would read it, and reveal those sweet nothings to the staff room or, worse, the headmaster, with who knew what repercussions? Perhaps Marrineau planned to elope! My imagination raced with possibilities.

You might only wonder what satisfaction I took from Marrineau's unexpected fall, I who had so recently been the victim of his harsh words and manhandling. And yet, for all Marrineau's imperious disdain for his inferiors – perhaps because of it – this humiliation at the hands of Mr Stamp now cast him in a tragic light: a broken, blinded Samson; or a lion in chains, dispossessed of its roar. A tense, nerve-tingling silence hung over the room for the rest of the period, as if with one last superhuman effort our adored and feared captain of everything might suddenly burst the powerful bonds of his ingrained respect for authority, hurdle the line of desks and devour Mr Stamp whole. Who could not have wished it?

In fact, Marrineau sat motionless except for an angry pulse, visible in the outline of his clamped jaws, his ears red with shame. When the tea bell rang, he hung back to speak with Mr Stamp. Loitering outside the door, I couldn't hear his mumbled plea, but Mr Stamp, in a high barking tone that indicated little respect for Marrineau's obvious wish to keep things hushed, said, 'And shouldn't you have thought of that before you decided to read it in my history class?' He looked up with a long, pained expression at the towering Marrineau, waiting for him to yield to the logic of this unarguable position – as if the punishment was now nothing and only submission would fully satisfy. But Marrineau said nothing and Mr Stamp dismissed him, his face angry and stiff but his eyes full of sadness.

Marrineau scowled at me as he passed in the corridor, though he could hardly blame me for his ignominy – or rather, he could hardly guess that if I hadn't been watching his clumsy subterfuge with such rapt curiosity it was quite possible that Mr Stamp would never have noticed what he was up to at all.

Poor Marrineau. Where were his large-thighed, laughing cronies now who daily insulated him from the buffetings of mortal inconvenience? Who were they against the might of the diminutive Mr Stamp?

The truth was, only I had what it took to save this day. Was it in the hope of winning Marrineau's gratitude at last, of creeping into his affections, that I loitered outside while Mr Stamp closed his briefcase and switched off his audio-visual equipment and vacated the history room, the letter still peeping out of his jacket pocket? I cannot deny it. I had invested more than I ought in trying to get my nostrils closer to the elusive Marrineau essence to be indifferent now to this turn in his fortunes. But there was more. Think of the philatelist's sudden, gut-quivering glimpse of a rare Treskilling Yellow in a bundle of nineteenth-century Swedish correspondence; or the birdwatcher's sighting of a nesting corncrake; or the climber who discovers a harder way up the mountain. Here, in the very opportunity to close in on the *grande bouffe* of Marrineau, was an unexpected appetizer, another beckoning of the never-had experience, the never-before-encountered quarry, and it was at least partly this that drew me after Mr Stamp, who was already quickening his step along the corridor, thinking perhaps of jam and toasted crumpets, but unwittingly trailing an altogether sweeter scent.

But I might as well tell you right now that things didn't go well; that I let myself down with a moment of what I can only call inattention; and that before the week was done I had bidden farewell to Mr Stamp and Marrineau and his fools and indeed the whole place for ever. I was out.

3

MY FATHER HAD DIED the year before, so it was Aunt Lillian who
arrived at school to pick me up, having parleyed with the headmaster and agreed that the best thing would be for me to leave
without further discussion or consequence. It seemed rather a
waste after all these years of trying hard for my dead mother.

'But what did you expect, William?' she demanded. 'What
else could we do? What on earth were you thinking?'

So many whats. I couldn't imagine Aunt Lillian put up much
of a fight. The headmaster had surprised her when he described
me as normally quiet and hard-working, though he added that
his hands were tied, in view of evidence from eye witnesses and
my own inexplicable refusal to explain myself (I had reverted to
the trusty tight-lipped defence mechanism of childhood).

'You were lucky they didn't bring charges,' Aunt Lillian said.

In fact I had ridden my luck in all sorts of ways in this final
episode at school.

My absence as duty prefect on the Minors' teatime rota
went unnoticed as I shadowed Mr Stamp to his own tea at the
Servery and afterwards to his rooms as housemaster on the

second floor of Winter. And then he didn't keep me waiting but reappeared ten minutes later wearing a different, lighter jacket – clearly minus the letter – and casual trousers. He walked briskly, slapping a folded newspaper against his leg. I followed him out to the hard tennis court beyond the pond and founder's statue, where a quartet of mid-schoolers were playing doubles in the late-afternoon sun. He settled in one of the summer chairs on the lawn, crossed his legs and opened the paper. He didn't seem to read it very closely, scanning the headlines and licking his thumb as he turned from one page to the next. He kept looking up smilingly to watch the game, and every now and then would call to one or the other of the boys, offering praise or advice. The boys cheerfully shouted something back, though it was hard to see how they could actually hear Mr Stamp's remarks. Two or three times he returned a ball that sailed over the fence.

There wasn't much I could do. It was warm rather than hot. It seemed unlikely Mr Stamp would take off his jacket. And if he did, what then? Should I start a fire in the trees or some other diversion? Across the lawn in the mid-school block I could see Miss Stiles, the secretary, moving about in her office. A scenario popped into my head in which I watched myself retreat from my cool spot under the colonnade and call Miss Stiles from the payphone outside the hall using my adult voice ('I'd like to speak to Mr Stamp, if I may. Yes, it *is* rather urgent, I'm afraid. Yes, it's Doctor *Bluther*'). There would be some enquiring in the background, during which someone with eyes in their head, perhaps Miss Stiles herself, would see Mr Stamp sitting not a hundred yards away. By the time Miss Stiles had sent some Minor duty boy scurrying across to summon Mr Stamp, I would be back in position, ready to pounce, and then, provided Mr Stamp didn't take his jacket with him, which of course he might well do . . .

But now the scene in front of me was changing. The tennis players had stopped for a drink, and one of them had flopped on to the grass, red-faced and panting. Mr Stamp immediately leapt to his feet. 'I say . . .' he shouted. 'I say . . . Perhaps *I* could take Thomson's place.'

The boys looked at one another and politely mustered the will to match Mr Stamp's enthusiasm for the idea. Only then did I see that Mr Stamp was actually wearing tennis shoes – that, clearly, he had come prepared for precisely this moment. And now he pulled off his jacket and threw it excitedly over the chair before jogging stiffly off to join the boys.

Sod Miss Stiles. The moment Mr Stamp had his back to me on court, his brown, balding pate catching the afternoon light, I sauntered towards the court, paused by his chair, waited until he tossed a yellow ball in the air to serve . . . then fished his keys right out of his pocket.

I hurried to Winter House. There was barely a soul around. After tea, boys would be in their dorms or watching TV or out practising sport. I unlocked the door to Mr Stamp's rooms and locked it behind me. The interior was very different to our own rooms – older and darker and woodier. There was a sitting area with an armchair, and a kitchenette, and I could see a study with a desk and books. It was no problem to find Marrineau's letter. Mr Stamp's shabby school jacket was on a hanger in his neat bedroom. The envelope was in the pocket, presumably untouched. I took out the yellow sheet inside and quickly read it.

'Dear David', it began in rounded, girlish handwriting, his name crowned by floating hearts pierced by arrows. It spoke of a night out at the cinema and of 'giving me a ride on your bike' and 'the lovely time we had!!' There were more exclamatory endearments and references to friends and schoolwork, then it concluded, 'I do hope you can come Friday! Sarah x x x'. Also in the envelope (it had been hand-delivered, I now noticed) was an invitation to Sarah's eighteenth-birthday party. Ha. Now I saw Marrineau's dilemma. The party was that night. The address was a country hotel some miles out of town and underneath was an illustration of how to get there. At the bottom of the invitation it said (and here must have been the killer torment for poor Marrineau): 'Admission Strictly By Invitation Only'.

I quickly replaced the letter in the envelope, and the envelope in Mr Stamp's pocket. The invitation I put in my own. Obviously this was the moment to flee with my treasure. But how could I, with Mr Stamp's cosy life at my mercy – his tobacco-smelling wardrobe, his drawer of Argyll socks, his desk piled with exercise books, biscuits in a tin? A framed wedding photograph stood on his chest – an unmistakably younger Mr Stamp arm in arm with a taller woman carrying flowers. They looked so happy. Was she now dead? In another country? With another man? These ghosts of old circumstances cried out to my nosiness, but I had no time. I rifled through Mr Stamp's briefcase, which contained homework for marking, two small oranges, several textbooks and his rolled-up map, taped at both ends. There was also a ball made out of rubber bands that he would bounce gently on his desk when he was pondering a problem in class. In his study drawer, beneath letters and bills, a tube of confiscated wine gums (I'll take those, I thought), a cigarette lighter and two or three holiday postcards, I found a snapshot of a grinning boy in PE kit. He couldn't have been older than nine. I didn't recognize him at first, but then when I looked more closely I realized it was Marrineau. How extraordinary! Why would he keep a picture of Marrineau? But of course – everyone loved Marrineau. Even Mr Stamp, childless and alone. How especially disappointed he must have been to have to confiscate Marrineau's letter. I considered taking the picture, but closed the drawer and took the rubber-band ball instead. I emerged from Winter House. I was elated but congratulated myself on my composure. It wasn't until I was out in the breeze that I felt the sweat steaming off me.

At the tennis court, Mr Stamp was standing in his shirt sleeves with his arms folded, watching the play now from the grass verge at the side. Two other boys had joined them and were hitting balls on the second court. I walked briskly past Mr Stamp's chair, dropping his key on the grass beside his newspaper, as if it had fallen out of his jacket. But this time, he saw me. 'Heming!' he shouted. 'What are you doing there, boy? Come here!'

My legs, I confess, turned to jelly. I took my time, steadying the rubber-band ball in my blazer pocket while I walked towards him.

He squinted at me impatiently. 'Now,' he said, 'you must run along to the Servery for me and have the ladies send someone out with a jug of lemonade or squash for my young friends here. On my account. Could you do that?'

'Indeed, sir,' I said. 'Right away. Lemonade, sir.'

He looked at me and blinked uncertainly. It was impossible for a small, imperious man like Mr Stamp to know if you were mocking him or doing as you were told. I hurried up the grass verge and away, my heart pounding.

I gave his order at the Servery. In the far corner, at the only occupied table, Marrineau and his friends were watching me. Marrineau was leaning back in his chair. They looked at me with the lazy regard of jungle predators appraising a distant film crew. Far from looking away, I returned their stares, moving my gaze from one glowering face to the next until I was staring into Marrineau's belligerent eyes. I had his invitation in my pocket.

I had done what he would not have dared. And now? Only two hours earlier it would have been enough to abseil into his room and tape the invitation to his wash-basin mirror – reward enough just to think of his astonishment when he returned. But I had also imagined a scenario like this, in which I strode boldly into their midst with the words, 'Hold off your dogs, Marrineau. I think I may have something to interest you . . .'

What did I want? To be one of his dogs too – to track him at heel, to sniff his hand, look into his face, await a kind word or gesture?

One of the four suddenly kicked the chair away in front of him and I stepped back hurriedly. I was off, as they knew I would be. No one followed, or even laughed, but I ran to my room. I was exhilarated. I felt something had happened to me, some change, and that the momentum was suddenly with me to push this day as far as it would go, with whatever means I had and however long it took. Did I have it in mind to *be* Marrineau? Who can say. But at seven o'clock, as I stood in front of the mirror in my admittedly unfashionable sports jacket, checked shirt and black school trousers, I had a taste of how that might feel.

I took an unlocked cycle from the sheds and pedalled the three miles or so out to the hotel. Here I left the bike in a corner of the car park and stood aside to watch the guests arriving. Some were being dropped off by a parent, some in groups, arriving in taxis. Music thrummed from upstairs. It occurred to me that Marrineau might turn up anyway, but there was no sign of him. I waited another half-hour then showed my invitation to the bouncer on the door and went up into the noise. Everybody seemed to be dressed in cool clothes. Some boys, already half drunk, were dancing. The girls wore heavy black eye make-up and short, figure-hugging dresses and socks up to their thighs. I headed for the girl at the centre of attention. She was pleasant-looking and her blonde hair was piled up on top with wispy bits falling at the sides.

I touched her arm. 'Are you Sarah?'

She looked at me blankly. 'Yes . . .'

'I have a message from Marrineau. I'm afraid he's not going to be able to make it tonight.'

'David? He *promised* he'd come.'

'I'm afraid he has rugby tomorrow. I'm here instead.'

'Bloody hell,' she sighed.

I pretended to look a little hurt.

'Oh, sorry,' she said, laughing. 'I didn't mean that.'

'I'm not meant to be an exact replacement.'

She looked around. 'Do you know anyone here?'

'Only you.' I stuck my hand out. 'I'm William.'

'Oh.' She smiled, shaking it exaggeratedly. '*Very* formal.'

I smiled back at her. I do have a good smile. And I should say I am by no means physically repellent, having what my aunt (who was often to be spied upon reading film or fashion magazines in an idle moment) would call 'regular' or 'pleasing' features.

'Do you play rugby, William?'

'To tell you the truth, I'm more of an indoors sort of person.'

'You're not drinking,' she said. 'Have a beer.'

'Do they have orange juice?'

'I suppose so.' She smiled at me again, uncertain. 'You're funny.'

'Am I?' I smiled back.

Her friends came to drag her away for a dance. I took a glass of juice from a tray at the bar and mingled a little. It wasn't my kind of thing but I was interested to be there. It was amazing, I thought, how much people were prepared to tell a complete stranger after one or two drinks. All I had to do was ask someone how they knew Sarah, and in no time I had half a biography – how she liked drama and owned a horse and was a day girl at school, and that she had a twin brother called Robin who had gone to university a year early. All kinds of things. One boy, perhaps hoping for a little reciprocation, tried to sell me some Ecstasy. I told him, rather cleverly, no, thanks, I'd had enough for one day.

I picked up a second drink and wandered out to the landing, then took the lift up to the next floor. When the doors opened I found myself facing an open store room stacked with linen and spare pillows. I popped in to check it out. It was warm and white and fragrance-fresh. I stayed just long enough to rest my cheek on a pile of towels. When I came out there was a maid in the corridor, but she had her back to me and was just disappearing into a guest room. I skipped away to the lift doors and pretended to wait. She came out a few moments later and moved along to the next door, which she unlocked with a cardkey attached to her waistband. I watched her as she worked along the corridor, marking her schedule. She didn't go in every room and I noticed she didn't lock the doors when she came out, just let them swing shut behind her with a heavy click. But they were locked all right, I found when she'd gone.

I continued to scout around. On the next floor I saw a trolley parked outside one of the rooms. The door was open and there was a man up a stepladder. I said hello and pointed with my drink towards the ceiling and asked what he was doing. He told me, in a friendly foreign accent, he was replacing a bulb. I peered into the room. No bags or clothes in sight. It smelled of air-freshener but also just very slightly of the man.

'Are you a guest, sir?' he asked, glancing at my drink.

'Yes,' I said. 'I'm just along the way there.'

'Ah.' He smiled and came down from the ladder and went into the bathroom. He'd propped the door open with his trolley wheel. What was needed, I saw, was something that would just stop the door fully closing, so that the man would think it had locked when it hadn't. A bit of cardboard? A tissue? Ah! I dug in my trouser pocket and found the wine gums from Mr Stamp's drawer. They were perfect, being both small and not too easily squashed. I bent down and wedged a couple at the bottom of the door frame. Now I just had to distract the man at the right moment.

I waited just a little further down the corridor for him to come out. Five or six minutes passed before he emerged. He yanked his trolley out of the way and the door started to close . . .

I bellowed down the corridor – 'Hello! Hello!' – just when the man might have expected to hear that final click of the door swinging shut, the everyday seal on a job done. He actually looked alarmed.

'Sorry, could you give me a hand? I seem to have locked myself out of my room.' I tried to look just slightly drunk.

'Ah, yes, sir. You have locked inside the key?'

'Yes, my key, inside.'

'You must speak with Reception, please.'

'Of course, of course. That's *exactly* what I'll do.'

He was relieved to see the back of me. I took the lift back down to the party. It was noisier now, with throbbing music and plenty of real drunks, mostly of my age, with their arms in the air. The dance floor was packed. I put my empty glass on the bar and joined the throng. Two girls latched on to me at either side and had me copy what they were doing.

But now Sarah swam into view holding a cocktail.

'Happy birthday,' I said.

'I was looking for you,' she said.

'I just had to slip out to my room,' I said.

'You're staying *here*? At the hotel?'

'It seemed easier,' I said.

'What – and your school's OK about that?'

'Strictly speaking? Probably not.'

'Woo, hoo,' she said. 'Aren't *you* full of surprises?'

'And you?'

Reader, she never left my side (except for a quick call to her parents to make her excuses). In the quiet of the downstairs lounge, we talked about *Romeo and Juliet* (our favourite Shakespeare) while she smoked cigarettes, and she almost cried when I told her about the pony I'd had that collapsed and died when I was eight. And imagine our astonishment, in the early hours, during our post-coital whisperings in room 313 of the Pike Rhydding Hotel (the wine gums had worked a treat), when we discovered that we were both twins, she with a brother and I a sister.

'Oh God, what's her name?' she asked, sitting up, moonlit and naked like a scene from a film.

'Isobel,' I said, stroking her arm. 'To tell you the truth, I think my parents have always liked her more than me. She was always the brainy one.'

'Oh *God* . . .' Sarah said again.

Yes, it was as if we were made for each other.

I don't remember pedalling back to school. My mind whirred with forebodings. Things were going too well. I imagined my room ransacked and the headmaster and board of governors waiting to confront me with my spiral notebooks and assiduously detailed records of fellow pupils and scrapbooks of their family snaps and greetings cards, not to mention Mr Stamp's ball of rubber bands and the souvenir Chinese soup spoon from my visit to Uncle Richard's lady friend's flat years earlier. But no. All looked normal for a Saturday morning, with perhaps a little more animation among the boys, some kitted out for the inter-house sevens to be played throughout the day. I walked on air to the dining room. Breakfast was almost over but there was bacon left and some watery scrambled eggs and toast. I was fabulously hungry. I had the place to myself, but had barely applied the brown sauce when I felt my arms grabbed from behind and was aware of Marrineau's looming presence in house rugby colours, the studs of his boots scraping on the tiled floor. Did he even mention Sarah? He didn't need to. There was a punitive and sudden quality in this that spoke it. Everything was a blur. I was aware of some painful roughing-up and swearing and a chair going over, and I suppose I must have pulled free somehow because the next thing I knew there was screaming and commotion and grown-ups running, and at the centre, like a rearing, dancing horse, was an injured Marrineau holding his face, roaring displeasure at the heavens.

And so the luck ran out. There was hell to pay, as Aunt Lillian was fond of saying – notably in the demand from Marrineau's rich and influential parents and their lawyer that I be instantly withdrawn from school. It was either him or me. In return, they agreed not to involve the police. In fact, of course, it would suit no one to have me up in court on an assault charge – not me, certainly not the school, certainly not invincible Marrineau, whose reputation as a Goliath of cool would suffer the glare of public display. But I responded to all enquiries with an enigmatic smile that transported me back to room 313. In the immediate storm of events I felt strangely out of myself, as if I was looking down on this tiny hullabaloo from a celestial height. I was banished to my room while the adults argued it out via faxes and phone calls.

That should have been that. But there was one last thing I had to do. And it was surprisingly easy. There was no guard on my door. This wasn't Soviet Russia. And with Marrineau not yet back from A&E and the story of my infamy not yet fully broadcast, there was nothing to stop me simply walking out of the house and across the playing fields – the pitches busy now with thudding tackles and cheering boys – and straight into the first-team changing room. No one challenged me. Marrineau's black tracksuit, with its yellow captain's stripe, was not hard to find. His keys, along with a few coins, were in one of his trainers, under the seat. I guessed Marrineau would come straight back to the tournament, and I was right. I watched from beneath the trees as he eventually arrived like a returning war hero to the cheers of his supporters, a bandage and sticking plaster across his face, his eye bloodshot. Now I saw that he was negotiating with Mr Frith, head of games. He couldn't play, it seemed, but he could referee. He pulled on an official's bib and swung a whistle on a ribbon while he talked. Mr Frith assigned him two teams of Minors and he ran off with them. The smaller ones struggled to keep up. How proud they would be to be refereed by Marrineau. His supporters watched him go, uncertain whether to follow and be obliged, like him, to stand among the Minors, or save their roars for the Majors of Hooke and Bentham. He was on his own.

With Marrineau pinned down by the nonsense of rugby, I walked calmly to his room. And what satisfaction to turn the key in that lock, to push open that forbidden door, to breathe the stale odours of that sacred place as if they were pure mountain air. There were things to see and appreciate. From all surfaces came the dull gleam of sporting trophies. On the wall were framed certificates, and a photograph of Marrineau shaking hands with a sporting personality. In a drawer I found the tan crocodile-skin shaving kit he deployed with such nonchalance in ablutions, drawing the razor smoothly through his enviable stubble with that natural grace only athletes have. I lay on his bed, leafing through a rugby programme, several years old, for a match between South Africa and the British Lions. I tried to feel its value to him. I prised open the staples and removed the double-page photograph at the centre – a final school souvenir. The last thing I found, hidden carelessly under the bed, was the chess set. I clicked it open to find a label taped under the lid inscribed with the name of its rightful owner – it belonged to one of the boys from the chess club. I guessed that Marrineau had taken it from the boy in some act of spite or bullying and simply kept it. I vowed to return it.

And now I opened the wardrobe. Here was the handsome tobacco-coloured rawhide cowboy jacket I'd seen him wear at weekends in the town with his gang and those excitable girls – perhaps Sarah herself had been there – who gathered around the games machines in the café.

How disappointing that Marrineau proved so lacking in imagination and substance. How little of him there was to cling to. The trick, I saw, was to step away before you felt the heat of a person. In the afternoon sunshine I could see the crowds of players running around and hear their distant shouts. I tried to pick Marrineau out, but he was too far away and much reduced. I put on the jacket, heavy and worn. It was too broad in the shoulders and yet in a way felt right and fitting enough. I stood at the window like the giant statue of Jesus above Rio de Janeiro, arms stretched wide, as if ready for crucifixion, long leather fringes hanging from the sleeves. To be honest, I felt like a king myself. And, of course, I too would rise again.

4

AUNT LILLIAN FOUND A private sixth-form college for me, starting in September. In the meantime, undoubtedly out of fear of having me creeping around her house for months, she fixed me up with a summer job at a firm of estate agents, Mower & Mower – two relatives with distant links to the family. It didn't surprise me to learn that they were located a hundred miles away from Norfolk, or two hundred if you went by train. Old Mr Mower – the other Mr Mower was apparently long dead – picked me up from the station and drove me to my accommodation, a fragrant guesthouse run by a nice Mrs Burton whose bedroom, I discovered (some minutes after unpacking), was home to a vast collection of ceramic farm animals.

Mr Mower picked me up after breakfast. I was almost entirely ignorant of what estate agents actually did. But, oh my, when I found out – when we arrived at his client's house and Mr Mower didn't knock on the door but simply unlocked it and ushered me in . . .

'The owners just give you their keys?' I asked.

'Of course,' said Mr Mower, taking off his trilby in deference to being in someone else's house. 'If they're working, or on holiday, or too busy to be around. It happens often. Then you have to make sure you arrive in good time, ahead of the prospective buyer. Make sure everything is ship-shape.'

We made our way round the house, Mr Mower pointing things out. Upstairs, he opened a door to a large study with an old-fashioned writing desk and swivel chair and bookshelves and two small paintings on the wall. We went to look out of the window.

'What can you tell me about the garden?' he said.

'The lawn has been mowed?'

'Excellent. What else do you see?'

'Trees? Bushes?'

'Good boy. Which means it's not overlooked by the neighbours. People like their privacy.' Mr Mower tapped the side of his nose. 'When the buyer arrives, that will be one of the first things I shall tell them.'

When the buyers turned up, a married couple with twin girls whom they left in the car busy plaiting each other's hair, he gave them the same tour, but added things about the roof guarantee, low crime figures and good local schools. Then he drove me back to the office to meet his staff. Rita, his slow-moving secretary, explained the filing system and how to answer the telephone if everyone was busy. In the afternoon Mr Mower and I went out again to two more properties, one to measure it up for sale with the owners, counting the rooms and asking about the boiler and whether curtains would be included in the price. Mr Mower filled out a form as he talked. He introduced me to clients as 'young William'.

By the end of that day I knew there was no way I would go back to school; that my life must begin anew here in this leafy, bustling town, as Mower & Mower's sales literature called it, only forty-eight minutes by fast train from the centre of London. I instantly became the keenest, hardest-working employee the firm had ever had, and by the end of the summer Mr Mower was delighted, though taken aback, at my wish to stay on. Aunt Lillian, grateful for any result that kept me a hundred miles away from her, agreed to send me a monthly allowance, which I calculated would more than cover my meagre living expenses and allow my modest wages to mount up in the bank. 'And do you know what you need?' said Mr Mower, beaming. 'Driving lessons.'

Although he had two sales consultants, Guy and Stella, I was the one Mr Mower took under his wing. Guy, who was probably in his late twenties, glowered, and would invent menial tasks for me to do, or send me to the café to queue for his lunchtime sandwich and various unhealthy snacks. He took pills for a mood-altering stomach ulcer. But I brought out the mothering instinct in Stella, the senior of the two, who occasionally brought me in a baked edible from home and twinkled with quiet amusement as I followed Mr Mower hither and thither, carrying his bag, but also internalizing the nuanced lessons of mortgaging, conveyancing and consumer law, or helping him dream up new marketing strategies and ads for the paper. He taught me how to read detailed blueprints and always to look a man in the eye. On my nineteenth birthday, in front of the whole staff, he presented me with a pair of opera glasses. ('For roof inspections,' he explained. 'A crucial part of the agent's armoury.') He decided that I had a creative bent and had me accompany Cliff, the photographer, to clients' houses as artistic director. Perhaps he feared that I would get bored. Perhaps he thought, as a young man who had forfeited the chance of university – renounced, as Mr Mower saw it, the life of the mind – that I required every last intellectual stimulus that selling houses could offer. In fact it was all the stimulation I needed.

It was months, however, before I found myself alone with a house to plunder. Rita tended to arrange visits when the client was at home; Cliff would pick me up at the office in his van and then after the job would drop me back there. It was a while before I realized that Cliff, who worked at a photographic supplies shop in town, could simply be sent on his way once we'd done the job. So, when Rita announced one day that I would have to let myself into a property with a set of keys, it was as if I had spent my life preparing for it. I worked with Cliff as usual, pointing up the most saleable aspects of the house, taking the dustbins out of shot and so on. Afterwards I told him I had other errands, and would walk back to the office.

'Ah, I get it,' he chuckled, in his Welsh accent. 'A bit of time off, is it? A bit of truanting? Well, don't worry, I won't tell.' He winked.

How perfect. Perhaps he had errands too.

Once he was out of the way I doubled back and let myself into the house again. I didn't have much time and I didn't know much about the couple who lived there, but I'd been round the house once with Cliff and knew which cupboards and drawers I needed to get into. I sat on the sofa in the front room and popped grapes from the fruit bowl into my mouth while I leafed through photographs and bills and letters. They had a piano, and a son not much younger than me to play it. I imagined they were nice parents. And I envisaged a teenage boy they could be proud of. But who could know?

I know now that you can't know everything about everyone. You have to think of it as a thrilling, ongoing project. Crossing the threshold of a strange house is like the opening line of a gripping story. At its best, penetrating deeper, it is like falling in love.

So, even as I locked the door, I knew I had to go back. I had a copy of the key made at the shoe repairer's on the high street (these days any outlying supermarket will do it without so much as a good morning, and certainly without wondering what you need it for), and handed the original back to Rita. By the time I went into the house again a week later I had my own camera – an expensive Polaroid bought out of my savings from Cliff's shop ('Oh, it's your own camera now, is it? I'd better watch out!'). I took pictures of everything, and I borrowed documents – contracts, scribbled notes, bank statements, payslips, passports, birth certificates, address books – which I then photocopied in the library in the evenings. I took a file from the stationery room at the office and filled it with their secrets. How I came to adore these people! When I sat down with an album of photographs they had taken one summer in the Canary Islands, I felt the sun on my own face; heard with my own ears the cries of their fellow holidaymakers across the blue pool. It delighted me to follow their busy schedule, chart their routines gleaned from the calendar hanging from a magnetized hook on the fridge or from the grey desk diary in the sideboard drawer in the hall where I left my mark (the first of many in this town) scraped inside the walnut case of an old chiming clock. One morning I watched the family leave their house at 8.20 in their blue estate. The next morning I saw them arrive at Wengham Grammar, where the boy got out (8.32) without a word and stomped up the drive carrying his flute case. The morning after, I was at the station in time to see the estate turn into the car park (8.39), where the man of the house got out and, pausing to plant a kiss on his wife's offered cheek, took the 8.55 to London, where I happened to know he worked as an accountant for GGV, a French-owned insurance company. The next morning (8.45), equipped with my opera glasses, I watched his wife arrive at the upmarket Aube Massey store in town, where she sold soft furnishings on the second floor. That lunchtime, I saw her at work, showing customers bolts of fabric in her saleslady's white blouse and black skirt and fashionably tousled hair, clacking back across the sales floor in her heels to answer the telephone. As she passed I recognized her perfume from the master bedroom. It almost came as a surprise to hear her speak.

So there we are. I squeezed the juice out of them, though they didn't know it. Simon and Jennifer (Jenny) Finch and their young Thomas, 45 Holland Road. They were my first subject. The first butterfly pinned to my board. There would be rarer and brighter ones, but they were the first.

And so we love, we tire, and we move on. Eventually the house was sold, of course, but I didn't mind. I knew where they'd gone (3 The Maples, on the north side of town). And who could say that I wouldn't get a hankering to see them again one day when the world had turned a few more times and the adventure seemed fresh and thrilling once more.

The new people, incidentally, were equally fascinating. That's another story, but also the point. They are all other stories.

In case I haven't said, this was the job from heaven.

But, you ask, what does this become? I can say that it grows and evolves and makes its own idiosyncratic demands; that it's a faith or master that will not be easily spoken against by ordinary reason; that this faith or master is a joy to serve; and that you proceed from first principles.

To start, there is the easy pleasure of the kind you might

describe as 'entry level' – i.e., that arising from access gained via legitimate means. The client hands you the key, you arrive at the house an hour or so ahead of the buyer, you absorb the atmosphere and carry out a little groundwork, you leave your mark and you open a file.

But then the challenge. The day comes when the view from the foothills has grown too familiar and you feel the lure of higher, bracing air, the urge to add a layer of complexity. You feel your breath quicken. You bind yourself to the category of uninvited guest. Now comes the question of weighing the balance of elements peculiar to a property. What are the chances of getting in and out without being noticed? What does the interior layout present in terms of risk and reward? Are you going to end up on a roof, looking for a drainpipe? Are you looking for relaxation today, or danger? Novelty? Endurance? Degree of difficulty? Or the sublime euphoria of full immersion? (I should say that the latter, though it can and surely must be done – more of which later – is not for the faint-hearted or the unprepared.)

For now, let us say there are varieties of hazard. Here lies the frisson of apprehension and planning. But also calamity. What would be an obvious act of madness in ordinary circumstances assumes, in a dazzling burst of enthusiasm, the shape of a reachable, ripe desire. Any fool, for example, might work out that a flat is much easier to get into when the owner is out than to get out of when the owner is in (having arrived back unexpectedly and slammed the door and sighed with relief, perhaps at the thought of a well-earned cup of tea). So I should mention the day I most resembled the other sort of fool. I thought I was being daring, opportunistic – and, to be frank, with a few years under my belt I would have seen what to do, would more instantly have balanced those elements before me and turned what looked hopeless into an opportunity of a rarer kind. What followed, instead, was ignominious and sudden flight, which no doubt distressed the poor owner (a woman and her grocery shopping) in the midst of filling her kettle. Don't ask what I would have done if she had seen me. All I know is that, though I had barely started out in this admittedly singular endeavour, I already felt I had everything to lose. But I took the lesson to heart. After seventeen years I can count on the fingers of one hand the times I have been surprised in the act, if not physically caught – mostly from expecting too much pleasure from too little thinking. I have only once been challenged face to face (again, more of which later).

If anything, these days I suffer from a superabundance of alertness to hazard. I know where the exits are. Over the years, I have become birdlike, wary of minor fluctuations. For the most part, the daily crumbs of bread are there for the taking – nothing more menacing than a breath of wind shakes the leaves; a change in shadow signifies only the movement of cloud. But still one prepares for an earthquake.

And so what it becomes, to answer your question, is second nature. Here, among strangers' belongings, is where I am most at home, moving quietly and surely. I know where they keep their private things, how they arrange their lives. I follow their plans and make mine around them. I try not to enquire deeply into the why, but humbly accept my gift, the exhilaration of being here, of breathing the air at this altitude. I will confess there is ritual. I leave my mark using the key to a red moneybox my mother gave me. I will eat or drink something, perhaps take a small keepsake – a teaspoon, a sock. But I also have my standards. No hidden cameras, wires or microphones are used in the making of my 'art'. I don't peep through windows. Where is the pleasure in that? I am not a stalker, or a voyeur. I am simply sharing an experience, a life as it happens. Think of me as an invisible brother or uncle or boyfriend. I'm no trouble. I may be there when you are, or when you are gone, or more likely just before you arrive. I agree it is an idea that takes some getting used to. But do we not all have a life to make, to mould it somehow around that of others, to search for the dovetail that seems best to fit?

Who could argue with that?

5

TWO THINGS HAPPENED WHEN I was twenty-one. The first was that I inherited what was left of my mother's money and invested it, along with my savings from Mower's, in four acres of disused railyard that ran along the wrong side of the river, facing the backs of a stretch of derelict, boarded-up commercial properties.

The second thing was that Guy left the firm. For some months he'd been ill, having managed to poison himself, as Stella told it, courtesy of a thawing chicken in his fridge that had dripped into a dish of cooked pasta on the shelf below. He kept threatening to get well but then got worse again. He lost nearly twenty kilos in weight, and at some stage it was not unreasonably decided by Mr Mower that Guy's recovery was likely to keep him off work for longer than a middling family business could reasonably bear. Obviously we all sympathized, but he had no alternative, he said, but to wish Guy well and pay off his contract with the firm.

In view of Guy's often high-handed treatment of me, I couldn't say I was sorry to see him go. At first it had been low-level sniping dressed up as teasing, usually out of earshot of Mr Mower. That much might have been expected. But things had begun to change. Although I was still officially the trainee, I had long since done my day releases at college and passed my driving test and by now had handled and completed a number of sales in the way Mr Mower had taught me – adopting his old-fashioned manners and the tweedy dress and thick-soled brogues of the country town professional, courtesy of Hilde & Son, local gentlemen's outfitters. I was the coming man. Perhaps I shouldn't have been surprised that Guy would take it so personally.

It was some weeks before his first spell in hospital that he engineered a crisis in the office that led to a rift between Mr Mower and me. The first I knew of it was when Mr Mower stormed furiously into the office one morning, having just called a client from home with regard to their imminent exchanging of contracts on Brierley Grange.

'Mrs Wendell was *very* puzzled,' Mr Mower said, looking at us all. 'Can anyone guess why she was very puzzled?'

No one could guess.

'Because it turns out that the Wendells pulled *out* of the Brierley Grange sale two days ago.' Mr Mower waited for the import of his words to sink in. 'Yes, I'm astonished too. But it seems she left a message on our answerphone first thing Wednesday morning. And when no one called back, she rang again in the afternoon. And spoke to a young man . . .'

It was now that Guy looked pointedly at me – indeed, led the others to look at me – causing me in turn to pause for a second, as if . . . *could* it have been me? No . . . no, I absolutely *hadn't* spoken to Mrs Wendell. Had I? The seed of doubt was sprouting and blossoming because Mr Mower, while not quite actually accusing me, was addressing me directly on how the devil *anyone* could be capable of such blatant negligence, that it *simply* wasn't good enough, and that the collapse of this sale had now derailed four of our other properties down the line, leaving a fine old damned mess. 'I'll get on to it,' Guy said, wedging the phone between his jaw and shoulder. While Rita dug out contact numbers, I continued to protest my innocence – pointing out that in fact I now distinctly remembered coming in on Wednesday morning to find no messages on the answerphone and thinking it was unusual. But no one cared about the answerphone now, and the more I protested, the more Mr Mower said, with some crossness, that the damage was done, and soon everyone was busy on the phone while I stood by until Guy completed my public shaming by suggesting I make myself useful by running out to the café for doughnuts. 'I need fuel,' he said importantly.

It was him. I knew it was him. I could tell by the way he sent long, warning looks in my direction the rest of that day and the following week that it was him. He had wiped the answerphone clean of Mrs Wendell's message, then failed to act on her follow-up call, with a view to nothing less than making me look like a schoolboy halfwit.

Then two weeks after the Wendell debacle, three rival buyers on the brink of making me offers for an unattractive but extremely well-priced house with conversion potential rang within an hour of each other to count themselves out. None of them was able to give me a convincing reason for their change of heart. Was it bad luck? Was it something I'd said? Mr Mower pursed his lips at the news but remained silent.

I brooded for half an hour then jumped in my car and sprang a visit on one of the buyers who I knew worked at a motor dealership on the town bypass. At first he thought I was a customer and came sauntering out when he saw me browsing the used models in the forecourt. He became flustered when he realized who I was, and gibbered about the weather and market conditions in auto sales until I eventually pinned him down on the question of the house. After further humming and hawing he said he had been put off buying by reports about the neighbour.

'The neighbour?'

'Look,' he said, 'I'm not against people with mental problems. It's a tragedy. My gran's in a home, but you know . . . we've got kids. And they've got this guy wandering in the street in his pyjama top? He's not even that old apparently. And I hear he's pretty full-on when he gets going. A lot of disturbance, night and day, shouting and banging and crying. Once they saw smoke pouring out of the window.'

Was any of this true? I'd heard nothing about it.

'I'm pretty sure there's nothing in this,' I said. 'Why don't you let me look into it? Perhaps arrange another viewing. I'm sure the vendors would be able to reassure you.'

He grimaced. 'Sorry. I don't think so.'

'I really think whoever told you this might be pulling your leg.'

He looked at me. 'I can tell you it's from the horse's mouth. People in the business. With respect, that's the trouble with you guys. You only give us half the story.'

I drove back to the office and called the man selling the house. No, there had never been any problems with a neighbour. Yes, there were one or two families on the street caring for elderly relatives but there had never been any trouble. I believed him.

Guy was the trouble. This had his paw-prints all over it.

But I could be trouble too. A couple more weeks went by, and I heard Guy hissing at someone on the phone one afternoon, saying they had to call him later at home. This was suspicious in itself – when Mr Mower and Stella were out of the office, Guy was more than happy to spend large portions of what he called 'down time' purring down the phone at impressionable shop girls or cackling with his drinking chum at the builders' merchants. But then later he hung back in the office when the rest of us were leaving and the cleaner was just arriving. 'I've just got a couple of clients to catch up with,' he explained.

I stood in the entrance to the shopping arcade opposite the office where I could see him hunched over his desk talking on the phone. Then he put the phone down and waited by the fax machine. For the next fifteen minutes he shuttled urgently between the fax and the photocopier. At last he came out with his briefcase. I stepped back into the shadows and watched him get into his car and drive off.

The next morning I was first in the office, with Rita, who had opened up. When she went to put the kettle on, I had a look around. There was nothing of interest on Guy's desk. But there were clues: an activity report on the fax with a phone number; the photocopier was set to magnify at 200 per cent. I pressed the redial button on Guy's phone. A woman answered. It was the district council – the planning office. How could she help? I asked her for the fax number there. No problem, she said. It matched the last number logged on the activity report. Oh, Guy, what are you up to? I can't pretend I wasn't just a little excited.

I waited until Friday, when Guy usually spent the afternoon in the office clearing his paperwork ahead of the weekend rush. After lunch, while he was taking his customary endless lavatory break, I lifted his keys from his jacket. I told Rita there were a number of outstanding For Sale signs that needed picking up around town, and that I'd be out in the van if anyone asked.

Guy's rented two-room flat was a five-minute drive away. I left the van somewhere out of sight and let myself in. I stood for a moment, just to test the atmosphere. The door to his bedroom was ajar, leaking his sour sleep-odours into the air. I pushed open a second door to reveal a bachelor lair, dark and untidy, with a leather sofa and an outsized TV with video player and a collection of action movies. Near the window was a dining area, and there, spread on the table with Guy's unwashed coffee mug, were sheets of photocopied A4 paper arranged in a large rectangle.

This was it – a draughtsman's plan, rubber-stamped with the council's logo and marked RIVER DEV 1. At first glance it looked like a layout of the town centre, not very different from the ones that had accumulated over the years in a cupboard at the office. But in this version the main road with its stretch of small run-down businesses had disappeared, freeing up space for 'pedestrianized retail'. There were shaded residential blocks, and a 'walkway' now snaked along the waterside. The reason for Guy's furtive activity was highlighted in yellow: a wedge of land between the station and the river. I knew this plot – an eyesore you could see from the bridge across the railway line, piled with stones and gravel and dotted with ramshackle buildings and rusting equipment. It looked unsellable. But here it was arrowed excitedly with a pair of question marks. Obviously Guy and his friend at the council were hoping to make a killing with inside information, snapping up this land before this scheme was made public and then selling it on to a developer. But did Guy even have money? That seemed unlikely. A search through his drawers turned up nothing but old pay cheques from Mower's and motor insurance and utility bills and overdraft statements. No tell-tale applications for mortgages; no hidden investments. Maybe his partner was the one with the money and Guy was in for a cut, presumably for reasons to do with Mower's.

My first thought was simply to expose Guy, but then in a

glorious moment of clarity, I saw instead what could be. I saw the future. I was twenty-one and I saw it right there, in Guy's kitchen.

His breakfast dishes were still in the sink. I opened his grubby fridge. He'd done some shopping for the weekend. I remember helping myself to a mini apple pie from an open pack. And then there was the raw, thawing chicken – an invitation in itself, sitting there in its pool of pink meltwater, and requiring only a tilt of the plate (the top shelf of the fridge was conveniently full) and a minor rearrangement of the food on the deck below. What could be more perfect? It was easy to imagine Guy arriving home that evening having stopped off at the Cutters for Friday beers with his foolish friends, too tipsy to swear with any certainty that he had clingfilmed that dish of leftover pasta, just lurching in, starving for his supper, tucking instantly into the first thing he found. And don't they say revenge is a dish best served cold? Myself, I had never cooked at home. This wasn't the kind of accident that could happen to me. But Guy. You had to shake your head at him.

I left his flat as he would expect to find it, drove across town to copy his key, then slipped it into his pocket while he was on the phone, no doubt planning his evening. If Rita ever wondered where those For Sale signs had got to, she never mentioned it.

I wasn't too surprised when Guy didn't turn up the next morning, or even when he didn't pick up when Rita rang him. 'That's odd,' she said.

'Perhaps he's eloped.' I grinned. 'With Stella.'

Rita didn't see the joke. 'Stella has appointments this morning.'

I needed to move quickly, but the weekend would buy me some time. I made sure to go out to the site, a neglected, debris-strewn yard next to the station, a high perimeter fence erected against vandals, a locked gate. There was nothing to suggest the site was for sale, just warning notices from a security firm that guard dogs were patrolling the grounds. I took down their phone number and called it from a phone box. The man who answered didn't know who owned the yard but gave me the contact number he was supposed to call in case of problems. 'Ask for the divestments office,' he said. 'But there'll be no one there till Monday.'

Next morning, Mr Mower called me at my digs at Mrs Burton's to ask if I'd mind coming in and standing in for Guy on the Sunday rota. Stella had been round to Guy's place but there was no one in. It wasn't until Monday that she found out what had happened: that he'd been sick after eating something; that things had worsened and he'd gone out for air in the early hours and fainted in the street; that he'd had to be taken to hospital. 'He's pretty ill,' she said. I copied Rita's anxious expression. Stella smiled. 'Don't worry, he'll live.'

That afternoon I went into Guy's flat again. Not only did I find the faxes from the council but also one of our enquiry cards ripped out of the office file. Back at the office I found the property listed but dormant, with a line through the entry. There was no sign of it having been worked on or the vendor having pursued a sale. The price, of course, would be rock-bottom. I called them to ask if they were still selling, and told them I might have an interested buyer.

'These are the buyers we talked about a couple of weeks ago?'

'Ah, that would be Guy you spoke to,' I said. 'He's away at the moment. But now the people are asking if you could move a little on price.'

It took a while, but I bought the site, using an out-of-town lawyer as a purchasing agent. By then, Guy's absence – prolonged, it turned out, by complications arising from his chronic stomach complaint, an added bonus – had given me a chance to shine again for Mr Mower. I got one of Guy's moribund properties moving by persuading the vendors to amend Guy's unrealistic valuation down a notch or two (by asking how they felt about the whispers going round that nearby common land was being earmarked as a stop-over for travellers). Mr Mower was certainly surprised at my instant success with what he remembered to be an unpromising brownfield site by the river that Guy had taken on a year ago. Imagine his delight when I announced that I had found a firm buyer.

'That really is excellent news.' He beamed. 'Who has taken it?'

'Damato Associates. They want to build a skateboarding park.'

'Skateboarding, you say? Splendid.'

This was a long time ago. It was early days for skateboards, at least in our town, but it made me smile to imagine the alarm on the faces of council officials at the prospect of scores of rowdy youths hanging out opposite their new development. But of course that was just mischief. I sat on my investment. I waited. Then just when I was starting to fear that I *would* have to open a skateboarding park, the council went public and things took off. It was an exciting time. In the years that followed, every middling town across the country was looking to turn its stagnant, weed-clogged waterways into a valuable environment for sleek apartments, shopping and private gyms. Ours was one of the first.

Oh, Guy. I never saw him again, though I went back into his flat one more time. I half expected to be greeted by the smell of stale vomit and diarrhoea, though I knew Stella had sent one of our cleaners in to spruce the place up. I was in there barely thirty seconds when I heard a bang at the window that made me jump out of my skin. I listened hard. Nothing. I waited a few minutes then crept to the window. A smear of blood was streaked across the pane. I pulled back immediately. There was the faintest stirring outside now. I moved to the door and listened, my heart thudding. Nothing. Then I went back to the window and waited. At last I risked opening it a fraction and inching my head out. It was just a bird lying dead on the ground. I almost laughed out loud. Before I left I took a few pictures – of Guy's suits, hanging in the wardrobe, and of his fridge, now empty, fresh and gleaming whitely. Then on his answerphone in the hall I found two old messages, both saying the same thing. 'Guy, it's me. Where the hell *are* you?'

6

TIME HAS FLOWN, SHALL we say. My life is as fixed as the stars. I feel a bond of kinship with the town that took me to its bosom, and now, in turn, I watch over its interests. But I have always had to look out for myself first, to find a position of strength. I knew this long before the trouble with Guy, long before my name eventually replaced Mr Mower's above the door. The unseemly tussle for money has to be seen in that context. Money gave me the best seat in the house, and that was all I needed. You wouldn't guess I was well off. I don't sit on committees; the local Rotarians don't know me; I have no active interest in the Chamber of Commerce. But a decent amount of my income is quietly siphoned into good works – schemes to keep youth occupied in our less salubrious housing estates. I fund a community centre and three toddler groups and Heming's sponsors local schools and adult evening classes. I won't go on. The people around me in more recent times – Zoe, Katya and the others – have even probably wondered at my own frugality: my modest car; my reluctance to take a holiday; my sturdy but unchanging wardrobe. Even if they found these signs of moderation consistent with my other small eccentricities (my insistence on being called Mr Heming, perhaps), they would doubtless be shocked to discover that my small flat, located in an unassuming development near the Common, was a furnished all-in rental listed in our own books and paid for in cash every month by a Mr Luckham (yes, a name borrowed from doughty Mrs Luckham at school), a quiet, anonymous tenant and low consumer of power and heating. The truth was that, as much as I loved this nurturing town that gave me purpose and happiness, I could pack all tangible evidence of my existence into two suitcases and leave in half an hour. I could disappear and start again. I lived with the knowledge that it could come to that.

Even Zoe, with whom I'd had a brief personal dalliance, knew nothing of my domestic arrangements – though I should say that keeping her in ignorance was far from easy, and required a level of tact and guile disproportionate to the rewards. In the end I had to choose between the benefits of everyday sexual convenience and the practical need to keep my personal self from the intimate gaze of others.

No doubt you are shocked to discover that I am drawn to the benefits of everyday sexual convenience. It is true that I have stood in a stranger's wardrobe with my head in their clothes, but I'm not the sort of man who gets his thrills from masturbating in their pockets. Far from it. Indeed, you may infer from my coup long ago with Marrineau's girlfriend Sarah that my impulses in that respect are within the usual spectrum. If I smile at a woman, I am aware of a response. In my earlier days at Mower's there were one-night stands, though these were generally out of town, and always at the girl's place. In substance nothing much has changed, though responsibility and position have made me more circumspect. There are one or two ladies I see discreetly, straight in and out, as it were, with cash changing hands. I can afford a hotel room, thank you. A massage will often do the trick. Essential maintenance, you might say. But there's nothing that would frighten the horses. A casual observer – perhaps someone in my own wardrobe! – would see nothing of unconventional interest.

Zoe was the sort of mundane error that follows from the proximity of men and women in a small office. I was her boss, but not much older than she was. Her green eyes and helpful smile followed me often. She offered a certain allure, a mystery, as it seems to me all women do. It lasted six weeks, though in truth her appeal in those romantic terms began to wilt from the moment she invited me into her house. This, of course, was a turning point: the removal of allure and mystery. Perhaps I might have admired her more if I could have just had a scout round the place without her there to complicate things with her questions about my background and taste in music, or eagerly watching my face as I spoke, trying to read my thoughts. What can I say? Invisibility has for so long been the linchpin to my favourite, most memorable moments. This was the opposite as dear Zoe tried to coax me out of my hole and into the light.

My secrecy was a joke that became an issue. 'But where do you *actually* live?' She would laugh, as if I were merely teasing her. There was no doubt that if I took Zoe back to my place, she would get the wrong idea, or worse, the right one. She was hurt when I called it a day, and quite rightly found my reasons uncompelling ('This isn't really working . . .'; 'It's not you, it's me . . .'), inspired as they were by the three romantic comedies I had watched in her company, snuggled too closely together at the cinema. I assured here there was no one else. The truth was that rampant sexual relationships are all very fine and necessary but, for me, real intimacy is elsewhere. It is something to impart and absorb, something to be filled with, quiet and slow. It soothes. It fires the senses.

I expected Zoe to leave the agency, but she stayed, perhaps to convince herself that I didn't matter, or just to prove me wrong about whatever it was about her open heart and easy laughter I didn't like. Perhaps, too, she enjoyed the fact that we had an unspoken shared history – as if we were keeping something from Katya, my senior sales consultant and a practical woman who I am certain couldn't have cared less. Whatever her reasons, Zoe was as bright as ever around the place, often so bright – so cheerful – as to be worrying. There were dates with other men after work, generally telegraphed by the nonchalant application of lip gloss at the close of business. Most recent was an entanglement with some dream man, which she unsubtly dangled under my nose until it crashed and floored her for weeks. Katya gave me a warning glance when she came back, but said nothing, as is Katya's reserved Lithuanian way.

The mess with poor Zoe taught me how much of a distraction she had been from the job in hand. My general wish, as ever, was to keep people happy and life rolling smoothly. A fairy godfather. A ministering angel. To this end, as I said, I keep my eyes open. In my meanderings through the homes of my fellow citizens, I'm more than happy to change a lightbulb or rewire a hazardous plug, or sort out a dangerous boiler. Way back, Mr Mower indulged my instincts for a holistic approach to estate agency, and paid for night classes in various aspects of building care, basic then intermediary. I was a passionate student. I am quite advanced now. I know how a house fits together, its wiring and plumbing, its bricks and joists and ventilation, its risk of structural collapse or infestation. People can be scatter-brained. There's always some chump going off for the weekend and leaving half the windows open or a faulty cistern clocking up ruinous expense on a water meter.

But there are people, too, who need to be firmly dealt with. I keep a hammer behind my back, so to speak, for loudmouths and show-offs. I suffer them, as everyone does, on busy trains (I travel to London once a month), shouting into phones and spreading their important belongings over the seats; or in town, heaving their giant ostentatious cars on to the pavement rather than finding a place in one of our numerous reasonably priced car parks. They are the same people who allow the spreading branches of their trees to darken and shed leaves and fruit on their neighbour's lawn; their raucous dinner parties go on into the night; they are a voluble presence on town committees and loudly spur on their poor children from sports-field touchlines or the front rows of school entertainments. We know them because they demand to be known.

Yes, what I describe is a composite villain, an identikit social grotesque. But how perfectly some people seem determined to fit its silhouette!

I knew Preece Gwyndyr from several years back. We had sold him and his wife a house in the leafy Pipers, a horseshoe of luxury new-builds, each with a landscaped quarter-acre, on the site of the old hospital. I saw the couple from time to time, alerted by the distinctive hectoring tone of Gwyndyr's Welsh voice, then catching sight of his livid complexion through a crowd, perhaps at a school fundraising evening (local functions are excellent places to watch, hear and learn) or a summer fair. His wife, in a circle of listeners, would watch him speak with a fierce pride, her eyes blinking like a bird as she balanced a cup and saucer or clutched a glass of wine. Like most former clients, they didn't know me. I was as invisible to them as the day I showed them round their house and persuaded them that our town was just the place for their growing family. (I wished I hadn't, and indeed there have been newcomers whose tempting offers I failed to pass on to vendors on the grounds that a small town can only accommodate so many citizens of monstrous self-esteem.)

Late one wintry afternoon I saw – or at least caught sight of – Gwyndyr when I was out walking. It had been raining all day, and I had my head down, but I recognized his car – a silver behemoth with ski carriers on top and a dragon sticker in the rear window – and made out his profile as he swept past me on a country lane heading back into town. I didn't quite see what happened, but a percussive clatter sounded in the air as he reached a stretch of road facing a cottage on its own. I saw that the rain had flooded the road on one side and on the left was a small car, parked hard against the grass verge. I assumed it belonged to whoever lived there. Clearly Gwyndyr had clipped the car, trying to take the narrow gap at speed. Now he had stopped in the middle of the road, his brake lights glowing in a moment of doubt, perhaps wondering if I – fifty yards away and closing in – could read his number plate in the drizzle and failing light. I hoped he'd do the right thing but suspected he would not, and, sure enough, in an instant he lurched off again until he was out of sight. No one came out of the cottage as I quickened my step to inspect the damage: the mirror casing was hanging in space, and there was broken glass on the puddled tarmac. The car was a cherry red and, though dulled with age and bearing the odd scar, looked well cared for.

I carried on home, where I wrote out a note giving Gwyndyr's name and address, then drove back to the scene. It was dark now and a light was on in the cottage. I slipped the note – in a plastic bag to keep out the rain – under the car's windscreen wiper, then went home. Early next morning, on the Sunday, I drove back and found a spot down the road with a view of the cottage. Some time after nine a woman emerged and locked the door behind her. She was probably in her sixties and neatly dressed. She saw the note first and then, with dismay, the smashed mirror. She read the note and looked up and down the lane. Then she folded the note with what I saw as an air of resolution, got into the car and set off. I ducked as she passed my own car, then followed her. It wasn't difficult. She was a slow driver and there was little traffic in town. But instead of taking a left in the direction of the old hospital site, she turned right and up the hill, eventually pulling up behind a row of parked vehicles outside St Theobald's. She was going to church. I might have guessed.

But in a way this made things easier. I drove home, put the kettle on and found out the times of St Theobald's services. Then I walked across town to the Pipers. Finding a spot with a view of the Gwyndyrs' front door wouldn't be easy, but I knew there was a wooded area surrounding the development, and a pathway where people walked their dogs and which provided a scenic route past local shops and a primary school and cemetery back to the town centre. From here a narrow public right of way cut through the Pipers. It wouldn't be a good idea to loiter, but if I timed it right I would be able to see the woman if and when she arrived. Last night's rain had cleared. To kill time I walked slowly to the shops and bought a newspaper, which I pretended to leaf through as I dawdled back along the path.

I checked my watch. The parishioners would be out of church now. If she was coming at all, she would want to get it over with sooner rather than later. Maybe she needed to go into this encounter spiritually fortified. I waited at the top of the path with my head in the paper, as if halted in my steps by an engrossing football story. I didn't have to wait long. Within minutes I saw the woman's cherry-red car turn into the crescent but then pass out of sight. A car door slammed, and immediately I heard Gwyndyr's barking voice. And now, as I made my way down the path between the fences of adjacent properties and out into the horseshoe, I could see that the woman's car was blocking the exit to Gwyndyr's drive, where his own massive vehicle stood with the engine running. I walked slowly down the side of the street facing the house. I could barely hear the woman's voice, but I could see she was showing Gwyndyr the note and the damage to her wing mirror. I could tell by Gwyndyr's tone ('I can *assure* you, dear lady . . .') that her protests would come to nothing. His wife emerged on the doorstep of the house wearing a housecoat and slippers and holding a Siamese cat (a second one peered from between her bare calves), and watched approvingly as her husband dismissed the woman's claims and insisted she move her vehicle. The woman stood helpless for a moment, then got back into her car, switched on the engine and struggled to make a clean three-point turn while the couple looked on.

She passed me on the corner, her face pale with upset. My heart went out to her, this elderly woman of the parish. My imagination was already busy conjuring her widow's habits and domicile – an inglenook fireplace with poker and coal scuttle; a tabby cat curled on the hearthrug; biscuits; a coronation toffee tin containing her savings; a black-and-white photograph of her husband on the sideboard, killed in the course of some noble service.

What could a mirror like that cost to replace? Just under forty pounds, as it turned out. The unit was available at a local stockist and it wasn't difficult to find a young mechanic willing to come out and fit it for a generous hundred in cash after his Saturday morning shift at a local auto repair. You might ask how I knew that Mrs Wade would be absent that weekend at her daughter Rachel's house in Ely (a good train ride away) – or for that matter how I came to know her name. Instead, picture her astonishment when she returned and saw justice restored.

By then Gwyndyr was also finding his life unexpectedly rich in mystery, albeit in a less welcome way. I can only imagine how frustrating it must have been for a busy man such as himself to wake up on successive mornings to find his shirt buttons pinging off as quickly as he tried to fasten them – or, worse, as he was perhaps eating that second breakfast on the train or in the office. And his shoelaces – why, it was almost as though someone had cut them three-quarters of the way through with a scalpel (I always carry a scalpel). Gwyndyr had a fine collection of watches, which he kept in an old-fashioned rosewood display case on his dressing table. But where was his 1970s Rolex – his favourite? Where indeed! (In my mind's eye I saw Gwyndyr turning the marital bedroom upside down in search of his precious watch, buttons flying off his shirt, giving his wife merry hell.) I had no idea of the watch's value, but a dry-lipped pawnshop owner in Bethnal Green said he'd give me a hundred and fifty for it. 'Excellent!' I said, with a brightness that probably surprised him.

The following Wednesday, Mrs G arrived back from her weekly appointment with her hair stylist to find water dripping through their sitting room ceiling from a spurting joint in an upstairs radiator. She called the plumber. On the Friday, it happened again, this time a faulty connection on the compression tank. Oh, the drip, drip of steady mischief!

On Saturday, a delivery truck appeared with a new washing machine they hadn't ordered, and in the evening two fuses blew, plunging the house into darkness during dinner with the Ericksons. On the Monday, a rowing machine arrived, followed on Wednesday by a suite of teak garden furniture. In a state of alarm, the Gwyndyrs cancelled the credit card that had seemingly, somehow, called up retail suppliers and ordered these goods, though that didn't stop more arriving (did they forget they had other credit cards?): they were soon the bewildered recipients of an electric piano, a wedding dress, ornamental statuary, and a handsome leather dressage saddle from an equestrian superstore. The police could only scratch their heads. The morning post, meanwhile, brought daily confirmations of holidays booked in Mauritius, New Zealand and the Norfolk Broads, along with tickets for London musicals and a festival of traditional sports in the Highlands.

For weeks the Gwyndyrs lived in fear of the doorbell. After an Easter break visiting relatives in Wales, they arrived home to find the house full of miaowing cats, which had gained entry via the cat flap but hadn't been able to get out again, not even to pee. Had Mrs G mistakenly switched the cat flap to 'in-only' before driving their own two Siameses, Pootle and Ming, to the kennels? In the absence of alternative evidence (all traces of inducement – fishy baits, free kitty dinners inside – had of course been removed), who could the Gwyndyrs blame but each other?

During their next absence, an out-of-town firm of landscape architects, paid in advance (in cash, their records would show, by a Mr P. Gwyndyr, who had personally come into their office with instructions and had even greeted their chainsaw-wielding operatives on arrival), removed a handsome yew hedge that bordered their property to the north. A few mornings later, Mrs Gwyndyr rushed out in her bathrobe to challenge a team of contractors from the travelling community who told her in the roughest of terms and most impenetrable of accents that they had been hired to rip up the couple's semicircle of stone-paved driveway and resurface it with plain tarmac.

Unsurprisingly the Gwyndyrs were almost afraid to leave the house. In the autumn, Gwyndyr made the local paper when he was fined by magistrates after pleading not guilty to the theft of a tankful of diesel at a filling station. His explanation – that someone must have stolen his car, filled it up, and then returned it to his house – lacked credibility, and one assumes his solicitor wisely talked down the chances of a successful appeal. After all, where was the evidence? Forecourt CCTV cameras, as everyone knows, are positioned to monitor licence plates rather than drivers. There was no sign that anyone had broken into the car – and I had no doubt that the spare keys were still in the top right-hand drawer of the antique French tallboy in the hall where he and I had left them.

In the spring the Gwyndyrs put their house on the market. Zoe took the call, but of course I was more than happy to handle it myself. I sat on the sofa in their almost familiar sitting room – an invited guest now – with a clipboard folder on my knee. It was a beautiful day. A day for looking forward, I thought. Preece Gwyndyr stared right through me as I prattled on about the buoyancy of the market and how this lovely weather gave one itchy feet. His wife was nowhere to be seen.

'Will you be staying in the area, Mr Gwyndyr?' I asked.

He wouldn't, he said, adding nothing.

7

IT'S EASY TO SAY, now, that I wish I'd drawn a line under 4 Boselle Avenue, but there are some things you cannot let go. Certainly there was something about the man with the small incontinent dog that continued to rankle. Perhaps I felt that my honour – the *town's* honour – had not quite been satisfied. Or maybe I was still in the grip of excitement after the disappointment of the farcically unreliable Cooksons earlier that day. But in the great chain of things – and in view of what happened afterwards at 4 Boselle Avenue and other sites of disquiet around town – I shouldn't understate the influence of Aunt Lillian, who has become forgotten in all this talk of property developers, wing mirrors and unwanted rowing machines.

The last time I'd seen her was some weeks before my twenty-first birthday (and a couple of months before Mr Mower shook my hand and gave me a box of cards printed with my name and the words 'Sales Consultant'). She wrote to Mr Mower, enclosing my train fare and asking that I come to her house in Norfolk. I hadn't been there since leaving school, though she had visited me at the office twice in that time, with Mr Mower present, beaming and pouring coffee and relating details of my progress.

The town hadn't changed much, though it seemed smaller. She surprised me with a stiff embrace, and we sat in the garden, where she smoked one cigarette after another and looked across the lawn as we talked. The point of my visit seemed to be about my mother's legacy, though I'd already been contacted by the solicitor and there was little to add. She said she was glad things were turning out well for me at Mower's, and praised my mature outlook, which was clearly the result of independent living. From this, though, I sensed she wanted me to know that I was on my own now, that her duty in respect of my late parents was discharged. She didn't actually say it was a relief, but neither had she invited me to stay over. There was an evening train, she said, that should get me back to Mrs Burton's before eleven.

We went inside for tea and sandwiches. There was a small gateau from the bakery and she had put out napkins and silver cutlery. Over my teacup I glanced at the windows of the house across the street where the Damatos used to live, and I remembered the kitchen there with its cakes cooling on the wire rack. Aunt Lillian eyed me, and I said she looked well and complimented her on the new wallpaper. She went along with my new-learned charm but her wariness spoke sharply when I asked after cousin Isobel, of whom she said nothing more than that she had married an army officer and was living abroad. She wiped a smear of cream from the corner of her mouth, laid her fork on the plate and reached for her cigarettes. The fork sat gleaming in the soft light. I looked from it to Aunt Lillian. Inevitably it called to mind that dramatic finale at school, Marrineau roaring with shock, staggering backwards, my breakfast fork embedded in his cheek, blood dripping from the handle. It was a breathtaking sight. Yes, a pity it had to happen, of course. But what else could

I do? What else must a boy so unexpectedly cornered do if not *fight* his corner?

I felt my aunt seeing into my thoughts. When I went upstairs to the bathroom, she followed and pretended to be busying herself on the landing. I admit I would have liked to have a look around. I had wondered what had become of my school chest. Was it still in the loft, filled with my treasures – the letters and cards sent to my schoolmates, my jaundiced scribblings, Mr Stamp's rubber-band ball, the willow-pattern spoon? There was still an hour to kill before the taxi arrived to take me back to the station (my aunt was taking no chances), but my mind, as ever, idled with thoughts of opportunity. Perhaps she would have a heart attack, or be called away to a local emergency. Or I could pretend to take a train, book in at a B&B and (somehow) steal back into the house the next day while she was at a meeting of her neighbourhood widows' coven, or – what the hell – just beat her to death right now with the barometer at the bottom of the stairs, which once hung in an alcove of my mother and father's front room before all this started. I did nothing of the kind, of course. The fact was I had bigger fish to fry now. If anything, I wanted my aunt to see that she was right – that I *was* my own man, and had shed what traces of juvenile madness she might think me still capable of.

And yet, of course, the past was all that remained between us. Back at the table, she steered the conversation to my mother. The day she died, my aunt said, they'd had to physically drag me out from under the Victorian day bed in Grandma Browne's parlour. I wasn't crying. Just mute and defiant. My aunt paused with a frown, as if inviting me to explain my behaviour all those years ago. But no; it seemed she wanted to clear up whatever 'misunderstandings' I might have.

'Misunderstandings?'

'Your father and me.'

I took a sip of tea and said grandly that that wouldn't be necessary.

She gave me a vexed look, and said my mother (her dear sister, as she reminded me) had been ill for some years. Since I'd been born, in fact.

'Do you remember Riley?' she asked.

'The cat?'

She opened her bag and handed me a photograph she had clearly unearthed for this occasion. It was a picture of my mother as a surprisingly young woman holding a cat. It was a close-up but you could see signs of a falling coastal path and the sea below. I had seen the picture before, but now it reminded me of how little I remembered my mother's face – that it was her closeness I always sought to bring back when I visited her memory. More shocking, though, was that the person in the photograph resembled, more than anything, a slightly finer version of myself in a wig and make-up.

'The resemblance is so exact. You can see it now. Do you understand? Afterwards your father could barely look at you.'

Taken aback at first, now I almost laughed. What – because I reminded him of his dear dead wife? Because I was somehow the cause of my mother's illness (I loved the way she slipped *that* in). How foolish I had been all these years, thinking that the reason he couldn't look at me was that he was too busy looking at Aunt Lillian! Ha. I should have seen that coming.

I wondered afterwards whether my aunt had some sort of illness herself; that this attempt to get my father off the hook, and thereby herself, was part of some final spiritual cleansing. She would get no shrift from me; not because I didn't accept her version of events but because in fact I *had* thrown off the adolescent burden of wondering why some things happened to you and others you could make happen yourself.

She continued. I had to understand, she said, how difficult – *delicate* – the situation was. Things were not always what they seemed. She had always been on call to help, had always been there for us, meaning my father and me, sometimes at the expense of her own child. And worse, in those last months my father had suffered from mental exhaustion. What else could she do?

'Of course,' I said brightly. 'You fell in love. While I was out at the football with Uncle Richard.'

'Your uncle was not a victim in this,' she snapped.

'And me? Wasn't I a victim?'

She lit another cigarette. Her hand was shaking. Her fingers had always been stained with nicotine. 'You know what you did,' she said, smoke hanging between us over the table. 'Perhaps you'd best just take the money.'

I never saw Aunt Lillian again. I came back for her funeral the following year (coincidence, I think, rather than the power of wishes), travelling alongside Mr Mower in his car under the wide skies of wind-flattened Suffolk and Norfolk. He was, I remembered, a friend of the family, though I didn't know how (and, come to think of it, still don't). Cousin Isobel spoke to him at length but greeted me without warmth. We didn't go back to the house afterwards. Isobel's husband, a man in uniform, looked hard at me. I can't imagine what she might have told him.

8

MORE THAN ONCE DURING the afternoon Zoe caught me staring over my coffee cup into the street and asked to the point of solicitousness if she could help with something. Zoe in her most helpful mood can be trying on a slow day. It was quiet. Katya was out seeing clients. I set Zoe to work supervising young Josh in our long-term project of embedding our web pages with video of neighbourhood facilities and street-view links.

The man's name, I had discovered from the electoral roll, was Douglas Sharp, and he lived with a Judith Sharp – presumably his wife, the Judith Bridgens who had bought the house on Boselle Avenue some years before. On successive days I found myself wandering down Boselle at around the same time in the morning I had seen him that first morning. Most dog-walkers fall into a routine, but I didn't spot him. I could have watched the house (I am an extremely patient watcher) or I could have taken my key and gone back in. I *was* interested in him, and now I was interested in his wife, whom I must have met at least once before, when she bought the place. I wondered at the circumstances of their marriage. Perhaps some women were just attracted by rude oafs, I thought. Or maybe he was a powerful and charismatic rude oaf who was good in bed and had bags of money. But then wasn't she the one who owned the property? They seemed to offer all the ingredients for a short project.

My curiosity would no doubt have eventually got the better of me, but a week later I almost physically bumped into the man, coming through the swing doors of the library as I was going in. In his hurry he didn't look at me – just edged his angular frame past with no word in response to my muttered apology, and strode towards the centre of town. I won't say I wasn't caught in two minds. I love the library. I had long been in the habit of taking refuge there from time to time. Understandably I made use of its research facilities – for one thing, the local paper is archived there – but I was drawn too by its homely warmth, its shady isolated corners, its soothing, dim corridors of books where a man might browse and pick up the murmurings of the two or three librarians who pottered around: Margaret, who had been there as long as I could remember, and her interchangeable younger colleagues who came and went, I learned, from a librarianship college course in Cambridge. I knew by heart (from patient watching) the pin number that granted access to the librarians' secret room marked 'Private' beside the front desk where I assumed they made coffee and hung their coats and bags.

Today, though, I turned instead to follow Sharp. He was some way ahead, ducking into the ground floor of the multi-storey. If he had a car, I was wasting my time, but he was just taking a short cut, and continued past the rows of parked vehicles, exiting at the other side. Now he crossed the road, and was heading for the Common, where he had walked his dog the week before. He wasn't out for a stroll today, though he still seemed to be a man impatient to be somewhere else. Tall, in a suede jacket and casual trousers, his longish, thinning hair flapping in the wind, he might have just stepped out of some workplace, perhaps to run an urgent errand or grab a sandwich. It wasn't far off lunchtime, though he was nowhere near the shops now. There was a firm of self-important architects near the library. Maybe he worked there. Or at the council offices. But where was he going now? He followed the river path as he had done last time, hurrying but also furtive, trying to keep out of the puddles. I kept my distance, but after one of the bends in the river he disappeared – presumably, I realized, up a steep set of stone steps that led to a section of Raistrick Road, one of the main routes circling the town. By the time I reached the top of the steps he was nowhere in sight.

He hadn't had time to get very far. Facing the wall and the steps down to the river was a terrace of substantial Victorian houses – four or five bedrooms with serviceable attics and cellars – flanked at one end by a used-car showroom. The stretch of houses ran half a mile to the Fount Hill crossroads with its bakery and newsagent and other shops. I'd once had a key to the house adjacent to the showroom, but the buyer, to my dismay, had immediately converted the property to bedsits. I knew nothing about the other houses, except that Sharp – unless he had jumped on to one of the buses that passed here – must now be in one of them.

I kept my head down and walked slowly along. Judging by the array of doorbells on the top step of each address, it was evident that the entire stretch had been converted – probably, I now surmised, for student lets, this being on the bus route to both the art school and the teacher-training college, twenty minutes away in East Wickley. Only one house, the one with the blue door – number 84 – towards the end of the row, was intact, though it had seen better days: the marble steps were chipped, with weeds coming through, the fanlight was broken, the sills were peeling and the sash frames were probably rotten. As I passed, my eye was drawn by the movement upstairs of someone drawing the curtains.

I walked along as far as the used-car showroom and stopped to inspect the vehicles on the forecourt. The proprietor appeared in the doorway and asked if I was looking for anything in particular.

'Just browsing,' I said.

'Go ahead, sir. If you need anything, give me a shout.'

I walked up and down for ten minutes, then called the man back out. I had him explain the merits of one car versus another, keeping one eye on the house as we talked, until eventually I'd run out of questions and he'd run out of answers.

'It's actually for my wife,' I said. 'Perhaps I should fetch her down to see for herself. She'll probably go for the lime-green one,' I joked.

'Ah, quite so, sir,' he said, laughing.

Now, as I retraced my steps back towards the crossroads, I saw a figure surfacing at the top of the riverside steps. I carried on walking. It was a girl – a young woman, rather – in a red cagoule and boots, pushing a bicycle. We were approaching each other now. She seemed breathless, having hauled her bike up the steps, but a smile hovered in her expression like that of a child fresh from the playground. She didn't look at me as we passed each other, not even when I turned and saw her chaining the bike to the railings outside the house with the blue door. She still wore the innocent smile as she skipped up the steps and let herself in.

Do you believe in fate? I can't explain it, but I felt caught up in hers. It was like opening a door on a bursting torrent. My heart flew to her – this lovely Red Riding Hood to Sharp's wolf, no doubt already lying in wait, under the covers, his eyes ready to devour her. Ignoring my own cast-iron rules of discretion and hazard, I loitered an hour or more in the immediate vicinity (no one has referred more often to an estate agent's sales précis in the street or inspected the small ads in a newsagent's window more thoroughly), but neither of them emerged. I was exhilarated but also disoriented. And almost sickened. From a distance, I have loved couples, even illicit ones, in their joy and insularity. They say something about a town and its life. But here was something profoundly wrong. And this girl's cares were instantly mine. She was devotion and duty in one.

The episode had ruined all thoughts of a quiet hour in the library.

Back at the office I found Wendy, my admin, cutting a cake for Josh's birthday. 'I did tell you, Mr Heming,' she clucked. '*Friday.*'

Josh grinned as uncomfortable a grin as an eighteen-year-old could muster in the circumstance of being fussed over by three women at various stages of what he would consider old age.

'So you did,' I smiled, 'and indeed here I am. On Friday.'

Zoe gave me a doubtful look and poured me a cup of coffee, brushing my fingers with hers as she handed it to me. I said a few words about Josh's excellent progress, that he was a credit to his parents (whom I had once seen from a distance), and that the firm's long-standing policy of providing our trainee with a course of driving lessons – generously inaugurated in my own time under old Mr Mower, about whom no one present but me had more than the vaguest inkling – would be set in motion the moment someone, perhaps Wendy, got round to arranging it. To the surprise of no one but Zoe, who feared I had forgotten, I reached into my desk drawer and presented Josh with his own pair of opera glasses. Everyone clapped, no one more than Zoe, who shook her head as if I had been teasing everyone all along. The brief celebration petered out when a young couple came in off the street looking for a starter home. The phones started ringing, and Katya took the opportunity to debrief me in the back office on the day's viewings and new business.

But my mind kept returning to Sharp and the young woman with the bicycle. Sharp was a textbook philanderer and predator, the house in Raistrick Road his secret love nest. Indeed it seemed more likely now that this house, too, had been divided into flats, and that Sharp rented one of them for precisely this purpose. I thought of the girl's face – hopeful and eager, and yet innocent too. Perhaps she didn't know he was married.

But then perhaps he *wasn't* married. Maybe the Judith Sharp the man lived with was his sister, who had previously been married but had reverted to her maiden name and asked her brother to move in – perhaps following the break-up of his own marriage – to help pay the mortgage.

I knew nothing. And wasn't this what Aunt Lillian meant when she said things were not always as they seemed? That I had made something of nothing? That the glimpse of a woman laying her hand on a man's was as likely a sign of sympathy as passion? Indeed. Which is why I have made it my business to look further into things, to do good and put things right that are wrong. Perhaps my aunt would have died more peacefully had she condemned a little less and loved a little more.

9

THE WEEKEND IS NOT ideal for snooping. People come and go more randomly but less interestingly. It is only good for following someone if you want to see the inside of a supermarket or garden centre. So, as the next day was Saturday, I decided to leave things a couple of days, waiting till Monday before taking a chance on an early-morning stakeout of Boselle Avenue.

I arrived at 6.45 and edged my car under the trees just in time to see a woman – presumably Judith – closing the wooden gate of number 4. It was barely light yet, but I saw she was a redhead, mid-forties and dressed for the City in suit and heels, and carrying a cream raincoat and a laptop bag. There was nowhere she could be going but the station, presumably for the 6.55 to Liverpool Street. An hour later, the postlady arrived pulling her red cart. Another half-hour passed before Sharp himself emerged, dressed as he had been on Friday but wearing a scarf and carrying a backpack. I got out my phone and took a picture of him. There was a new white 4×4 parked in front of the garage but he was walking. I got out of the car and followed. He too went to the station, straight through the barrier with a season ticket. Was he travelling south or north? South, I guessed, scanning the timetable: three minutes. I bought a return that would take me three stops down the line, went through the barrier and crossed the bridge. There he was, buying a Danish. I sat on the bench and sneaked another picture of him. The train arrived. Sure enough it turned out he was only going as far as the next stop – nine minutes away at East Wickley. From there a short walk took us to the art school and teacher-training college. But between the two small campuses on the same road sat the town's further-education college. Here he stopped, unlooped his scarf and plugged earphones in from a music player, clearly turning himself into a jaunty lecturer showing a youthful profile to the students of hairdressing and leisure management who attended here alongside A-level dropouts and adult learners taking IT classes.

I took the next train back up into town. I supposed that Sharp worked part-time, hence his being free on a Friday afternoon. Judging by the timing, he would have caught the train back to town after his morning shift. But why take the train, which then meant coming through town and walking across the Common, when there was a bus service direct from his college to the house in Raistrick Road? But then I remembered the library. Of course. He must have been returning books.

Back in town, I called the college office, approximating my voice to a younger person's (I'd heard enough of Josh to carry it off). 'Yeah, hi, really sorry to bother you but, like, I'm supposed to see Douglas Sharp about my essay after his class, but I can't remember what time he said it was?'

'Would you like to speak to him?'

'God, no, I'll be in more trouble if he thinks I've forgotten.'

'OK, well, he has a lecture at ten and a class straight afterwards.'

'I think it was this afternoon . . . History, yeah?'

'History? He teaches English.'

'English. Yeah, that's what I mean.'

'Well, Mr Sharp has nothing timetabled for this afternoon. He's just Monday and Friday mornings and his Wednesday afternoon lecture.'

'Cool. That'll be it. Thanks.'

I supposed I had at least two hours. I headed back to Boselle Avenue and let myself in. There was a lingering smell of toast and cigarette butts. I leafed through the morning's post in the hall, all of it addressed to Judith – bills, a catalogue, junk mail – then I put the kettle on for tea. I flicked through a diary on the kitchen table and a file of papers I found in a writing desk in the dining room. Here was their marriage certificate – dating from two years ago – plus bank statements, mortgage documents in her name and a credit agreement for the 4×4 out on the drive. There were divorce papers from Judith's previous marriage, and various older letters to addresses in London, where it seemed she had lived and worked back then. A photo album showed snaps of the couple holding champagne flutes in some island paradise, draped in garlands and displaying their wedding rings. I moved from room to room, taking pictures and video. Upstairs was Sharp's study, piled with books and papers. The desk was littered – pens, CDs, a pack of paracetamol, a brown apple core, a globular paperweight recycled from green bottles. On the wall were photographs taken at bookish functions and a chart showing garden birds. Under the desk was a pack of flyers for a reading he had hosted the previous July at the bookshop in town.

I sat low in his chair, my feet planted on the laminate wooden floor as I scrolled through his emails and checked his bookmarks and browsing history – news providers, internet porn, a 'salon' celebrating modern literature, a dating site, online poker. Amid a shelf of movies were three or four homemade DVDs in plastic sleeves labelled with their subjects – Forssinger, Gates, McLarrily. These I copied on to my memory stick and replaced on the shelf.

Of course I had no idea what I was looking for, but I did feel I was getting some measure of this Sharp. He was working in a job beneath his qualifications; he had married a woman eight years his senior; he was a magnet for debt; he was a philanderer . . . what else?

How did the girl on the bicycle fit in? I'd only seen her once, but her image floated into my mind again and my heart turned to marshmallow. I wondered about her own place – a flat, I guessed – and tried to imagine her in it, moving from room to room, relaxing in front of the TV, dancing in the kitchen to music. I closed my eyes. I felt that if I lay on the bed here for one moment I would be lost in the dream of her – that the Sharps would arrive back and find me there, an unwakeable estate agent, like someone in a fairy story.

Had I forgotten something? It wasn't until I came downstairs and saw a vet's leaflet among others on a chair by the phone – 'National Flea Month' – that I realized what it was. Where was the dog? There was no sign of it: no bowl out in the kitchen, no dog lead or rubber chew or other doggy paraphernalia. And, come to think of it – I sniffed the air – no doggy smell.

I opened the side door that led to the utility room and then another door to the garage. I switched on the light. Here was a chic pale-blue car, a stepladder, a golf club, shears, a lawnmower, a tree-saw hanging on the wall. The car would be Judith's. The mower and shears, judging by the state of the garden – both back and front – were not often used.

I turned off the light, washed and dried my teacup and left the house as I found it: frustrated. Strangely – or strangely for me – the more I knew about Sharp, the more I wanted to know about the girl. And, of course, the more I wanted to see her again.

10

At MIDDAY I DROVE to the flat in Raistrick Road. What else could I do? No one showed up. I sat in the car watching for signs of life – a window opening, a shadow behind the curtains – but there was no one there. I returned to the office only when Katya called to remind me that we had a meeting at six with O'Deay's, a firm of developers with a gated estate of retirement bungalows coming to market. I nodded my way through the meeting, allowing Katya to steer proceedings. Afterwards she suggested a drink, perhaps a bite to eat; we had other items of business to discuss, not least a proactive new strategy for the Cooksons. 'They're going to the Seychelles for ten days. We could get some buyers in while they're away,' she said.

I shook my head. 'They won't do it. They're afraid that we'll walk dead leaves into the house. They think we won't be able to switch their burglar alarm on and off. Anyway, selling isn't their problem.'

I pleaded tiredness and raced in desperation back to Raistrick Road. My heart leapt when I saw that a downstairs light was on. But there was no cycle chained to the railings. Perhaps they had taken it indoors. I took out my opera glasses and hunkered down in the car. Some time after eight a pizza delivery man arrived, his moped throbbing at the kerb as he mounted the steps with a box and rang the bell. At last. I rolled my car window down. A light went on in the hall and the door opened. The pizza man was in my line of vision as business was transacted but I distinctly heard a female voice and laughter as the box disappeared into the house and the door closed again. I waited. I felt nauseous as I imagined the two of them on the sofa sharing supper. At 10.35 the light went out. Then a landing light appeared, followed by a lamp in the bedroom. It wasn't a flat then, as I'd thought, but a house. It somehow made things worse. The curtains glowed a deep red. But seconds later the place was in darkness. I wondered what excuse Sharp had given his wife. An educational conference? A sick friend?

And the girl? All I could do now was return early in the morning, then follow her home – or, more likely, to her place of work.

I drove home and started copying the images I'd captured at the Sharps' on to my computer. What puzzled me was that if the Raistrick Road property was not a flat conversion but a house – a three-storey townhouse offering leafy views and riverside walks – how could a part-time lecturer afford to rent it? Or rather, I thought, how did he disguise the expenditure? I ran through the couple's bank statement. There were no outlandish cash withdrawals – the mortgage was the single biggest outgoing, followed by a monthly instalment for Sharp's white 4×4, courtesy of Judith's substantial salary as HR director of a City insurance firm.

One thing I could do was find out who owned the property. I logged on to a land registry search, paid the fee and keyed in the address. It would take a few hours to come through, probably midmorning. Now I looked at the DVDs I'd copied on to my memory stick. I set the first film going. It showed some event – heads bobbing, glasses chinking – held at Warninck's, an independent bookshop near the arts cinema. The event looked well attended, bright-faced people milling around with wine amid light chatter and expectant mirth. Then Sharp himself came on to a small stage with a microphone and introduced a guest author, J. L. Forssinger. Sharp was quite the host, suavely interviewing Juliet, as he called her, as they sat facing each other in striped armchairs. Afterwards she put on glasses and read an extract that was followed by questions from the audience. And now here was red-haired Judith – planted by Sharp, no doubt, to get the ball rolling – asking Juliet when she'd first had the idea that she might one day become a crime writer.

The next video produced a similar scenario. This time after the reading Sharp moved among the audience with the microphone. Judith was there again, volunteering with the inaugural question, followed by one or two others. Then, miraculously – almost as if I'd dreamed her into the film – there she was . . . a lovely young woman in the crowd, speaking into Sharp's microphone, her bushy hair tied back. It was the moment they met. It had to be. As she made her contribution I watched him regarding her, smiling with a narrow-eyed, undisguised animal longing.

How my heart soared for her. How I hated him. Was this love?

I took a fresh scalpel from my box and sharpened my coloured pencils while I watched. 'The theme of loneliness is very strong in all of your books, Mr Gates,' she said. 'Where does that come from?'

I wondered whether Sharp even remembered now that this occasion was on film, this fine literary evening with his older wife fading into the throng of laughter, replaced by this fresh new blossom. The camera moved away to another questioner and I fast-forwarded the video for further glimpses of her, but there were none. I rewound and replayed the moment over and over. The girl's cheeks had the beginning of a pink glow. Her voice was more confident and resonant than I'd imagined (and, believe me, I had imagined) – a voice accustomed to speaking out, in a classroom, a debating chamber, a public arena. Far from being cowed by the proximity of minor celebrity, she seemed merely to be acceding to the assembled will to make a success of the evening, expressing solidarity with this town event using nothing more forceful than good humour and clear intelligence. I'd been looking for her all day and now, as if heralded by the stars and the planets themselves, she had come to me.

I left her image on screen and watched her, mid-question, from my couch until the screensaver kicked in. Even then, I felt her presence in the room. She seemed, at least for this moment, to belong here. I don't have the conventional comforts – I rarely watch TV, for example, and own only the most basic furnishings. But this is the place I sleep, surrounded by my keys, of course – shimmering on every wall under the dimmed lights like gold and silver, each opening a lock in a portal to pleasure and adventure. I go to sleep counting sometimes. I have no idea how many hundreds or thousands there are – randomly scattered, you might think, some out on their own, others hanging in twos or threes on their little hooks – though together they are a collage of the town, every pendent shadow a house and a way of life.

I lay down for a moment, closed my eyes and saw her again.

11

SOMETIMES YOU'RE JUST LOOKING at things upside down. It can happen when things are moving fast. I'm not perfect, though I realize that in the service of brevity I might have given the impression of super-efficiency, of one thing following rather too easily on the heels of another. Needless to say (though here I am saying it), I have edited out the hours of preparation, or even the hours of *not* doing something – of *not* jumping to the next ledge in a high wind; of beating an undignified retreat. Or, as I say, of just not seeing what is in front of me. I'm just saying, bear it in mind.

There I was next morning, waking fully dressed, my mind slow to free itself from a dream in which I was being pursued by assassins along twisting corridors of falling books. Light streamed through a crack in the curtains and I reached for my phone. It was 9.17. There was – aha! – an automated message in my email. The house in Raistrick Road last changed hands in 1976 and was owned by Giles (deceased) and Agnes Rice. There was no mortgage held against the property. It sounded like a renter.

I took a shower and put on fresh clothes, then pondered my

way to one of my favourite breakfast spots: the Wilsons' place, a detached flat-roofed house that stood above the railway line overlooking the sports centre and surrounding sports fields on the other side. I'd hardly eaten the previous day, so I made some eggs and toast (the Wilsons and their four children lived in the sort of homely chaos you could hold a wrestling tournament and hog roast in without making any discernible difference) and called the office to tell them I would be in later.

I had missed my dawn vigil at Raistrick Road, but today was Tuesday – Sharp was free all day, so the chances were he was still in bed. If his wife was at work and thought he was out of town with some legitimate excuse, he would be unlikely to return too early and risk being seen by a neighbour. More likely was that he would stay at Raistrick, perhaps waiting for the girl to visit during her lunch break. Oh, where was she now? Presumably she worked in town – hence her bike ride along the Common and riverbank last Friday. None of this helped. I sat at the Wilsons' big window and munched my way through breakfast, leafing through the local paper. In the property pullout were our multiple spreads of ads, with photographs of Katya and Zoe explaining the 'Heming Pledge' and our discount on all sales from now till Easter. Zoe in particular was an asset in the paper with her unforced smile and trendy looks, Katya more serious, but the two of them putting out a combined message that was friendly and professional, perhaps even a little sexy. Nice contrast: traditional, modern. Heming's.

I prefer to keep my own face out of the advertorials. Practically no one in town knows me, despite the fact that I attend many public events, concerts, black-tie fundraisers, quizzes and fêtes. I have learned the skill of being likeable without being memorable. I wear no cologne. Where some stand out, I stand back; remote from the performance, I am part of the applause. Events such as these are meat and drink to a local paper, of course. Here were typical ones – a cancer fun-run, a jumble of pictures from last week's folk and blues festival held at the arts centre.

And then a thought struck me. I finished my second coffee, washed my dishes and cleared them away. Warninck's was only ten minutes away, in the old part of town. It occupied the old corner Co-op – a large premises for an independent bookseller's but resourceful in the way it drew business in. Even this early on a dull weekday there were customers, one or two sitting with a coffee in the rear of the shop. I could see now that this raised area, with its comfy seats pushed back, formed the stage area for their literary events.

I approached a woman wearing a manager's badge.

'I'm looking for a book,' I said.

'Well,' she beamed, 'you've come to the right place.'

'The author did a reading here?'

'Our evenings are very popular. Was it travel? We had Moira McLarrily in November. She was marvellous.'

'No, this was a novel.'

'Barrington Gates? *Suit of Coins*? He was excellent.'

'That's the man!'

'He *is* popular. I think we might even have a signed copy, let me see . . .' She led me into the fiction aisle. 'E, F, Fleming, Gaskell . . . Oh,' she said, her eyes re-scanning the shelf, 'he's more popular than I thought. I'm afraid we're out of stock. Can I order you a copy?'

'No, don't worry. It was just a recommendation from someone. You must have done too good a job with your literary evening.'

'Have you been along to one yet? It's quite jolly. And of course there's always a glass of wine thrown in, so to speak.'

'So I gather. And who's the chap who does the interviews?'

'Oh, that's Doctor Sharp. Douglas. We're *very* lucky to have him. He lectures at Cambridge, no less, but he lives locally. It was his terrific idea to bring these events into Warninck's. They used to have them in the library from time to time, but not with a great deal of success. We have a better position here. More footfall, I think he said. I'm sure I have his card here somewhere . . .' She went behind the counter and rummaged through a box. 'Yes, here he is,' she said, holding the card to the level of her tinted bifocals and announcing his name and college.

I didn't need to go to the library at all but as if to follow the woman's cue – as if knowing what I really wanted – my feet took me there. I didn't usually need a book to ground me here; I preferred to browse, move around. But I was drawn now to Barrington Gates. What was the theme that had inspired her question . . . loneliness? I found a hardback copy on the shelf and read the blurb: the redemptive tale of a self-made millionaire who returns to the village of his birth following the accidental death of his brother by drowning. I found a quiet place to sit, and was soon absorbed, though not for long.

It was her laughter I heard first – abrupt against the general quiet but quickly curtailed as if she couldn't help herself. Then I heard her speaking close by, in local history – discussing something with a colleague, Margaret, her voice still full of stifled gaiety. I knew, even before I stole a sideways glance at her profile and the dark wavy hair that made her look like an English wartime film starlet, that it was her. This was why Sharp had come here the previous Friday – to let her know he was free and to urge her to join him at the house as soon as she could. I wondered now about her hours. Maybe she worked part-time herself, or was able to take a couple of afternoons off in lieu of weekend shifts. But how long had she been working here at the library? It couldn't have been a month since I'd last been in, perhaps two.

I kept my head down, but watched as she moved happily to and fro, her skirt swinging lazily as she walked, offering a glimpse of knee above her black boots. I inhaled the fragrance she trailed as she passed the back of my chair and I shadowed her on adjacent aisles when she left the desk with a trolley of books to replace on the shelves. I could hear her humming to herself as she worked. I could hear her breathing. At the desk, she wore glasses to check finer print and turned on a sunny smile for customers as she hit her computer keys. There was a beauty in her method and efficiency. Even the way she sat down or rose from a chair in a single movement was something to admire.

But now she glanced at her phone from time to time, and the reason for her buoyant mood became evident. Sharp arrived, hovering at the swing doors until he caught her eye. I saw his raised eyebrows and her embarrassed smile in reply. Then he left. She murmured something to Margaret and ducked into the room marked 'Private' for her coat. On the way back she took off the lanyard she wore round her neck and left it on the counter. She had put on a little lipstick. I abandoned my post and hurried out after her. Sharp was not far ahead, swinging his keys like a 1970s playboy, his trousers unnecessarily snug, I would say, for a man in his late thirties. He was heading for the car park. I paused in the concrete shadow of the entrance. I could get my own car in five minutes, but that would be four minutes too late, and there was no taxi rank between here and the high street. There was nothing I could do except wait – and then watch as they passed moments later in Sharp's hideous white 4×4 with the darkened windows. Dr Shark, charlatan.

Feeling the chill spring breeze now, I realized I'd left my

scarf in the library and I retraced my steps. I could see it still hanging on the chair, the book open on the table. Why the car, I wondered? Perhaps he was taking her out somewhere. But at least I had found her.

I pushed through the revolving door of the library. As I passed the front desk, I saw her lanyard with its laminated name-tag coiled on the counter where she'd left it in her eagerness to leave. Margaret was busy in the aisles. I retrieved my scarf, and on the way out again scooped the lanyard into my pocket. I didn't look back, just kept walking. I reached the corner that would take me into the town square and the office. I felt the cord and the plastic card. My step quickened. I was impatient to know her name, but I also wanted to savour the moment.

But when I walked into the office I was immediately beset by Zoe and Katya, both of whom had been trying to reach me.

'Ah, apologies,' I said, checking my phone. 'I turned it off while I was with the Curries.'

'But it was the Curries who just called, wanting to speak to you.'

'Did I say Curries?' I shook my head. 'Cooksons. I meant the Cooksons.'

Katya looked even more puzzled. 'You've been to see the Cooksons? Are they back on track? What did they say?'

'Oh, you know, the usual. I think they said they had plans for a spring break.'

'I told you that yesterday.'

'Indeed. And you were right.' I beamed at her. 'I suggested your idea of lining up some buyers while they're away in . . .'

'The Seychelles.'

'Indeed. They seemed, well . . . cordial.'

'Cordial? Does that mean they'll let us in?'

I was saved from Katya by a call from the Curries, which took some time to deal with. After that, Zoe ambushed me with her own anxieties, not least of which was the tale of a tenant from one of our riverside studios who had disappeared owing a month's rent.

'That's one of the Damato flats?'

She nodded.

'Just arrange to have it cleaned. I'll deal with it.'

At last, in the privacy of the small back office, I took out the lanyard, its orange cord wrapped around the white laminated ID. I flipped the card. Her name was Abigail. Abigail Rice. I sounded the name under my breath.

And then it clicked. *Rice*. I almost laughed out loud. The house wasn't Sharp's at all. It was hers.

12

ABIGAIL, OH, ABIGAIL. I waited and watched her now in the mornings on her early run, huffing down the steps to the river path, crossing the bridge and on to the Common and making a circuit of the town centre – alternating her choice of streets, as if to keep me on my toes – before coming back up via the news-agent and bakery at the top of Fount Hill. By now she was pink-cheeked, sipping from her water bottle, her lovely wiry hair held back in a red elastic hairband. The air had cleared, the clouds swept from my mind. It seemed more likely than not that she had been alone the night I watched the pizza delivery man arrive. And the Friday I'd bumped into Sharp coming out of the library? He hadn't been returning books at all but picking up the key to her house. *Her* house.

What wouldn't I have given for that key now.

But I hadn't been idle. It had taken a while to find her mother's name in the Death notices of a year-old copy of the *Sentinel* in the library (Abigail herself was only feet away when I uttered a silent 'Eureka!'), confirming that she was an orphan like myself. Still in mourning, what a vulnerable lamb she would have presented to a sly fox like Sharp, a performer with a microphone, plausible and charming, wheedling his way into her life as he had with his wife, Judith. He couldn't love Abigail. Not as I could (my scurrying, worrying heart told me that much).

I visited the house, approaching it methodically as I distributed a handful of our leaflets along that stretch of Raistrick Road. It was a big house. Too big for her mother (who, according to the notice, had died after a short illness), and now too big for Abigail. She must surely sell it in favour of a cosier place (I could picture her in one of the Victorian cottages on the hill opposite St Theobald's, stooping in the small back garden among rows of peas or snipping at some unruly floral abundance that matched her hair in its beauty and abandon). Pushing a leaflet through the letterbox of her blue door in the afternoon chill, I allowed my fingertips to linger in the warm interior – a taste of things to come.

I loitered then, hoping to catch a neighbour who might tell me something about Abigail or her mother, but saw no one. And then I reached – of course! – the newsagent's. I made a show of bumbling amid the stationery until I had the attentions of the owner and his wife, to whom I found myself explaining how I had foolishly fled the office without so much as a pen, and with clients to see! After some deliberation I chose the most expensive brand they had, alongside good envelopes and a book of standard sales forms. 'Ready for business!' I laughed.

'Business is important,' grinned the man with a faint bow of the head. 'We must *all* do business. Otherwise . . . poof!'

'Precisely,' I said, taking this opportunity to stress the importance of quality service and the building of trust if local business people are to retain the continuing confidence of the community.

The couple agreed wholeheartedly. 'We too must do this,' said the man. 'Every day we work. It is hard, but . . .' He smiled.

'But we must show people that we are always here, ready to serve? Everyone needs us sometimes. If not today, then tomorrow. Or, in my business, sometimes even the following year. But it becomes personal, don't you think? Each customer is important.'

They both smiled, though less certain of my meaning this time. The man once again gave a slight bow. 'Thirty-two years we are here now.'

'And that tells its own story. I mean, especially in your line of business, you know your customers. You take a pride in knowing what they want.'

'Ah yes,' said the woman. 'We know, we know.'

'For me, for example, in my replacement-window business, I have a note in my diary to see a certain customer. A courtesy call, you understand. But there is no answer. I come twice, still no answer. Should I call again? I don't know. Perhaps I should cross this lady off my list. But perhaps she is ill?'

The woman looked worried. 'She is your customer?'

'Not exactly. I spoke to her last year. Mrs Rice, at number eighty-four? Perhaps you know her. *Please* come back in the spring, she said. Perhaps I shouldn't say this, but her windows are in a worse condition than ever.'

The woman looked grave. 'The lady at number eighty-four?' She conferred briefly with her husband in another language.

'The lady passed away,' said the man, shaking his head. 'Many months ago. Her daughter, she came home to look after her, but the lady passed away. And now she lives here. We see her.'

'Her daughter?'

'A lovely girl,' said the woman. 'She came from London. At first she cancelled the papers, but now every day she comes and buys!'

I added a chocolate bar and a drink to my purchases. 'Keep my strength up,' I said.

'Ah,' said the man.

The doorbell tinged, heralding two new customers and bringing an end to our friendly babble. The couple wished me a good day.

It was a common enough story. The child who moves away – to university, to work, to establish herself in a new place – and then has to return to her home town to nurse an ailing parent. Would Abigail stay now? She had a job. Perhaps she had hopes of Sharp.

My heart sank at the thought. Was it possible to drive them apart without driving her away again? What else would keep her here in this town? The leaflet I posted would remind her of her choices – the opportunity to cash in her inheritance and return to her life in London. She'd be able to buy a smart flat in a good area. It was likely that she already had a flat in London she was renting out. And yet my hope had to be that she might sell. That her key would one day fall into my hands. There seemed no other way. Though of course there was, and always had been.

13

As I said, I feel lucky at this moment just to hear myself breathe. The air is thin, and I ally myself once again with the spirit of those who dare themselves into hazard, who scale those heights where oxygen is shortest in supply – though this story would be best told from a higher prospect still. I'm never quite far enough up the hill to discern a safe ending. I see the broadness and detail below, but what lies in the misty above? Perhaps oblivion. One slip! It seems there's always one more twisting path, narrowing upwards and slippery underfoot, with some horned beast barring the way, giving me the eye. It's always the story so far.

Hearing this, you might assume my worst dreams are about falling. In fact they are about disclosure and pursuit and swift extermination. A less attractive metaphor altogether. They are about having my roof ripped off. And in this hour before dawn, that fate has never felt more real and threatening. I feel my pursuers upon me. I lie in dread awaiting their loud cries and horrified triumph. Here! Here! The pest beneath the floorboards!

It was probably true what Aunt Lillian said about the day my mother died. I do love an enclosed space. A small stairs cupboard is ideal. Surrounded on all sides. The muffled quietness. In my aunt's barely used back room I made a den under the oak dining table, draped in the big Christmas tablecloth out of the drawer and heaped inside with cushions. It was here, in the green shade, that cousin Isobel once discovered me with the fashion dolls she no longer played with – Sindy, plus Sindy's boyfriend Paul, plus two larger pink babies in nappies. I had swapped their clothes round so that Paul was wearing Sindy's short gingham nightie and carrying water skis, while Sindy wore Paul's sheepskin coat, her white nurse's mask and nothing else. Together they took care of the children, though of course really it was me who decided who was punished and who had jelly and ice-cream. It was a game I could have played all day, had Isobel not arrived, screaming and punching and bringing the adults running.

'You're too sensitive,' Aunt Lillian said to Isobel at tea.

'But *you* . . .' she said, glaring at me. She didn't finish her sentence; just laid down her butter knife, thin-lipped, and wiped her mouth.

Was it the troubles with Isobel long ago that pulled the final lever that sent me on this track rather than that? Or was it little Anthony Damato? Or something entirely lost to memory? I don't blame you for wondering. What is strange, thinking about the time around my aunt's death, was how attending two funerals in quick succession didn't seem peculiar, even though I'd never attended one before – not even those of my parents. (I might add that I haven't attended one since, though that will soon change.) Strange too that Mr Mower was also present at both. But in fact – outside of my mind, which understandably always wants things to make sense – the two events are entirely unconnected. After all, things don't actually conspire to give you this life or that. Life may look like a pattern from the inside (no doubt a rat will think it wondrous that Nature has gone to the trouble of building it a maze of underground pipes to live in) but no one is really pulling levers. I prefer to see myself as author of my own fate. I am looking for no one to blame. Or indeed thank.

And even as I work here, the clock ticking, blood pumping wildly through my veins – and the situation far from ideal – I cannot in my heart wish things otherwise. The truth is that death is never far away. It cannot be helped. I have learned that much.

One of the troubles was how much Isobel adored that new baby, and bound him instantly to her dreams when we came to live at Aunt Lillian's. How she would love and care for him, with his mother dead and buried! I knew nothing, but watched in vague wonder as she cradled him and whispered to him, overseen by my aunt or distant father.

I step now into the wondering mind of my six-year-old self who knew nothing, open my eyes on his vague world. Everything has changed. Riley isn't allowed in the baby's room, my father says. We must let him sleep. The baby is always asleep, or crying for our mother, who is gone, everyone says – my father, Aunt Lillian, Mrs Holt from next door.

Mrs Holt looked after me and gave me a biscuit when the cars came, and let me play. The curtains are always closed now, even in the daytime.

I stand behind the curtains while Isobel is out at Sunday Club and Aunt Lillian feeds the baby with a bottle. He doesn't have a name yet. We will choose one soon. The baby is wrapped in white and blue and has the tiniest red hands. Later, when he is fast asleep in his room with the pink pigs, I stand next to his basket. His tummy goes in and out. He has his new soft yellow kangaroo beside him. I go to ask Aunt Lillian what is the kangaroo's name. 'Kanga,' says Aunt Lillian. When he is older the baby will love Riley and his soft orange fur.

Later, I see Aunt Lillian washing her hair without her blouse on. She pushes the door closed so that I cannot see. My father is digging. I watch him from behind the shed. I can smell the mud on his spade.

Riley is asleep on the warm blue metal of Aunt Lillian's car. 'Riley!' I call. I make a 'ch-ch-ch' sound like Aunt Lillian does when she wants Riley to come for his tea in the kitchen. Riley moves his ear but keeps his eyes closed. There is a wasp. I am afraid of wasps and wait for it to buzz off as my father has told me. In the kitchen I rattle Riley's empty bowl on the hard floor. In he comes quickly now with his tail in the air. He sniffs at the bowl and looks up at me with a wondering face. I pick him up. He is big and heavy but I can carry him. His fur is soft and warm. I climb the stairs with him to see the baby. Just one look. When I hear Aunt Lillian, I drop Riley on to the carpet and he runs away. In the room I sit quietly behind the door. The baby is dreaming, hidden deep in his basket. And now Riley is here again. He looks at me and then at the baby's basket. He waits, then springs up. I can't see him. But we are all quiet, the three of us, breathing together in the room. I close my eyes. Then I hear Aunt Lillian call once and then again sharply. Quickly I am out on the landing, closing the door. I feel my face is hot.

'What are you up to?' asks Aunt Lillian, and takes me downstairs. Her hair is bundled in a towel and there is the smell of the bathroom.

Afterwards there is hell to pay, as my father sometimes says. Aunt Lillian is screaming, which makes me cry. My father now is shaking me. The television is on behind me, showing the programme with monsters. Later Mrs Holt takes me to her house for a biscuit and some milk. Later the baby is gone, and Riley too. My father's face, which is nearly always red, is as white as my mother's when she was lying still on the bed.

Riley has mothered the baby, I hear someone say. Because the baby has no mother. That is why they have both gone.

14

A DAY PASSED. AT THE LIBRARY, Abigail and Margaret – or, occasionally, their younger temporary colleagues – came back and forth. My eye was drawn to the room marked 'Private'. I knew the security number, but of course it was mad to imagine I could get in and out without being seen. It would be mad to try. The door was adjacent to the desk but faced the public part of the library that housed the computer terminals. But there it was, daring me. The urge was great. The thought of it triggered memories of my schooldays – the frisson of expectation that preceded that deeper thrill and pleasure of occupation, transgression, possession and, yes, love of a sort.

Once or twice I have walked that line between foolishness and valour, knowing that the secret to taking on risk and beating it is nothing more complicated than a raw willingness to act, to seize the opportunity, without hesitation, the instant it presents itself. I gave myself the best shot I could. I waited for a day when Margaret was away and Abigail was holding the fort, aided by one of their students, and walked into the library wearing a tweed jacket from a charity shop and glasses. To the library staff, I was an anonymous browser. But to the distracted visitor – especially those using the computers, and these were mostly students – my aim was to look at least not unlike a librarian. From my belt I hung an ID card (based on Abigail's and mocked up on the office laminator) that would pass muster from a distance. Thus armed, I entered the field. I took off my jacket and hung it on the back of a chair as far from the front desk as possible. Whenever the staff were safely behind it, I stayed out of their line of vision and busied myself in a low-level way: walking with purpose in my shirt sleeves, opening and closing microfiche drawers or tidying the newspapers and magazine area; I even helped someone operate the photocopier. When Abigail or her assistant were out on the floor, I melted into the depths of the reference section.

Lunchtime brought a steady trickle of people returning books, which gathered in piles on the desk before being categorized and transferred to the trolley. At last there was a lull. Abigail's assistant disappeared behind the door marked 'Private', reappearing moments later pulling on her coat. She was taking her break. Abigail handed her some money, presumably to bring her back a sandwich from the high street. She'd be gone at least fifteen minutes – substantially longer if she herself was lunching out or had other things to do. The queue at the desk had dwindled to none. Abigail came out and pulled out the loaded trolley. She always started with fiction, which took her furthest from the desk. She would have to work her way down one aisle and up the next before she came within sight of the door marked 'Private' again. I had no idea how long that would take. I did know, though, that the moment had come.

I watched Abigail and the trolley disappear slowly into A–L, then strode casually up to the door, punched 5-1-5-9-4 into the grey metal panel and pushed it open. The door closed behind me.

A wave of urgency hit me as my senses took in the scene – a yellow bowl in the sink, tiled counter, kettle, smell of scattered coffee granules, two library chairs around a bandy-legged table. On the table were mugs, teaspoons, a grey scarf, a small pile of books. Two umbrellas stood in a corner, and hanging alone was Abigail's red cagoule, her backpack on the rack below. My hands went to her pockets, rifling, thrusting – here were tissues, gloves, a red elastic hairband, clip-on cycle lamp, a battery in its packaging. Inner pockets: a glove, another glove. I shook the coat. Nothing.

I took a breath and the hush of the room was shattered by a piercing ringtone. It was the phone outside. I froze, then went to the door. The desk was feet away. It would only take a few seconds to dart out, unplug the phone and get back. But I didn't have a few seconds. I opened the door a crack. The trill of the phone now filled the library. People turned their heads. And there she was, walking briskly, wearing a professional smile. The phone seemed to be shrieking now. What sort of call might require her to come back here to this room? The pile of books on the table – had they been put aside for some colleague, now calling about them? There was nowhere to hide. But she would have to key in the number to get in. It was a heavy door. I could block entry from my side. She'd be puzzled. Try again. Give up until her assistant returned. She reached the desk, but now the phone abruptly ceased its clamour, its last half-ring echoing out. She paused. Then she turned on her heel, back towards the trolley.

I clicked the door shut and resumed my search with renewed anxiety. The backpack now – its top pocket containing paperback, earphones, shopping list. Bundled inside, a yellow jumper. Another compartment. I unzipped it. And now, here on its own, wedged into the fold, was a single key with a circular wooden fob painted green. I squeezed it tight then slipped it into my pocket. I didn't think about it yet. What it meant. My head felt compressed, as if in an aircraft with sound baffled and time suspended. I knew I needed to get out, but some other instinct took over. I opened the fridge, saw milk, yoghurt and most of a large chocolate bar. Dark. I snapped off a generous oblong, freed it from the gold foil, and crammed it in my mouth.

It seemed to trigger a buzzing noise nearby. I whirled round, ready to flee. The scarf on the table was twitching and then I saw the phone, its screen flashing. I pounced on it. D CALLING. I pressed the reject key. My nerves screamed at me to get out, but I couldn't. Here was her phone, in my hand. I couldn't take it, but nor could I just leave it there. An idea came to me. I took out my own phone, switched it to video and began to cycle through the contents on Abigail's handset – her 'favourites', her recent calls and calendar, her reminders and photographs. My heart was thumping – and now the phone thrummed with a text from 'D'. I carried on. What were the chances of her walking straight in here now, before she'd finished her trolley round, remembering she'd left her phone on the table with her scarf? Sharp probably called or left a message every day at this time, especially days when she was in charge and couldn't meet him. Or he would try the landline again. She would be listening for it. She would be hurrying through her task to get back to the desk.

I could sense her coming now. I darted back to the door and peered out. The front end of the trolley was visible at the end of M–Z. It was motionless, but even as I watched it started to move. I closed the door. If I came out now, she would see me. I thought for a moment, then reopened her favourites page, found her number for the library (helpfully marked 'Work'), keyed it into my own phone and hit 'Call'. The loud trilling started up again outside. I knew she would respond more quickly this time, hopeful, expectant. I stepped away from the door and waited for her to answer on the other side, my lips close to the phone.

'Hello?'

'Hello, is that the library?'

'Yes, this is the library.'

'Ah. I'm so sorry to bother you, but *please* tell me I left my jacket there. It's a sort of brownish tweedy jacket. I was sitting just outside the microfiche cubicles. I just got out of the car and realized.'

'One moment, I'll just check.'

I replaced her phone on the table, opened the door and walked out, her hairband squeezed in one fist, my phone in the other. I saw Abigail out of the corner of my eye just re-emerging to the left. I pushed through the swing doors and clapped the phone to my ear just as she spoke.

'Hello? Hello? Yes, it's here. I have it.'

She sounded so pleased to be helping me, I fell in love with her all over again.

'You've saved my life,' I told her. 'I'll come straight down.'

'No problem at all. It'll be behind the desk.'

Sweat poured off me. The taste of the bitter chocolate lingered in my mouth. I waited. After ten or fifteen minutes Abigail's assistant rounded the corner carrying a striped paper bag. I waited till she'd gone in then watched for the switchover. They spoke briefly as she handed the bag to Abigail, who then vanished into the room marked 'Private'.

Now I walked into the library and retrieved the jacket.

And I was gone, across the road, up the hill, walking quickly until I reached my flat. I changed my clothes and drove to Raistrick Road. This was as good a time as any, with Abigail safely at the library for the rest of the day. I parked as near as I dared to the house, though the chances of being challenged were slim. There was no Neighbourhood Watch. It was a main road populated mainly by students, who came and went and minded their own business. My heart was booming. But as I approached the door I felt the fear. Perhaps the fear was there all along and I had pushed it to the back of my mind in the rush of triumph and escape. But now it rose again. The fear, of course, was that this was not the key. That the key to this house would never have been hidden away in Abigail's backpack – that the key to this house had been in her purse, which I had seen with my own eyes when she gave her assistant money for a sandwich. I knew now as I had then that this was not the key. I inserted it into the mounting plate and tried to turn it, hoping to feel the mechanism shift and fall.

It might have been set in stone.

15

I AWOKE ON MY COUCH at first light with Abigail's velveteen hairband curled in my hand, strands of her dark wiry hair twisted into the fabric. I fell in and out of sleep, as if in the grip of a fever, images of Abigail and Sharp rising and falling in my mind. At nine I forced myself to get up. I shaved and showered and called Wendy to say I would be out for the day.

But doing what? There was no point following Sharp to and from work. It would only end in my sitting outside the house in Raistrick Road simmering with desire and hatred. For a while I sat among the cabinets and drawers in my back room. I had neglected my filing and maps – the work that was so vital to the smooth running of things, and which always gave me so much satisfaction. I collated photographs and notes. I downloaded files from my phone, used the printer. I loved the effort of having everything on paper, tied up, tangible, accessible, classified. But I couldn't hold focus. What I needed was another strategy, I thought. I needed Abigail to see for herself what kind of man had cheated his way into her bed. He was no Cambridge lecturer, that was for sure. That was the place to start. I thought of the card the woman in Warninck's had read out and after some deliberation called the university's faculty office.

The woman who answered had no knowledge of a Dr Sharp. 'Let me just check our records.' I heard her in the background consulting colleagues, then she came back on to the phone. 'There *was* a chap called Douglas Sharp, two or three years ago, but he wasn't on staff, he was a postgraduate student.' She paused as if looking further. 'It's possible he taught one or two classes.'

'Do you have a forwarding address?'

'Just one moment.'

Off she went again, but then after a minute a man picked up the phone. 'I gather you're asking about Douglas Sharp. May I ask what this is about?'

'Yes, of course, thank you. This is his brother. I'm trying to track him down. I'm afraid there's an illness in the family and I need to let him know.'

'I see. But I'm afraid he left the college some time ago. I really have no idea where he might be now.'

'But he was studying there?'

'He was a PhD student. What did you say your name was?'

'Sharp.'

'Of course. Brothers, you say?'

'We're not very close. He doesn't keep in touch. But our mother is seriously ill. You said he left some time ago.'

'Perhaps I could ask his supervisor to call you.'

'That would be kind. What's his name?'

'*Her* name. Greening. Professor Greening.'

'Obviously, it is quite urgent . . .'

'Of course.'

I gave the man a fictitious number and then hung up.

Something was afoot. I waited an hour then called the porter's lodge and asked to be put through to Professor Greening's office. 'She might have been trying to call me,' I said. 'The name's Sharp.'

There was a beat of uncertainty. 'Douglas Sharp?'

'This is his brother.'

'I see. One moment, sir.'

I was in luck. She was busy, but on a break. 'I'm afraid I can't help. Your brother had rooms here at the college, but left no forwarding address. I sympathize, of course, but as you may know, he left under a cloud – and, I might add, in a hurry.'

'So he didn't finish his doctorate?'

'I should say not. You might conclude, if only from the newspaper reports, that that was very much a diminishing option. And we do have discretionary powers. He brought the college a great deal of unwanted media publicity. Let's leave it at that.'

'But what happened?'

She paused and then sighed. 'If you don't know, I have probably already said too much.'

'The porter's lodge seemed to remember him.'

'As well they might.'

'And this would be what – two years ago?'

'Just over three years ago. I really can't add more. But good luck with your search.'

I didn't yet know what I was looking for, but I had an inkling where to look, and within half a minute was logging into the *Cambridge News* online archive. A search for 'Douglas + Sharp' produced zero results, but after five minutes the name of the college served up a feast worth waiting for: 'Brawl at College Dinner over Don's Sex Trysts with Student'.

The 'don' description was over-egging it, but this seemed to be the report in question: in a nutshell, the story of a furious

Muslim father who arrived late in the day all the way from Glasgow with two equally furious companions, possibly brothers, demanding to speak with the man – an English adult in a position of trust – who had made his daughter, an undergraduate under the man's tutelage, pregnant in her first term at Cambridge. It was not made clear whether the wrongdoer – unnamed and downgraded to a junior lecturer in the story – was actually available to meet his accusers. It transpired only that there was a fierce argument between these men and the head porter and his assistant that quickly flared into a scuffle, drawing in a number of academic staff arriving at that hour in full regalia for a college dinner. Their intervention, intended to calm matters, understandably made things worse, the suspicion being that one of their number was actually the defiler himself, though there was no evidence that he was even in the city. Fists flew, blood was spilt, a crowd gathered (several witnesses were quick enough with their camera-phones to capture one of the dons bleeding vividly down his white frontage, possibly from a punched nose), the police were called, arrests were made and a 'long-bladed weapon' was recovered at the scene. Charges were made and, reportedly at the behest of the university authorities, dropped.

The outrage of the violence was compounded with lurid details gleaned from the girl's acquaintances, revealing twice-daily lovemaking sessions between the 'thirtysomething Don Juan' and the eighteen-year-old he had met and seduced at a literary reading at a bookstore in town. The man, thought to be studying for a doctorate in English, had taken the girl, a teetotaller, to a wine bar. Once, the couple had been seen together in a punt on the Cam.

There were links to subsequent opinion pieces on the dangers for first-year female students, the university's failure to screen casual teaching staff with access to vulnerable young adults (though in fact he had not been the girl's lecturer at all) and the general betrayal of ethnic and working-class undergraduates by 'unthinking and unrepresentative elites'. Final mention of the scandal consisted of a brief report that the miscreant had been removed, reportedly for some ancient but occasionally revived offence of 'moral turpitude', and the supervision agreement on his research thesis formally rescinded. The fate of the disgraced girl was not divulged.

So how did it end? Had she been put to death by concerned relatives as punishment for dishonouring the family name? Were her father and brothers still theoretically in pursuit of Sharp? It occurred to me that I could tip them off if only I knew who they were. But perhaps they had let bygones be bygones. The girl might still be at Cambridge right now, foetus long aborted, happily ensconced in a higher-rated college with full no-strings bursary and furiously revising for her finals having learned a valuable lesson in life and moved on.

Don't we all do that?

16

I HAD ERRANDS TO run that I'd been neglecting: rubbish for the recycling bins, shirts for the laundry, a suit for the dry cleaner's. I drove to Fairley, a sprawling neighbourhood at the edge of town where I sometimes had keys cut. Here was an estate of affordable housing, a big supermarket and parade of local shops – newsagent, pharmacy, bookie, aquatic supplies, hairdresser, fried chicken franchise. I deposited my garbage and laundry and sat in the supermarket café with coffee, juice and toast. The events of the previous day – its high adrenalin rush and crashing disappointment – were only now swimming back into focus. All I had to show was the trophy of Abigail's hairband, a memento to hold close to my cheek like a saint's relic.

I took out my phone and ran through the video I had made of her phone's contents at the library. The light was dim, but most of the numbers in her directory were legible. 'D' for Douglas, of course. Home – her landline at Raistrick Road – Mum, Solicitor, Work. Other London numbers, mainly girls' names, were probably friends. Her photographs included a series from what looked like a girls' night out, two or three of an older woman

– her mother, I guessed – holding an old ginger teddy bear, and there was one of the author she had admired at the reading at Warninck's. There were two of Sharp: one with a chalkboard menu behind him and the other, presumably at Abigail's house – which of course made me want to kill him even more – with the ginger teddy in his lap. Disappointingly, there were none of Abigail herself.

I paused on her calendar: here was a string of entries, mainly marked 'D', one of them last Tuesday, the day they drove off in Sharp's car. It was Tuesday today, but there was no entry for it. But now her reminders file came up, and here he was again: today's date, 'D. 2 Swans Ebb 1.30' – clearly a reference to the Two Swans at Ebbidge, a thatched pub five or six miles out of town. I hadn't been there, but like everyone I'd seen its restaurant get three stars in a Sunday newspaper. A date, then, which seemed out of kilter with my perception of things. What sort of furtive extramarital fling was it that suddenly bathed itself in the aura of romance? Was love the new price of sex? Did Abigail want more than a casual involvement with a married man (if she knew he was married)? Was Sharp playing along to keep her sweet? I found myself growing hot with indignation at his clumsy subterfuge, this attempt to make the sordid resemble something tender and real.

The temptation to watch the two of them together was strong, but was it worth the risk? I'd spent too long in the library recently. No one notices a stranger in the street, but how many times do you see a passing face before it becomes familiar? Anonymity was my strength. Once lost, it was impossible to get back. Sharp had chosen this out-of-the-way pub to reduce their chances of being seen. If Abigail recognized me there, even as a local from the library, it was likely that she would notice me elsewhere in the future. I couldn't be confident, either, that Sharp wouldn't remember my face from our dispute at the gate to the Common if I were suddenly pointed out to him. And then what would they be thinking? Who *is* that guy? A private detective?

And what was there to discover? That the two of them had a mutual fondness for sea bass?

I put it out of my mind, finished my breakfast and thought about going into the office. I could catch up on some work and return fresh to the problem of Sharp in the evening. I might look again at his online gambling. Or maybe there was some harder evidence – something I hadn't spotted in his correspondence maybe – concerning the blow-up in Cambridge. Life is full of hope.

Katya was manning the office. Her eyes lit up when I walked in.

'Aha,' she said. 'O'Deay's!'

'Success?'

'I think so. They're asking for another quarter point, we're asking for another ten properties. I think they will agree. In the meantime, there's some more of their blurb to look at when you have a minute.'

'I'll do it right now,' I said. 'Any more news?'

'I spoke to Mr Cookson, but he just seemed cross when I suggested we try to get some buyers in while they're away. Didn't you tell me they were cool about it?'

'Cool? I may have said cordial.'

'Cordial – what is that? All they've done is given us permission, after months of hassle, to put a sign up on the approach road.'

'Well, then,' I said. 'That's a start.'

'How many starts do we give them?'

I went to the back office and buried myself in the O'Deay's project. Wendy made tea and gave me my messages. It was turning into a bright spring day. It really would be foolhardy to go out to the Two Swans. But by noon I could stand it no longer.

'I'm just popping out,' I told Katya. 'I thought I might cast an eye over the O'Deay's site on this lovely day. See how things are.'

She glanced up in surprise but I was gone before she could say anything.

Twenty minutes later I pulled into the Two Swans' car park. The pub hadn't been open long but two of the smaller outdoor tables overlooking the river were occupied by lone drinkers smoking and reading the paper. Inside there were no customers yet, just staff busying themselves polishing glasses or setting tables in the bar. I walked through to the restaurant. It was reassuringly large, the original low-ceilinged room with exposed beams leading to an extended sun lounge with waterside view and exit to the garden. I was greeted by the manager.

'Table for lunch, sir?' she asked.

'I was thinking of it,' I said. 'But later – about one-fifteen?'

'Let me just see what we have.'

I followed her to a counter, where she opened a folder showing a chart and reservations. I cast an eye over the list. No Sharp, but there was a Douglas. Table three. The last in a row close to where we were standing.

'Any chance of a table in the sun?'

'Ah, I'm afraid not. They're always the first to go. But I can put you by the window. Table for two, was it?'

'Just one, I'm afraid.' I smiled.

'That's fine then, Mr . . . ?'

'Williams. Thank you.'

I went back out to the car and called Zoe's mobile number.

'Hello?'

'Zoe, it's me.'

'Mr Heming, is something wrong?'

'On the contrary. I was thinking, if you're not busy, you might come out and meet me at the O'Deay's development. See what you think of it.'

'Well, no, I'm not. Busy, that is. I could, of course, but my car's in for a service and wax.'

'Ask Wendy to get you a taxi.'

She paused. 'But what about Katya?'

'Don't worry about that. I was just thinking it might give you some insight into this sort of development. Move you up a little. You don't have to mention it to Katya.'

'Move me up?' she trilled. 'I'm not sure I know what that means.'

When I arrived at O'Deay's, Zoe was waiting with her eager smile. We didn't spend long on site. We surprised the sales manager, who checked with his superiors and then took us on a short tour. The show house wasn't quite finished, but we got an idea of the layout and concept. I nodded and asked questions that I already knew the answers to. Zoe followed my lead in looking alternately fascinated and enthusiastic but didn't say much. Frankly, there wasn't much *to* say. Once or twice I caught her eyeing me curiously. It was true that I had spent very little time alone in her company – perhaps the occasional drive to see a client – since our 'romantic' interlude came to a difficult end two or more years before. She looked thrilled when I suggested lunch afterwards. 'It gets more and more intriguing.' Her voice was low.

'Not at all,' I replied. 'Just lunch. On this lovely spring day.'

In view of our history it probably wasn't the best idea, but the truth was I felt the need for camouflage. A lone diner in a restaurant could attract a wandering eye. People were far less interested in couples. Not very gallant, I know, but effective, I hoped.

When we were standing in the car park of the Two Swans, her eyes widened at the thatched roof and picturesque setting. 'Gosh, how lovely,' she said. 'We are pushing the boat out.'

'Only the best for Heming's,' I joked. As we both knew, a sandwich wolfed down at the desk was our usual style. Business lunches, I had always argued, were unproductive and took too much out of the day.

'It's not your birthday, is it?' she asked.

I smiled. In the office she had once asked when my birthday was, and I had held out, changed the subject, refused to tell. I'd made it seem light-hearted, but for me it was a matter of principle. But then she had dwelled on this 'oddity', as she saw it, returned to it and made a running joke out of it. She seemed somehow to enjoy calling me Mr Heming, as if – given our brief episode of familiarity – the two of us were now acting out some secret charade. On the whole I didn't mind. Her occasional playfulness was an endearing trait, creating a little esprit around the office and providing a counterpoint to Katya, who was from Lithuania, and didn't think there was anything amusing about formality. The others had no issue with it, Josh being young enough to do as he was told and Wendy old enough to remember when all bosses were called mister.

The restaurant was busy now. Zoe went to the ladies' while I explained to the manager that there would be two for lunch after all.

'No problem. And we've had a cancellation, so I will be able to put you in the sun lounge if you'd still prefer that.'

Zoe reappeared and a waitress showed us to our table. I insisted that Zoe have the river view. 'How thoughtful, Mr Heming!' she said.

The waitress took our drinks order.

'Just tonic water for me,' I said. 'Best keep a clear head.'

'Oh,' said Zoe.

'You go ahead,' I said.

'Should I?' she twinkled. 'Perhaps just a large glass of Rioja, then.'

She smiled, as though it was understood that I was trying to get her tipsy, which couldn't have been further from the truth. I had seen Zoe tipsy on enough occasions to be wary of its effect on her – one moment highly affectionate and the next saddened beyond help, especially when she rightly began to suspect a lack of enthusiasm on my part.

'How do you see me?' she had once asked on one of our candlelit evenings out, her eyes quizzical, her chin propped up in her hand.

'Like this!' I said, opening my eyes wide.

More than once an evening out with Zoe had ended in tears. As considerate as I tried to be, the most innocuous remark could set her off.

The surrounding tables were filling up now. Zoe flattened her napkin across her lap, flicked back her hair and sighed contentedly. 'I can actually see swans from here,' she said.

Of course I wondered if she might be getting the wrong idea, but it was too late to worry about that. The important thing was that she was sitting between me and table three. And if we looked like a couple delighting in each other's company, all the better. So we chatted about Josh's progress with the website until the drinks appeared, then detained the waitress while she decided what to eat. I had picked the first thing on the menu and was already shooting nervous glances at the door. Zoe, clearly delighted to make the most of the occasion, was more leisurely in her choices, and was still deliberating when Sharp and Abigail appeared across the room, setting my nerves on edge as they were shown to their table. Abigail was radiant and demure. Sharp guided her into a chair, his hand almost on her bottom. I suddenly felt sick.

'So what do you think, Mr Heming – langoustines or the soup?'

The print on the menu danced before my eyes. I couldn't say what Zoe or I finally chose, or what we found to talk about before it arrived, but bread and olives were somehow on the table followed by some sort of fish and we were eating, and babbling about the O'Deay's project – what Zoe thought about pricing on the bungalows, how we might squeeze O'Deay's further in exchange for a lower commission. My eyes flitted back and forth, from Zoe's mouth, alternately talking and chewing, to table three, where they were busy with appetizers and a carafe of wine.

I wished now I had taken a risk and tried for a table within range of theirs. I felt a desperate need to sample the atmosphere, the quality of their murmurings. The more I watched, the more I longed for it. And now Sharp was leaning towards her. Some unctuous endearment, no doubt. She smiled, her eyes downcast, as if inspecting her salad.

A trellis behind them bordered the greeting area and service hub. Would it be feasible to loiter there for a few minutes without being run down by waiting staff? Perhaps there would be an opportunity later.

We ate. They ate. I realized it was a mistake. I wished we

hadn't come. I felt I was drowning in the affable, tinkling hubbub of the place.

Zoe, on her second glass of Rioja, gazed across at me with ominous fondness. 'Do you remember that beautiful bistro we once went to? The little French place in Constable country? And we stopped the car on the bridge on the way back and watched the riverboats moored up under the moon, with their lanterns rippling on the water? The way the music came floating up, and the smell of barbecue?'

I smiled and couldn't find anything to say, though what I remembered vividly was the two of us squeezed into the front of my small car, Zoe's head on my shoulder and the smell of her shampoo. I remembered having to wind the window down. How romantic she had thought the boats were, with their little red curtains lit up cosily from the inside. How smoothly she had then skated into the subject of family holidays on the Norfolk Broads with her younger sister, who was now married and had recently given their parents a lovely granddaughter, and how sweet and adorable she was. 'I can't believe I'm suddenly an aunt,' Zoe had said, laughing. 'I'm the old maid of the family!'

'Congratulations,' I had replied, without quite meaning to.

Amid Zoe's reminiscing, my own thoughts turned to my anguished vigil in the street outside Abigail's, the glow of *her* room. In my dreams, I had conjured myself into that space I could see from the street, her red curtain the only thing between us, my cheek brushing the satiny fabric as I listened to her settling in her white feather bed.

Zoe paused. 'I often think of that evening,' she said.

Across the room the abominable Sharp was offering Abigail a spoonful of something toothsome. Even at this distance I could see his phoney, simpering, ultra-considerate expression, his suspiciously white smile as he helped Abigail to more wine, touching her hand from time to time and staring into her face. Perhaps there was some other point to this occasion. Doubt and sadness clouded Abigail's expression from time to time. Maybe they were breaking up! It was hard to see whether Sharp was trying to console or persuade. Perhaps a little of both.

'Who do you keep *looking* at?' Zoe said suddenly.

'Sorry, I was miles away. What did you say?'

She shook her head. 'Nothing. It really doesn't matter. Why would it? I need the loo.'

Was she cross with me? She left her napkin on her plate and weaved a path through the tables. But now I saw that Abigail had vanished too, leaving Sharp at the table. I tried to read his angular face, which had relaxed into a state of neutral watchfulness, off-stage but ready for its next cue. He glanced around the room. I kept my head down.

Zoe was taking for ever. The waitress came to clear the table and brought a dessert menu. Should I order? Perhaps just coffee.

But the waitress had no sooner departed with my order than Zoe returned, moist around the eyes and sniffing. She didn't sit down. 'I'm going to head back, actually. Sorry, and thanks for lunch. I'm just not . . .'

'But what is it?' Clearly I had upset her.

'Nothing. I'm just not feeling too good. And I need to get back to the office. I have a ton of things to do.'

'Do you think it might have been the venison, or—'

'No, I'm *fine*. Just . . .'

'But how will you—'

'It doesn't *matter*.' She waved away my concerns and headed for the rear exit leading out into the car park.

Now I saw Abigail and Sharp preparing to leave too and I

tried to catch the attention of the waitress, who seemed to see me but swept past twice. It was several minutes before I could cancel the coffees and get the bill. I paid in cash and hurried to the exit. I had to stop for a couple who were entering, and I got outside just in time to see Zoe leaving in a taxi. Abigail and Sharp, though, were nowhere to be seen. I started my car and pulled out on to the main road. They surely couldn't have got very far, but there was no sign of them on the almost empty road. I saw Zoe's taxi turning into a filling station, and sped past. Just when I thought I'd lost them, I rounded a bend and caught sight of Sharp's vehicle some way ahead, delayed by a large flock of cyclists. I kept my distance. After a few moments he seized the opportunity to overtake, somewhat dangerously, leaving me behind. He was getting further ahead, but then instead of staying on the road to town, he took a left turn. I reached the turning and followed, but couldn't see him. A narrow lane now took me winding through copses and fields. Perhaps he knew a short cut. I put my foot down but could see nothing on the bends visible ahead as the road ribboned down towards the valley. They seemed to have simply vanished, but then, as I passed a wooded area on my right, I saw a glimmer of white amid the trees and bushes.

I slowed and pulled into a gravelly bay some way down the lane, then walked cautiously back to the spot. There was a track into the woods, the entrance almost concealed with hanging branches and undergrowth. It was probably used – though evidently not often – by forest rangers. I crept in, not too badly camouflaged in my brown-green tweed suit. The track didn't go very far and I spotted it immediately through the thicket of branches and thorns, squatting darkly in the green shadows –

its mirror chrome, its curve of halogen lights set like precious stones, its inscrutable smoked-glass windows. I didn't dare get any nearer. I just waited and watched, until the body of the car began almost imperceptibly to tremble, and I could watch no more.

17

LET'S SAY I'M TEN years old. My father is at his office, so it can't be the weekend. Perhaps it's the school holidays. Directly below my window I see Aunt Lillian standing by the Austin calling for cousin Isobel to hurry. I don't know where they are going – it's too early for a dance class and her piano lesson is Saturday – but Aunt Lillian has said they won't be too long. I'm allowed in the park on my own. It's only a short walk, but I haven't decided whether to do that or not. The scariest part is the walled stone steps that turn halfway down so that you can't see what bigger boys or fierce dog might be coming up, or waiting at the bottom. A garden of evergreen bushes and shrubs rises to the side like a dark jungle. Beyond is the huge, bright square of the bowling green and the safety of its old men playing on Sunday. But today isn't Sunday. I sense its quietness from the top of the steps and decide to go no further.

At home, from my window I look down at the Damatos' house. Mrs Damato is busy upstairs. The bedroom window is open and, below it, the door is propped open, as it always is on a sunny day. I can hear music. The Damatos, my aunt has told me, are Italians. In the front garden little Anthony is playing. Who is that with him? I can't see because of the hedge, but they have toys with them.

When Aunt Lillian said 'You know what you did' in her dramatic way, I suppose this was the day she was talking about.

I steal into Mrs Damato's kitchen. There are no cakes cooling today but she has a huge biscuit tin. Distracted from his play, Anthony watches me enter and then re-emerge, a smile of wonder on his dark little face. His friend has blonde-white hair, white socks, new white leather sandals. Her name is Angela. She holds a small stuffed bunny-rabbit to her chest and looks up to Anthony as he looks up to me. I have a delicious coconut biscuit for them both. The sunny day is ripe for adventure. The street is deserted. I tell them to hold hands as we walk along. At the top of the stone steps I can smell the grass, hear faintly a motor mower. We skirt the empty bowling green, a forbidden square of perfection held by white stones. No one is using the putting green; likewise the tennis court, which has weeds emerging at the crumbling edge of its asphalt surface. On the distant field boys are hoofing a football, their cries just audible; and beyond them, in a dip of the land, the protruding giant 'A's of the swings and slide, too far away to discern activity.

We're not going to the swings. I have a little house, I tell them. We can play there. Excitedly they chat together as we walk, or rather they each issue small announcements about themselves.

'I've got a bunny-rabbit,' says Angela.

'What's for tea in your house?' Anthony asks me.

'Wait and see,' I say.

*

The truth was, my aunt knew little about what I had done. Guessing at it was enough to horrify her, to feed her imagination, her fear of what I might one day do.

18

THINGS STARTED TO MOVE. I saw Sharp's dog again while walking back to town on the Friday, having been to see a client. For no good reason I had decided on a route that would take me down Boselle Avenue, and there he was – Barney, a Jack Russell cross, cartoon-cute and staring from a fading poster fastened to a lamppost. MISSING, it said. REWARD. The Sharps' name and number was written beneath in marker pen. Further down I could see a second poster and a third, leading my eye to the uphill path that led off Boselle and eventually to the town's Victorian cemetery with its iron railings and shady trees. Even in their polythene envelopes, the posters were weather-beaten and sodden. Clearly they had been up for weeks. My hand automatically reached out to take one – an act indistinguishable from the routine, omnivorous collecting that had been a part of my life's work and pleasure since childhood. It was a scrap of colour in Sharp's blizzard of moments. How easily I was sucked into this. I thought about Abigail – a prize to be wanted above all others – and felt myself losing focus, allowing what I felt for her to be drowned in the mundane fact of Sharp. I felt the need for purity and my senses tingled at the thought of her. She was a pinhead of light, pulsing through the tumbling cumuli of events, constant but no nearer.

At the office, Zoe was working with studied care at her desk. She had barely spoken to me directly since our lunch together, and only two mornings before I had seen her perhaps twenty yards ahead of me walking past the entrance to the Common, quickening her step as if she had eyes in the back of her head. At work she maintained a level of cheer that hung around the office like static. Her behaviour reminded me of the time immediately following our break-up – the same grim scrupulousness in the brightness of her speech and demeanour that signalled one thing but meant another. I could say nothing to her that she would want to hear.

Wendy buzzed through with the news that a tenant had been found for the Damato flat.

'Let's hope he, or she, is more reliable than the last one,' I said.

'He's a he,' Wendy said. 'Name of . . . Mario? Something foreign. Contract's in the file, three months in advance, and the key's on my rack if I'm out when he comes. I'm on my lunch break soon.'

I waited till she'd gone, then lifted the key – labelled Marrineau – from the hook and headed for the riverside apartments. I rarely went down there. That whole affair seemed like something from a different era now. I had bought one floor of the development – or, rather, Damato Associates had – as part of the original deal, and had acquired the freehold to the building when the property company ran into trouble two years later. I still let out the middle floor, to single professionals or couples. This flat – an open-plan space with a view of the rear of the bowling alley and cinema – was shiny and anonymous and smelled of cleaning products. The furniture, now absent, had left prints in the carpet. I stood at the window. Another fine day. On the opposite side, people were eating at café tables the bowling-alley people had put out on a deck. It was a fine apartment. What had brought me here under this amusing alias? I could easily have re-let the place. Perhaps I sensed the need for a safer refuge from Zoe's inquisitive gaze. Standing there I thought about Marrineau and the time I had looked out from his window. Where was he now? What had become of his famous fringed rawhide jacket?

Perhaps you think I am haunted by the past. On the contrary, I draw from its proximity and heart. All the lessons I have learned are there. You will recall that I took Mrs Luckham's name for the tenancy of my flat; now Marrineau's for this one; and of course Damato for my company. It's not significant, but I cannot help but think of them sometimes. How we leave our passing imprint on the lives of acquaintances and strangers alike. I have woken from dreams of Mr Stamp searching in vain for his ball of rubber bands, or Mrs Wade flummoxed to find a new wing mirror on her dented but otherwise well-cared-for cherry-red car. It's not so much remembering as wondering how I am remembered, even as a phantom, by others.

My phone started ringing. Being caught here, it made me start, but it was Wendy calling about a valuation.

'What, now? Is Katya not around?'

'No, it's her afternoon off.'

'Zoe?'

'She said she would, but now she's too busy.'

'Well, is it urgent?'

'That was my impression. The lady wants to sell. But, no,

she's at work right now and I said we'd get back to her. She wants to know if we can come at seven this evening.'

And then she told me the address.

For a moment I was speechless. It seemed like a nonsense, or a trick. But then I remembered the flyer I had left on the doormat.

'Are you sure that's the address?'

'Yes, why wouldn't I be? It's right here, number four. And it's a Mrs Sharp – S-H-A-R-P. And, yes, I'm sure. And we've sold the house before. It's in the file.'

'Right. Fine. Excellent. Tell her I'll be there.'

I was smiling. I felt that something had suddenly dislodged and that the world and its possibility was in full flow again. I locked up the flat. I was gripped by an urge to walk. What the hell had happened?

I walked for over an hour, along the river, up on to the ring road and back into town. Abigail's cycle was parked in a bike stand outside the library and as I passed I could see her, seated amid a group of children, a book open in her lap. It was like a sign. Things were changing, and I would be close to her soon. Wishful thinking, you might say. But who says I couldn't make a wish happen? Hadn't I spent my whole life doing that?

I arrived ten minutes early and parked under the horse chestnut up the street from their house. Outside was Mrs Sharp's pale-blue car and behind it a liveried hatchback from Worde & Hulme – one of our rivals. An early bird. Perhaps others had been called too, but that wasn't among my worries. Who else would be willing to cut their commission to zero (or indeed buy the damn house themselves, as I had done in the past) in the emergency of shunting unwanted guests out of town? Heming's didn't get where it is today without being very competitive.

It was a mild Friday evening. I rolled the window down. Almost instantly, the quiet of the street was disturbed by voices – a man's shouting and a woman's raised in protest. I couldn't make out what was being said, but the door to the house slammed unmistakably and the figure of the agent – clipboard in his hand – emerged more abruptly than I might have expected, and almost backwards. I recognized him, a senior from W&H. Our paths had crossed once or twice at industry functions. He coughed, straightened his tie and looked up and down the street while he regained his composure. I half expected the neighbours to wonder what the racket was all about but there was nothing but the twittering of birds.

The agent got in his car and pulled away. But then he stopped alongside my car and leaned out, smiling. 'I wouldn't bother, if I were you,' he said, jerking his thumb towards the house. 'One or two domestic differences. It seems the lady of the house is selling out from under the feet of the husband. Unfortunately he arrived home unexpectedly. He's not a happy bunny.' He looked back again at the house. 'I imagine things are hotting up as we speak.'

I offered a world-weary grin to match his own. 'You may be right.'

'Take it easy,' he said.

I waited for him to drive off, then got out of my car and approached the house, wondering whether something might yet be retrieved from the situation. But even from the gate I could hear them rowing. I thought about ringing the bell, but figured that opening the door to another estate agent would be unlikely to improve Sharp's mood.

On the other hand, Mrs Sharp was expecting me. And I needed to stay in the loop. I looked in my record for their landline number and called it. No one picked up. When the answering service kicked in, I left a message for Mrs Sharp saying I'd been held up but that perhaps I might call round in the morning between ten and eleven if that was convenient. Somehow I didn't think it would be convenient but I guessed that Mrs Sharp would at least call the office to reschedule.

I went back home. After an hour I checked the office voice-mail. No one had left a message. I waited till midnight then called again. Nothing. In hindsight, you might argue, this would have been a good time to forget the Sharps. But I could no more do that than a bear can forget her young or a migrant bird its compulsive journey over land and ocean. I am driven by nature, unable sometimes to distinguish wants from needs.

19

NEXT MORNING I WENT straight to the office. I had it in mind to speak to Wendy about the Sharps but thought better of it and she didn't ask. I was thinking about Mrs Sharp. But was I worried about her at this stage? Perhaps a little. I was worried about how things were developing.

I grabbed my briefcase and walked to Boselle Avenue. The pale-blue car was still there but Sharp's 4×4 was not. I hesitated, then walked up to the front door and rang the bell. I waited and tried again. The house was quiet. I can't explain why the key was in my pocket. I hoped to find Mrs Sharp in, and yet I had prepared for the house being empty. I had no idea, of course, where either of them was – perhaps they had patched things up and gone off to the supermarket. Wherever they were, in the light of Mrs Sharp's determination to sell the house and her husband's determination to stop her, I couldn't assume that no one would be around. That being the risk, going into the house would be foolish. But here I was with the key now in my hand.

I slid it into the Yale lock, twisted half a turn, then carefully pushed the door open. I allowed it to close behind me and pushed the lock button down. As I stepped forward, something crunched underfoot, and as my eyes became accustomed to the dim light I saw that the parquet flooring in the hall was littered with fragments of glass and crockery. The handle of a vase lay on the bottom stair. I edged my way to the kitchen, where I could see an upturned chair through the half-open door. The blinds were down and the light was on. Here was more broken glass. There was blood smeared along the tiled floor. I crouched to touch it. It was dry. There was more blood on the work surface, and a trail of drops leading to the utility room. The odd thing was that even now I didn't suppose the worst. A badly gashed hand, perhaps, I thought – from the broken glass. The door was ajar. I pushed it open. An ironing board stood with a fallen pile of folded laundry nearby, one of the towels dark with blood. One of the taps was drizzling into a white butler sink stained red. I was aware now of the cooler air coming from the garage, the door to which was also slightly ajar. I opened it and switched on the light.

Foolish, I know, but everything I looked at in the garage screamed murder – the teeth of the hanging tree-saw, the golf club, the gleam of a spade leaning against the wall. Had there even *been* a spade last time? I took a step closer and peered at the earth clinging to the blade.

If Sharp had . . . *If* he had . . .

Obviously this was madness, but obviously I needed to look in the garden. Who wouldn't? I remembered there was a tall metal gate at the far side of the garage but it was bound to be locked. A more likely access to the garden would be via the French windows. I retraced my steps back to the hall. Here, on the table in the hall, next to the phone, were two rings – her rings: one with a diamond, the other a gold wedding band, both tacky with blood.

I admit I was trembling. I had to stay calm, keep focused. The house was empty; the door was locked. There was opportunity. I went to the French windows in the sitting room and looked in vain for a key. I peered out through one of the panes. The garden was as overgrown as ever. It was impossible to see beyond the belt of wilting lupins to its furthest reaches where the ground was higher. I had to see the garden. But not via the side gate. Even if it had been left unlocked, it was in open view of the street. Whatever had happened here, not being spotted now was a priority. I needed a vantage point. I crept back into the hall and up the stairs to the landing. Here was Sharp's study. I made sure I couldn't be seen, then looked out. There was perhaps something . . . I took out my opera glasses and trained them on the rear of the garden. I could clearly see freshly turned earth, though it was obscured by branches and leaves. It could have been the end of a vegetable patch, though the Sharps had no obvious horticultural leanings, and why had no attempt been made to clear the surrounding knotweed and brambles? I stared at it for some moments.

Was it? Could it be?

I needed to get out, but first I wanted to check the Sharps' bedroom. The door was wide open. The curtains were still drawn and the light switched on, spreading a glow on the snowy duvet of a kingsize bed, neatly made and hovering like ectoplasm in the room. Drawers had been flung open and emptied of their contents. A wardrobe door gaped on its hinges. My first thought was that Sharp had packed his bags and fled. But thinking about it . . . perhaps he had packed his wife's clothes and made it look as if she was the one who had left – walked out on him after their row. Then he would concoct a story of a secret wealthy lover, a tycoon she had met through her job in the City who had whisked her away to his love nest in a foreign city or on a tropical island.

What was I supposed to do? I could – I ought to – tip off the police; anonymously, yes, from the payphone in the train station. They would assume I was an opportunist burglar, up the line from one of the run-down suburbs of north London, who had stumbled upon bloody evidence of wrongdoing. The police would find Judith Sharp in her shallow grave without her wedding and engagement rings and apprehend Sharp at Heathrow or at one of the European ferry terminals. Doing nothing, or even hesitation, I thought, would give Sharp the time he needed to stage a more legitimate death for his wife – a fireball engulfing her wrecked car off a remote stretch of road, or at the foot of high cliffs out in Suffolk – before assuming ownership of the house as her legal spouse. Yes, they'd had a row, he would tell police – that much would be verifiable by the agent from Worde & Hulme he had thrown out. He had told Judith he wanted a divorce, and she had driven off into the night and not returned. Yes, of course, she seemed distraught. Was she capable of taking her own life? I imagined Sharp shaking his head ruefully – catching the eye of the sympathetic young policewoman, perhaps casting a habitual glance at the curve of her legs – confirming that in fact his wife had recently been suffering from depression.

And now I wondered how Abigail slotted into this. Perhaps it was a recurring facet of Sharp's life. Not that he necessarily killed his partners, but that he used each – invariably more financially secure than he was – as a stepping stone to the next. This one had gone wrong.

I heard a vehicle outside. I darted lightly to the window and drew back the curtain just enough to see the drive. There was no sign of anyone. I left the room and went quietly down the stairs, turned the latch and opened the door. All was clear. I let the door close behind me and heard the lock click. I was at the gate, almost back on the street, when I remembered my briefcase. It was still upstairs on Sharp's desk. Even now I didn't panic. I didn't even hesitate. I simply went back and let myself in again. This time, I didn't proceed with caution, but vaulted up the stairs. At the top I froze. Right in front of me – in Sharp's study – stood Sharp himself, facing the window. He was inspecting the contents of my case. I could not move. He should have turned at the sound of my pounding up the stairs, but he just stood there hunched over the case, his angular body filling out the small room. He was wearing running clothes – a tracksuit and trainers – and in that instant I became aware of the tinny sound of music. He was wearing white earphones.

I can't be sure what happened exactly. Perhaps he caught sight of my reflection in the lamp, or maybe the music stopped just as the top stair creaked under my weight. All I know is that even as he wheeled round I was upon him with all my strength and ferocity, shattering the silence of the house in a sudden, almost comic, uproar. My advantage was quickly lost. He was taller and stronger and had me in an absurd headlock but I propelled him backwards, setting in motion an awkward ballet of push and release as we crashed into the desk, sending papers and books and stationery flying. I tasted blood, and had there been room he would have had me on the floor, but he forced the back of my head against the bookshelves with a crash. I saw stars and tried to force him back, but he whirled me against the desk again. It was now that I saw the glint of something familiar, and my hand, remembering the cool, leaden glass of the green paperweight, reached out and grasped it. But I'd no sooner taken its weight than he twisted my wrist and it was gone, falling with a thud and rolling heavily across the laminated floor. I half kneed him in the groin but he was ready for me again, and punched me twice in the stomach. I felt the air go out of me but held on to him with both arms, as boxers do when they are tiring or playing for time or feel they're being beaten. Did Sharp lose his footing then? He staggered backwards, taking me with him on to the landing, and then he slipped – his legs tugged abruptly from under him. I threw all my weight against him now, and he flew back, striking his head with the sweetest shudder against the banister post. I felt his grip loosen as he tumbled away.

Apart from my labouring breath, a hush now fell upon the house, until they came rising up again, the electronic micro-beats, audible from Sharp's earphones, dislodged now, the thin wire of one of them looped across his cheek where he had come to rest, his body inverted at the foot of the stairs, one leg bent awkwardly beneath him. His head was tilted at an unnatural angle and it seemed to be over, but as I reached the bottom of the stairs he began to twitch quite horrifyingly, his eyes staring out of their sockets at the ceiling. It was a curious hiatus, panting here, watching him jerk and judder when I might still have called an ambulance, but I had already made my choice.

The inside of my cheek was bleeding where I must somehow have bitten it. I made my way into the kitchen and splashed water on my face. Then, regaining my composure, I went into the garage, brought back the golf club – a wood, judging by its bulging face (if memory served, from a summer camp in Scotland Aunt Lillian once sent me to) – took the measure of its heft and length and finished Sharp off with a single firm swing to the temple.

I swear I could hear the chimes of an ice-cream van.

You know what you did.

Oh dear God, if she could see me now.

20

THE HUT IS ONE of my places, but I've never been inside before. If adults see you alone in the cemetery (and most of those who do are taking a short cut from the park to the bus stop) they give you a look to let you know they've seen you there, loitering amid the black stones, some of them as old as the town itself. But I'm not loitering. I am just drawn to the hut.

The hut is on the far side of the cemetery from the park. From the hut you can see the flat roof of the whitewashed pavilion, which is always dark inside and has a wooden floor that echoes when you stamp on it, and smells of pipe tobacco and is the preserve of the slow-witted park keeper who issues tickets to the putting or bowls on busy days. Today is not busy. And the cemetery is deserted. All the loved ones of the dead people here are dead themselves and buried in a more modern cemetery across town or their ashes cast over the waters of the Broads. The man who rides the mower and looks after the cemetery is nowhere to be seen. This is his hut. I have seen him run a hose from the tap here or take his round-bladed spade and neaten the verges or the grass paths around the graves. He is friendlier to children than the park keeper or other adults are and wears a flat cap smoothed to a leathery dark finish with weather and grime. Some of his front teeth are missing. The hut sits against the cemetery wall. It is hand-built from unwanted lumber with tarry asphalt on the roof. It is inexpertly fitted with windows salvaged from other buildings, held in by nails that have been hammered in and bent over and left to rust. If you peep in you can see the chair and bench where the cemetery man eats his lunchtime sandwiches or reads his paper or has a cup of tea when it's raining. It's perfect. I loose the hasp and staple and with a tug the door is open.

'This is my house,' I tell the children (though strictly speaking nothing has ever been my house and may never be again).

We begin with a surprise. I take out a box of coloured matches we have had since Guy Fawkes Night and crouch down to strike one. Anthony's eyes widen at the sight of the red flame. I tell them they are my magic matches. I strike another, holding the match expertly until the flame goes normal and then dies. I strike another. I am happy to lie on the bench while the children play underneath. I have draped a dustsheet over the bench like a curtain and found some sacking for them to sit on and given them each a biscuit. Around us, in our sun-warmed space, are the tools of the cemetery-tending trade: gardening equipment, flower urns and zinc buckets, a bag of cement, another of sand, a third of gravel. There is a red can that smells of petrol and makes a pleasing hollow, sloshing sound when you lift it. I listen to their contented murmurings. They have made a baby of Angela's bunny-rabbit. Perhaps they are offering him some biscuit crumbs. I have no wish to disturb them as they care for him and settle on who they are in this game and what they want to be. Imagination is a fine thing in itself. Outside I hear bees where they move among the bramble flowers and dandelions, and in the distance, though I didn't notice it start up again, the whine of the mower. I close my eyes for a moment and listen to the children's low voices. The sound of the mower now ceases. I sit up sharply and scramble to the window, which has cobwebs on the inside. I ought to have gone by now. There is still time, I hope, to be present for Mrs Damato's horrified discovery, and to throw myself into the blaze, to feel the full heat of my mischief.

The man is some way off but I can see his bobbing cap as he moves through the cemetery in the direction of the hut. I am quick. The door scrapes the ground as I push it open and slip out, keeping my head down as I scamper across the path to the cover of the ancient gravestones and statuary, the smell of freshly cut grass high in my nostrils. Out here and free, it is an adventure to dash from stone to stone, ducking out of sight. After a minute or two I can't see him at all. Perhaps he has turned back, or has work to do in another part of the cemetery. I wait at the entrance, behind the pavilion for a moment, then cross the park, below the line of the bowling green, and take one of the unpaved cul-de-sacs that lead to the main road. From there I walk up the hill and turn right on to our street. I am lucky. All is peaceful at the Damatos', with its door ajar and garden empty of children. Mrs Damato is still upstairs. I hear the soft whirr and clatter of her sewing machine. I make myself small behind an armchair in the lounge, which is spick and span from Mrs Damato's incessant housework.

Minutes on end pass, but now she is at last calling the children. I hear her outside. There is shouting now and a scream. The voice of a neighbour joins in the hullabaloo, then a second. It fills me with excitement. I squeeze my eyes closed. Now a lady is in the hall, using the telephone. There is more shouting and crying. I crouch and hide and listen. I stay as long as I dare, and then at last slip out at the back, down the sloping garden with its roses growing to the wall and the unpaved cul-de-sac below, dark beneath the heavy trees. I glance once towards the park and pause. And now I run. I am blind to everything. I will stop for nothing, retracing this part of my earlier journey from the park, slowing at the end when I reach the main road. I can hear the ice-cream van somewhere. I look back down the cul-de-sac once more but I will not wait, and soon I am back on our avenue where I am safe.

Opposite our house is a police car, sky blue and white, and I can hear Mrs Damato's shrill voice. She is standing with the policeman, a neighbour at her side. The gate is open. Their heads turn at my approach. Asked if I have passed two children, I say I have not. Mrs Damato is urged to be calm. I am quizzed further. Where have I been? To buy sweets at the shop, I say. No one asks me to produce the sweets or indeed turn out my pockets, where they would find one of Mrs Damato's biscuits. Mrs Damato doesn't even seem to know who I am.

The policeman asks if Anthony has ever gone off on his own before.

'Never, never!' wails Mrs Damato. She throws up her arms and breaks into a flood of high-pitched gibberish.

Another neighbour arrives and is told what has happened. The ice-cream van turns on to our avenue with its sudden jolly peal of bells and the policeman steps into the road with his hand raised.

I take the opportunity to escape to our house, where I pour a glass of milk and watch from my window, eating the evidence of my involvement. I am waiting. Almost immediately there is a scream below and Mrs Damato dashes along the street, out of sight of my window. When she reappears, she is carrying Anthony, holding him tight and stroking his hair, his poor face streaked with tears. But relief on the faces of the other grown-ups has already turned to panic as they realize he is alone, and Anthony is now set down on the pavement to answer questions. Where is the little girl? Where is Angela? Where is she? He cannot answer. A woman is running towards the group outside the Damatos' and everyone turns towards her. Is this Angela's mother? I fear so. Certainly there are recriminations and more howling. Perhaps she has noticed that little Anthony is wearing Angela's white sandals. Perhaps Mrs Damato is demanding of Anthony why he is no longer wearing his blue cardigan.

At this point Aunt Lillian's Austin pulls up. She sees the commotion and crosses the street, followed by cousin Isobel, with shorter hair, cut into a neat bowl shape. The policeman speaks to Aunt Lillian and she looks serious and shakes her head. Isobel listens with her arms folded. Then, as if she knows something, Isobel turns and looks straight up at me. As if she knows that worse is to come.

21

FROM ABOVE, SUNLIGHT STREAMED through the study window, casting a green shadow on the wall of the stair from the paperweight balanced on the top step. From outside came the distant repeating beep of a reversing refuse truck. It seemed an age before I moved. I felt as though I were refuelling, and that the longer I stood there the more the power would surge into my body. At last I felt I might explode with energy. On the downside I had only the vaguest sense of what needed to be done. Clearly, somehow, I had to get Sharp out of here. How could I be certain that a neighbour or a passing motorist had not seen me arrive or even just seen me walking up this street? The house was filthy with my fingerprints and footprints and Lord knows what else from my recent visits. It had been bad enough to have the wife's body on the premises; now, with two bodies, even the least intelligent police detective would be looking for a third party. I imagined that to make Sharp's death look like an accident or suicide would exceed the skills of a man who buys and sells houses, even one practised to an intermediary level in electrical and plumbing work.

How much simpler, I thought, if they'd just killed each other.

I switched Sharp's music off by the control on the wire. He was wide-eyed, and pale as marble, but had no blood on him – just a great bald swelling where the golf club had hit.

I took the club into the kitchen, scrubbed it, wiped it and took it through the utility room to the garage. Here was Sharp's brutish white 4×4, squatting in the light from the kitchen. This was the way he had entered the house – driven into the garage, and then come straight through to the kitchen. Had he been planning to move his wife's body after all? Why else would he bring the car in and close the garage door behind him? I lifted the tailgate and, sure enough, the back seats had been folded down to create the necessary space.

But now, of course, Sharp had kindly given me the where-withal to move his own body. The key was in the ignition. I rummaged in the rear and found a travel rug and a blue tarpaulin in a side compartment. Ideal. Back in the hall I spread the tarpaulin on the floor, and manoeuvred Sharp's body on to it. Then I unclipped his music player and emptied his pockets – a wallet, a little loose change – and eased off his wedding ring and unlatched his chunky bracelet wristwatch. I put the ring with Judith's next to the phone. It wasn't too difficult to drag the tarpaulin with Sharp on it down the hall and into the kitchen; more so to get him past the ironing board in the utility room. Now, carefully, I rolled the body off the tarpaulin and down the step on to the ridged concrete of the garage floor. As I'd envisaged, the tarpaulin had swept along with it a tide of crockery and bits of glass from the hall and kitchen. This I redistributed randomly, shaking the tarpaulin to free any remaining fragments. Then I returned to the car and spread the tarpaulin in the back. I tried to haul Sharp to his feet. It was all but impossible. In the end I propped his legs up against the bumper, then – mustering all my strength – took the weight of his torso, gave it a quarter turn and heaved him in sideways. I stood panting, my hands on my knees, then covered him with it as well as I could. The tarpaulin wasn't big enough, but the travel rug obscured everything above his knees. I brought down the tailgate and looked through the dark windows. I couldn't see a thing. I went round the front. The windscreen and side windows were less strongly tinted, but ought to do the job.

In the front of the car I found Sharp's phone, which I switched off. Then I went upstairs and restored his study to a natural state of untidiness, wiping door handles and surfaces with my handkerchief and repositioning the glass paperweight on the desk. Then I gathered my own scattered papers and put them back in my case. There was one crucial thing. I clattered back downstairs, picked up the phone in the hall, and found my message from the previous night. I listened, waiting for the option to erase it.

Sudden movements, by definition, come at a time you least expect them, but none has made my blood race faster than the shadow, that very moment, at the front door's frosted window, followed by the rattle of keys. I had two seconds to do something. I do not remember replacing the phone receiver or even moving. And yet by the time the front door opened I was already in the utility room, pulling the kitchen door shut after me. In the last instant I saw the intruder pause at the entrance, and put down two carrier bags. I was close enough to hear her sigh. 'Just look at this bloody place . . .' came the murmur. It was, of course, Judith Sharp.

My heart was pounding. I couldn't think, just kept perfectly still.

I waited till I heard water hitting the bottom of a kettle, then

I slipped out into the garage, locking the door behind me. But now I was in the dark and the switch was in the utility room. Fearful of kicking something over, I groped my way along the side of the car until I felt the door handle, then slowly squeezed it. The interior light clicked on. I climbed into the front seat and turned on the side lights, illuminating the main garage door. All I needed to do was open it – and then drive like hell. If she heard the car, she would think it was her husband who had returned and then left quickly to avoid meeting her (obviously this would have to be a different husband from the one I had envisaged escaping to the Continent after burying her body in the garden; here I was again trying to turn the picture the right way up in an emergency).

The door was a metal roller, which probably meant it was automatic – and quiet. Hence Sharp's unheralded arrival. I found a thumb-size remote on the car's key fob and tested it with a double click. The door gave a preliminary, soundless jolt. Perfect. I steadied myself to go. But just as I was about to turn the key, I was hit by a terrible sensation. For the second time I had left my briefcase upstairs.

I cursed my idiot self. As before, but for greater reason now, I could not just leave it there. I got out of the car and listened at the door of the utility room. Nothing. Where was she? She had probably begun the task of cleaning up – maybe she was in the hall. But I couldn't just walk in while she was in the house. Or could I? The more I thought about it, the more it seemed obvious. But first I needed to distract her. I thought of my trick with the phone call at the library. I found the house number in my phone from the night before and hit 'Call'. I waited a moment, then got the engaged tone. I realized that that was almost as good. I darted back to the car, pulled the keys out of the ignition, locked the doors, then pressed the remote for the roller door. Sunlight poured in as it began its noiseless ascent. At shoulder height I ducked beneath it and set it closing again. No one was in sight. I went round to the front and rang the bell. I had just assumed the smile of my professional calling when the door opened and Judith Sharp looked out at me, holding the phone with a bandaged hand.

'Are you Mr Heming?'

'Indeed I am.'

'He's here now,' she said into the phone. 'Thank you so much.' She put the phone down. 'I just got your message, and called your office. I was hoping to catch you before you got here. You'd better come in.'

I followed her in.

'As you can see, things are a little . . .' She gave a wave of her hand. 'But we need to press on.'

'Of course,' I said. 'Was there an accident?'

'Accident?' She seemed confused.

'Your hand?'

'Oh.' Mrs Sharp ran her good hand through her mess of red hair. She looked terrible. I wondered if she was on medication.

She took out a pack of cigarettes and lit one. 'I had to stay at my sister's,' she said, inhaling smoke. 'She picked me up from A&E, but I called a taxi this morning. I didn't want her coming back here. Would you like coffee? I'm just making some.'

'Thank you, lovely. And do you think I might use your bathroom?'

I didn't wait for an answer but dashed upstairs. The case was where I'd left it and I crept back down, concealing it behind my back. She was still in the kitchen. 'I'll just need to pop out to my car,' I called to her. I stepped outside for a minute, then strode back in with the case under my arm. She was sitting at the kitchen table, surrounded by mess, one hand on her forehead.

'Please,' she said.

I smiled. I glanced at the utility-room door, which was still closed, and sat down to join her, taking out my valuation pad and unclipping a pen. She answered distractedly as we went through the formalities . . . the three bedrooms and study, the wet room, the new guttering recently fitted, the maintenance contract for the boiler. 'I bought the house through your agency. I don't know if you remember.'

'It does ring a bell,' I heard myself say, sipping coffee, but thinking of the body of her husband barely ten feet away. 'We've sold several down here. It's a very nice property. I'll need to take some measurements.'

She stubbed out her cigarette. 'Let me show you around.'

She was on her feet surprisingly quickly and pushing open the door to the utility room. She hesitated when she saw the mess and frowned, as if only at this moment recalling what had happened. 'This is our laundry room,' she said, sidestepping the ironing board, 'and the garage is . . .'

My stomach flipped and I felt the sweat spring up along my hairline. I prayed to God that I wouldn't have to kill her too.

'Oh,' she said. 'He must have taken the key. We'll have to get in through the front.'

'Please don't trouble yourself, Mrs Sharp.' I beamed. 'At this stage, a garage is a garage, is it not?' I pointed my laser tape measure in the opposite direction. 'Perhaps the other rooms?'

We went upstairs first. Mrs Sharp, her features etched with resolution, threw the curtains wide in the marital bedroom and closed the drawers in the chest, muttering beneath her breath. Then we went into the study.

'Will you be leaving the bookshelves?' I asked.

She stared out of the window, and I saw her blink back a tear.

'Mrs Sharp?'

She was sobbing uncontrollably. She perched on Sharp's swivel chair with her head tilted forward in her hands and wept. I gave her the handkerchief I'd used to wipe my fingerprints from the paperweight that had helped send her husband head over heels down the stairs, and made the soothing noises expected of any man in this situation.

'I'm sorry,' she blubbed. She dabbed her eyes and blew into my handkerchief. She sat shaking her head, her lips pressed together, for some time. I felt time ticking by.

'Was this something to do with Mr Sharp?' I asked gently.

She said nothing.

'To be honest with you, I saw the agent from Worde & Hulme as he was leaving last night. He seemed quite shaken. I gather there was unpleasantness.'

She remained tight-lipped. At last she said, 'I'll be happy if I never see him again. He's gone anyway now, I hope, and good riddance.'

'The agent from Worde—'

'My husband.' She raised her bandaged hand, as if to show me it. It had already come unravelled.

'Here,' I said, 'let me sort that out for you.'

I took out my scalpel, stretched and slit the fraying material and tied it back up smartly.

'Thank you. That's very kind.'

'Is it a bad injury?' I asked, in my kind voice.

'It's just a cut. And my fault. That's not to say he doesn't have a temper. He does.'

'Are you sure you wouldn't rather do all this later, Mrs Sharp?'

She looked alarmed. 'No, no.' She gave a sigh and looked at me. 'It's just that I hadn't told him I was having the house valued, and he walked in on it. There was a fight. Hence the mess. Cups were thrown. Saucers and plates were thrown. My wedding ring was thrown.'

'But the house *is* yours to sell?'

'Of course. I bought it before Mr Sharp came along. Your agency handled it. As I said.'

'Indeed. Well, these things happen. Though admittedly usually after a discussion.'

'He didn't deserve a discussion,' she snapped. 'He told me he was working late. I knew what he was up to.' She sniffed loudly. 'I know you don't want to know all this.'

'You have my sympathies. I have some experience of it myself.'

'You're married?'

'My ex-wife is married to my brother.'

She stopped sniffing. 'That's hard.'

'Life picks up again,' I said. 'That's what I have found.'

'But you'll understand why I did what I did. I had his bags packed by the time he got home. He drove me to the hospital but I refused to speak to him – except to say I wanted him out. By morning.' She looked at me with anxious eyes. 'I'm going to stay with my sister. Do you think you can sell it quickly?'

'If you're sure you want us to go ahead.'

'He put my rings near the front door. He left his own ring too.' She paused then nodded. 'Go ahead. Sell it.'

Mrs Sharp had calmed down now, but showed no sign of moving from the chair.

'Do you see the patch of digging at the top of the garden behind the trees?'

I took out my opera glasses and focused on the patch of bare soil again. 'Ah yes. And that's . . .'

'The woman was the last straw.'

You'll understand why I did what I did.

I went cold. Abigail?

'She's not the first. From his bloody reading group, no doubt. The younger woman, I suppose. Impressionable.' She bit on her lower lip, still staring out into the garden. I could barely listen, but on she babbled. 'I got home from work a few weeks ago. Barney's escaped, he tells me – that's my dog. Ran off when his back was turned, he said. Which is rubbish. Barney would never have run off. But he carried on with it. He even went out and put up some of those posters with Barney's picture on. Then a week or so ago I was in the garden and found him under a pile of old rubbish and stones behind the garage. He wasn't even well hidden.'

Of course . . . the dog.

'He said it was an accident. *What?* One of his *eyes* was missing. I screamed at him so much he couldn't even think of a lie quickly enough, and admitted it. Barney had done his business on the rug, he said, and he'd lashed out at him with his boot.'

'And that killed him?'

'He was having a fit, the dog. So in a panic he put him down with one of his golf clubs.'

She was silent again. Dogless. Dougless.

'So that's Barney at the top of the garden.'

She gave a hard smile. 'I made him go out and buy a spade. He refuses to do any gardening. The grass grows back, he says. Can you believe anyone would say that? I'm well rid of him.'

There was a long, loud ring on the doorbell. My heart jumped, but Mrs Sharp barely flinched. 'I know who that is,' she said.

'You do?'

She got up from the chair and went to look out of one of the front windows, then came back. 'I stopped paying for his car two months ago. In fact I stopped paying all his bills. They've been three times this week to repossess it – huge yellow removal vehicle crawling round the area. He's started locking it in the garage.' She gave a laugh. 'Serves him right.'

'So this other woman . . .' I said.

'You get tired of turning a blind eye,' she said. 'But when other people know too . . . well, let's say I got to hear about it. There was a note. Anonymous of course. And a picture.'

I paused. 'Do you know who she is?'

'I don't care who she is. Not now. I just want to get out of this life and this house, and make a fresh start.'

Of course I wanted to get out of the house too. I just needed to keep her upstairs long enough for me to free the car from the garage.

'Well,' I said, 'if we're moving on from valuation to sales, we'll need a few more details – and of course to arrange a time to come back and take photographs of the property. But first I'll have to get a set of contracts from the office. Do you think I could pop back later today? Give you a chance to sort yourself out?'

'I'll try to clean the place up,' she said.

She didn't move, but lit a cigarette, and gazed out towards Barney's grave. I wouldn't get a better chance. I took the stairs as quickly as I dared. The repossession men had left a card in the letterbox. I took it and let myself out. I only needed a few seconds. I raised the garage doors, darted inside and got into the car. All that mattered was to get out. I started the engine and rolled the car slowly on to the drive, closing the door behind me. I edged into the street and began to turn right. I saw a yellow recovery truck heaving into view from the main road. Instinctively

I pulled on the wheel and turned left. The driver had to have seen me but made no attempt to follow. I gained a little speed, took a right, and then another.

And now what? My plan – and I'm afraid I had no other – was to dump Sharp at the Cooksons' empty property, perhaps make it look like an accident. Why the Cooksons? Because I had the keys to their house in my pocket. And not *their* keys (which they had so steadfastly refused to part with) but *mine*, which I'd had on my wall since I sold the house for the previous owners sixteen years ago. I'd intended to drop in at some point during the week just for the hell of defying their attempts to keep us out. But now I had been presented with an opportunity that could hardly have been better served up by the Divine Provider himself.

22

THE COOKSONS' WAS LITERALLY the last house in town, a detached property at the furthest end of a picturesque access lane bounded by brambles, woods and fields. There was no through traffic. The two other houses on this stretch were themselves obscured by sturdy evergreens and set back from the road. I hadn't forgotten that Katya had it in mind to erect a For Sale sign at the bottom of the lane, and I approached with caution. But the sign was already in place, fixed with a plywood arrow, as if to direct me to the house. Although it was Saturday, there wasn't a soul in sight. I turned off the hill at the cricket club, and into the narrowing lane, the trees dappling the surface with shadow. It was a wonderful day, darkened only by the mischief I had in mind.

The property stood bright and empty. Out on the woodchip verge, two wheelie bins had been put out for the Wednesday pick-up. To the practised eye there is a stillness – an innocence – to a deserted house that shows itself to the world, as a happy duckling to a waiting fox. Even so, I paused for a minute or two, peering through the slim trunks of the silver birches and pines marking the property's front border. The soft crunch of shingle sounded beneath the tyres as I moved up the curved drive. At the top was a hammerhead turning space of finer gravel and a double garage with red doors came into sight. I had already decided not to enter the actual house. But to the side was a gate, accessible with the small iron key on the ring. I backed up, waited a moment, then got out. The key turned in the oiled lock. Inside, a crazy-paved path led to the Cooksons' familiar broad patio, limestone edged with blunt slate monoliths. Beyond was a covered swimming pool, and beyond that a split lawn, shrubbery, and fruit trees stirred by the breeze. The plot was squared off by thickets of trimmed blackthorn the height of two men.

Sharp's body had shifted on the journey, though his face was still covered. I was afraid, for a chilling moment, that he might still be alive – that he might suddenly leap out at me and grip me by the throat. I lifted the corner of the blanket. Some residue had leaked from his mouth on to the grey fibrous material that lined the car where his cheek was pressed.

I gripped two corners of the blue tarpaulin, judged his weight, then tugged. The torso fell heavily on to the gravel. I didn't want to leave a trail of gravel up the path, so I took Sharp under the armpits this time and dragged him. I got him as far as the patio and laid him face up with his head towards the pool – as if he'd been walking backwards and tripped over the decorative monoliths and smacked his head on the paving stone. There was still no blood. It *could* be an accident. Sharp was unshaven; he was wearing a tracksuit. He could be a thief. Or not. I could have supplied him with a tyre iron – some tool for breaking and entering – but decided against it. He could be anyone, his purpose here baffling, nothing on him but a set of house keys. Even when the police identified him, it would be a mystery. Confusion, I had decided – or rather realized – was the best strategy. I wiped the gate key on my shirt (Mrs Sharp still had my handkerchief, I remembered), pressed it against Sharp's fingers and slid it into his pocket. Here was the start to a dozen detective stories. But where would it lead? It was as bad to have too many clues as no clues. The police would find dots to join but it would never make a picture.

I pulled the gate shut behind me without touching the handle.

Now I folded the tarp and the blanket, and dumped them in one of the wheelie bins on the verge. But what, you may ask, about the car? Should I leave it and risk forensic experts finding microscopic bits of Sharp in the rear luggage compartment? Of course not. First I took the car back down to the lane and parked it under the silver birches while I smoothed out the tyre ruts in the shingle. Then I got back in, with the idea of leaving it a little further down beyond the lane, near the cricket club where the road was wider. Now I rang the repossession people, gave my name as Sharp, and told them where to find the car. I placed their reminder card on the seat. I knew a little about the persistence and cunning of car repossession operatives. I had heard how they would patrol all day, lurking in adjoining streets, waiting for their moment to pounce. There was no doubt they would come and claim their bounty. It wasn't beyond hope that the yellow truck loitering around Boselle could get here in ten minutes. By the time the Cooksons returned, the car could be platinum-valeted, resold at auction and be back on the road hundreds of miles from here.

But I'd no sooner pulled away than I had to hit the brakes. A car was slung at right angles across the lane, just after the bend at its narrowest part. The car was red and had a box-sign on top – a learner practising a three-point turn. I kept my distance. The driver, anxious at my presence, stalled the car. The instructor would be telling him to relax and take things slowly. He would be telling him that we all have to learn and that other road users generally show forbearance with new drivers. There was no rush. I nosed forward a little. The learner started up the car again. The back of his vehicle lifted slightly as he released the handbrake. I could sense his nervousness. I knew he would misjudge the camber of the road. The car stalled again and rolled backwards before the brake lights flashed on in panic. A little more gas, the instructor would doubtless be advising. The driver started up the engine again, revved loudly and began his procedure anew. Under renewed pressure, the driver was now neglecting to release the handbrake at all, leaving the car straining like a chained dog.

A minute had passed. Perhaps two. From his side window, facing me, the instructor acknowledged my patience with a raised hand and a smile on this sunny Saturday. I lowered my head. The driver was reversing in juddering increments, but there was no room to pass in Sharp's huge car. He stalled once more, restarted, and then at last began to edge forward. The lane seemed twice as long as I followed slowly at a distance. I had to get the car at least within sight of the cricket club.

At last we reached the end of the lane. The learner car indicated right, stalled once more at the junction and then chugged up the hill and out of sight. I pulled in at a spot just ahead of the junction, left the keys in the ignition and jumped out. I started to walk down the hill but then remembered Sharp's phone. It was in the compartment between the seats. I went back, pocketed it and slammed the door again. But now I could see the yellow truck, turning up the hill. The trees here offered no feasible cover. Back along the lane was a dry-stone wall, a barred gate and open land. I clambered over the gate and waited, ready to run. But there was no sound from the truck. I ventured a look. They had stopped ahead of the corner. Obviously they were wary. A skinny man appeared wearing overalls and a baseball cap pulled over his eyes. He saw the car and gestured to his unseen companion. He crept forward and peered in through the tinted window, tried the door, then leaned in to take the keys. The man in the baseball cap held the car keys aloft, signalling his colleague to turn round. I assumed he would then simply follow the driver in Sharp's car, but instead they laboured to manoeuvre, first, the truck into position, and then the 4×4, all the time with an eye on the house, still perhaps expecting the owner to come out from somewhere, perhaps brandishing a shotgun or waving a fist. No doubt they had the law on their side and paperwork ready to be exchanged, but they were met with nothing except the indifference of the quiet lane and its slender trees, their leaves moving in the breeze. The man in the baseball cap slid beneath the car and within a few minutes they had winched the gleaming white giant car half aboard and rumbled away in a rising cloud of dust.

I set off for town along the public footpath across fields bright with the green of an emerging crop. I walked quickly, Sharp's phone in one pocket, his wallet in another. His house keys were still on the ring. After half a mile I took the phone out. There were two voicemails. The first was from Mrs Sharp, the night before, in a state of barely suppressed emotion, telling him to be out of the house by the time she got back; the second was Abigail, made at just after one o'clock – fifteen minutes ago: 'Hi, it's me. I'm here, but where are you? I see you ate that second Danish! I knew you would. Do hurry. Lots of love.'

Her voice cut straight through me.

He had spent the night with her, of course. That's where his bags were. Perhaps still packed. The two of them had gone for a run in the morning. Then she had gone to the library, while he read the paper, waited till he thought his wife wouldn't be in. Then he had folded down his back seats and gone back to Boselle to clear out the rest of his belongings – his books, his papers, his computer, his golf clubs.

But she was in my mind now, supplanting him. I knew I was close. I felt his wallet, heavy in my inside pocket, swinging against my heart as I walked. I increased my step on the descent via St Theobald's. There was mud on my shoes – no doubt the distinctive sort that would add up in a detective's mind alongside the footprints made by a particular sturdy English brogue in this field. My suit trousers were muddy and somehow ripped at the knee too, I noticed. These were details to be dealt with at leisure. For now I wanted to get home. I skirted the town centre, the alley behind Warninck's bookshop, past Tiepolo's bread and cakes. I strode past the library windows without a glance, then up the hill, past the Common to the little courtyard where my car sat. I unlocked the door to my flat. I was almost dazzled by the sunlight pouring through the net curtains, the familiar, comforting room gleaming with my keys, arranged like a map of the town across the walls.

I took out his wallet, expensive calfskin, doubtless bought by his poor wife. Banknotes, receipts, credit cards, college ID, a few coins transferred to the zipped purse for safekeeping while he was out jogging with Abigail. I further probed the compartment with my thumb and forefinger. I knew it was in there. I shouldn't say I would have killed for it, but I had, and now here it was. I held it up, her key, an almost weightless chip of gold with a shiny red heart-shaped charm attached.

She was mine.

23

OF COURSE THERE WAS nothing conclusive about the unexplained box of coloured matches found in the cemetery man's hut. They could have been anyone's. And of course the police were happy enough to suspect the cemetery man himself, who after all was found in the cemetery carrying the boy's blue cardigan when the constable and others arrived to comb the park. It was the cemetery man himself who had seized upon the matches – found on the floor of his hut along with Anthony's shoes and one of Angela's socks – as evidence of an unknown third party. And what use would *he* have for novelty matches, he protested – a pipe smoker with a silver-plated pocket lighter he'd had since he was in the navy! You could ask anyone. But even to me this seemed a flimsy defence for a man found in a cemetery with the cardigan of an abducted toddler and unexplained shoes in his hut. He was a loner with no wife or family. And you only had to look at those teeth. These were the details that filtered out over the weeks. I can't even say for certain that it came to court. The evidence of 'interference' was circumstantial. And you could hardly expose a pre-school child to the ordeal of a police line-up. Still, the cemetery man was never seen again. It might seem unjust, but what if he *had* done something? We had all been warned about strange men in parks. It was a regret that the Damatos had had to move, though. They were indignant at the suggestion that their Anthony was the true owner of the matches and that he had escaped his playpen with the little girl in tow. But could anyone in the neighbourhood trust their children again with an Italian? That's what people were saying. In fact, as everyone knows apart from some snobbish and ignorant people in Norfolk, Italians are devoted to their children. I for one loved Mrs Damato.

Within my own domestic circle, I remained the only suspect. Aunt Lillian, ashen-faced, demanded to know that afternoon what I had bought at the sweet shop. She turned out my pockets and found biscuit crumbs. I denied having been to the park. I shrugged when, perhaps a week later, the issue of the matches arose, prompting my father, anger in his face, to take the cupboard in the utility room apart in search of *our* coloured matches, which Aunt Lillian distinctly remembered seeing in there alongside a box of ordinary matches, torches, batteries, an ornamental lantern and other paraphernalia that seemed to be the random remedial ingredients for some minor future emergency.

It must be said that my father and Aunt Lillian were often at loggerheads about me. How vexing to have such a boy maniac in their midst, curdling their love and happiness and future.

And yet in the end my aunt must have felt that things had not turned out too badly. Certainly she seemed pleased enough with my progress when I visited her just before she died. She knew that Mr Mower liked and trusted me, and it was hardly in her interests to scupper my blossoming career at Mower's (which was so reassuringly distant from her life in Norfolk) by casting doubt on my character, whatever she might privately have thought. But Isobel? I remembered seeing her conversing with Mr Mower at Aunt Lillian's funeral. If they had subsequently kept in touch, and it seemed reasonable to assume so, Isobel would surely have heard about Guy – especially when his funeral followed Aunt Lillian's so closely (and I'm sorry not to have mentioned this previously; perhaps I was waiting for it to become a footnote). Might Isobel now share her concerns?

My precise recollection of events is confused. But one thing I do remember – in fact it was *on* the day of Guy's funeral – was being asked by Mr Mower to fetch something from his house. He was expecting an important client, and because of the rush getting to the funeral that morning he had left a file he needed at home. It was upstairs on a lamp table on the landing, he said. His wife was away. I was wary. I found the file soon enough. I didn't intend to poke around in his house – and of course Mr Mower was back at the office waiting for his urgent file – but a half-open bedroom door ahead beckoned. I pushed it open. It was just a small spare room with nothing in it but a small bed and a chest of drawers. On the chest of drawers was a framed black-and-white photograph and a candlestick, hardened wax pooled in its cup. The photo was of a boy, probably in his late teens, though it was hard to tell his age. He was smiling, but you could see in his eyes and lopsided look that his awareness of the world was skewed. His face resembled those I used to see peering from the bus that took mentally subnormal children to school when I was a boy.

I knew little about Mr Mower, other than that there was a Mrs Mower and a married daughter who lived in Spain.

When I handed Mr Mower his file, he touched me on the shoulder. No doubt he was affected by Guy dying unexpectedly (which I admit even took me by surprise), no doubt feeling bad too for having paid off Guy's contract when he was sick. But was he also thinking about his own boy?

Stella knew nothing about the boy, but Rita, who had been with the firm for years, said his name was Malcolm and he'd died in his twenties. 'Handicapped,' she said. 'Died of pneumonia. Mr Mower thought the world of him, let him come to the office sometimes with his mother.' Rita took out one of our cards. 'Mower & Mower? That was Malcolm. He was the other Mower. Not many people know that.'

It occurred to me that one person who probably knew about Malcolm was Aunt Lillian – that she might have guessed Mr Mower would do his best with me, back at the start, when she'd sent me here for the summer. Perhaps she told Mr Mower I'd had difficulties at home, that this would be a big favour. What better way for him to seek a little purpose after losing his boy than to help another? And it could hardly have worked out better for everyone. How delighted they both were when I said I wanted to stay on and learn the business, to make a home of this town. And now with Guy out of the picture, what could go wrong?

Mr Mower did not speak openly about his plans for me, not even in the period of freshness following those two funerals. And yet I sensed a change of air, as if possibility itself was breathable and energy-giving. A year went by and then a second. Stella became accustomed to my growing seniority as Mr Mower handed me large projects he would normally handle himself. Meanwhile, I had been secretly working to put finance in place for deals of my own in the riverside development.

When Mr Mower called me into his office one morning to announce his retirement – along with the offer that I run the firm under his name for a small share – he was surprised when I said I'd have to think about it. He was even more surprised a few days later to find that I had the money to make him a generous counter-offer to purchase the firm outright. A shadow fell briefly over his face – as if, perhaps, I had gazumped his own idea, ungraciously seized my future before he could give it. But then he smiled. It was his turn to think about it, but he wasn't going to refuse. In the end he insisted on a smaller sum but also that he remain for a time in the wings, to aid the transition. After a year, the Mowers sold up and moved to Spain, to be near their daughter and grandchildren, Heming's was born, and all was happiness.

24

I GAINED UNLAWFUL ENTRY into Abigail's life a few minutes after I saw her leave for work the morning after the business with Mr and Mrs Sharp, her hair damp from the shower. I was surprised that she had been out on her usual run. Bumping her bicycle tyres down the front steps, she looked tired. No doubt she was anxious about her precious Douglas. Her last text to him was just after midnight. Perhaps she feared a last-minute reconciliation with his wife. I watched her cycle off, down the road, then dismount at the gap in the wall that led down to the river path.

I had no doubt that this time the key would fit, though I paused to enjoy a moment of calm before turning it. Then I closed the door behind me, shut my eyes and inhaled, holding that first taste in my nostrils. Of course, it's nothing more than molecular. But also how magical, especially at that time of day, when the slow lingering charge of a person is still in the air. It goes beyond the steaming aromas of morning – the mingling of coffee and shampoo and croissants. Here was Abigail in essence, arising from the rustle of clothes against her skin, the warmth from her bed, her spearmint breath, the brisk eruption of human dust in the simple tightening of a shoelace. Thus do we leave the signs of ourselves. Its seduction is narcotic. The dreamiest high, the thrill of newness. A fresh drug to try.

When I opened my eyes the first thing I saw was what I assumed to be Sharp's pair of matching holdalls standing side by side in an unused breakfast room. Not wanting to spoil the day, I moved on, capturing each unfolding scene with my small camcorder. The front room was full of heavy furniture, a bow-legged coffee table, vases, clashing patterns. Upstairs was Abigail's mother's large room, heavy with dead smells, a good-sized guest room, a box room containing a single tubular-framed bed, and then . . . Abigail's vast double with its light woods, girlish treasures, 1960s lamp and zebra-print rug, a desk, a laptop, the red curtains I had seen from the street glowing in the night, her mother's ginger teddy. Here was her music docking station, her TV set, DVDs and bookshelves of novels and poetry, popular psychology and philosophy manuals and travel guides. This was still her living space, a teenage retreat she had moved back to as an adult. There were boxes yet to unpack. More books. More poetry, old university books. It was as though, after her mother's death, she had not yet allowed herself to fully occupy the house. For now, I touched nothing, opened none of the drawers, searched for no diary or photographs or letters. This was not a day for greed but thanksgiving. Sometimes what you have is all you need. Having slayed dragons to be here, it was enough to be buried in the softness and earthy scents of her bed, its autumn leaf-patterned quilt left in a careless heap, the pillows creased and unshaken from her night's sleep.

O sweet, fragrant slumber!

By the time Abigail returned I was safely above, locked into the mustard-painted attic, with its cherished junk of memories:

board games, toys, a doll's pram, a walnut-cased stand-up radio, boxes long ago marked with their contents; the careful repository of a family shrunk to one.

I had unpacked, laid out my bedroll in an enclosing cell of heaped furniture, and raised the skylight blind to the starry blue heavens. I showed my moneybox key to the camera and cut my mark deep into a floorboard. She ate in the echoing kitchen (I was glad to discover that the gentlest jousting of knife and fork sounded through the house) and then came upstairs. Oh my. I lay quiet in the faintly starlit darkness as she moved around. I heard her speak (to whom?) on the phone. She listened to a radio talk programme. Perhaps she read a book, or sent one more anxious plea to Sharp's voicemail or inbox. At some point she went to the bathroom and used an electric toothbrush. She coughed lightly. Her mattress creaked as she rolled over to turn off the lamp or set her alarm. Perhaps she cried a little. Who could be happier?

I have had my moments of accident and adventure. I have filmed myself cowering in the dusty underspace of a bed while a man in a hurry to catch a train ironed a shirt in the same room. I have been illuminated without warning in the small back garden of a young woman after dark (I might as well tell you now that this was Zoe). My best moments have resembled feats of comic heroism. Imagine me, for example, at the Houths' of Anders Close – flight from Florida due in at six, taxi booked for 7.15 to whisk them home for, what, 8.15, 8.30? I was up with the birds, showering, hoovering, zipping my weekend bag, enjoying a relaxed breakfast. I washed and dried my juice glass (I'd brought my own juice), bagged my rubbish, swept up the cake crumbs (a good slice from most of a Dundee stowed in the larder), cooled the kettle, scrubbed and replaced the cafetière. Bang on schedule, the taxi was at the kerb, children clamouring to be let in. As the front door opened, I left noiselessly from the conservatory at the rear, slipped into the garden shrubbery and through a narrow but well-used gap in the hedge that gave on to the hospital grounds (where I happen to know Mrs Houth works in an administrative capacity). I am generally scrupulous in making a clean exit, though on this occasion it pleased me to think of Mrs Houth halting in her steps while her husband struggled with the suitcases. 'That's odd,' I imagined her saying. 'Can you smell coffee?' A small aromatic mystery getting smaller with each sniff of the air.

Folly, dread, victory – all might sharpen the appetite. Abigail was a career first. I ate, drank, dreamed and breathed her. She was that newest drug, that highest ledge, the rarest butterfly, all in one. The full immersion of my most ardent imaginings. It lasted five days – I could not risk more before the discovery of Sharp's body – but what days they were! During the day, I visited her at the library. I loved to watch her graceful movement along the aisles, her quick-moving hands as she worked at the desk. When circumstances allowed, I closed in and caught the trail of her perfume. She never looked at me once. It was perfect.

I turned up as normal at the office, though it's possible Katya or Zoe or Wendy might later have recalled (if asked, as they probably were) a greater sense of vigour about me in recent days and weeks. Zoe and I drove out to the retirement bungalows again with a contract to sign and Katya brought down the hammer on two properties that same day (a bottle of bubbly was duly cracked open at close of play, Zoe – revitalized, it seemed, after our misunderstanding – showing Josh how to ease out the cork without 'prematurely spurting', as she called it, making Josh grin and turn pink). It was Katya too – who knew nothing of the Sharps' differences of opinion the previous Friday – who returned to speak to Mrs Sharp, value the house and prepare the documents, sending Josh in afterwards to take photographs.

But meanwhile I barely thought of Sharp, staring up at the sun and the moon for those five days and nights in the Cooksons' back garden. At the time, what happened to him seemed the obvious outcome of a larger necessity. If I thought about him, it was only to hate him for involving me in his death. At other moments I clearly saw it was his character that had been his undoing; that he had crossed a road that hadn't asked to be crossed. I thought too (when I thought about him at all) about what had shaped his mood on the day we had first met. Perhaps he had already quarrelled with his wife about the dog, or with Abigail about his wife. Perhaps he had walked the dog to Abigail's house only to be refused entry. Imagine his fury when he returned to find Barney's shit on the rug! In such a confluence of events – even accepting my role in hastening the opportunity to vent Sharp's rage – Barney's death was inevitable. The only surprise, I thought, was that the poor creature had lasted so long. The pity was that Abigail would never know what I had saved her from. And most of all, that's what I was thinking when I thought about Sharp.

Sometimes, as I remember it now, those five days were over in a moment. At other times they seem like the endless school holidays of childhood, or the innocent summers one imagines before the onslaught of war. My senses held themselves out to her, swaying and falling like tides under the magnet of the great moon goddess. And then in the drowsy, breathing darkness, I tumbled through memory into my mother's bed. Here was her bathtime fragrance but also a rising sourness as she held my face to her belly. Can you hear? A brother or sister was inside her, where once I was. In the soft nest between the unyielding bedclothes and my mother's bare skin I heard and wondered at the nearness of this life and longed to be closer. But here it ended, an ear to the slow, pumping warmth. Here was love, eternal and pure. All I needed to do was listen and it was there.

And then, standing behind the curtains with my piece of bread, or behind the wicker chair in the garden room, hearing their voices, sometimes urgent or shrill, I would take her words as treasures and in my sleep amplify them into giant-size, like the ones in my book of rhymes, the black letters ornate, seriffed and towering. I would worm between the letters themselves – crawl beneath the enclosing roof and walls of an A or an H – and have her close to me in my dreams. What became of the baby boy after mother was taken from us? That was one of the secrets kept from me by Aunt Lillian and my father, who stared ahead and said nothing.

But love was here again, in a delicate balance, the unimpeachable Abigail, pure as a thought to hold safe in my head and never let go. Her pureness was in nearness, not in an embrace or a glance or in fond words. Here – even for five days – was something true and lasting. To expect more, to touch the prize and ask to be touched in return – to engage in full (and I knew this) – was an insidious sweet poison.

Eventually I descended into her private things, her Morocco notebook – she wrote poems in lilac ink; here was her fountain pen – and her social network secrets, left open one morning on her laptop. Here were some of the photographs I had already seen. Her girls' night out, I now saw with a jolt of recognition, was actually her book group, an arrangement of like minds round a table with bottles of wine, one of the women peeping coyly over the top of a paperback, her eyes flirtatious, showing off. Sharp was out of shot but present, his elegant fingers resting on the base of a wineglass, his chunky bracelet watch absorbing the light. In her Morocco notebook, Abigail had written:

Beast
Unseen (or so he thinks) beneath the painted ceiling
  dark of sky,
he nightly blinks indifference here to God in code
that only He can read (and that's the joke),
then dreams the tang of everyday desire.

Beast II
Was it my unkempt charm that caught your eye that night,
or my impressive grasp of metre, length and rhyme
that pleased your ear and lured you into sight,
that you might catch my scent and touch my arm,
and taste my cheek when it was almost time?

Poetry, I admit, is the locked room to which my mind cannot quite be relied upon to find the key, but I read and reread with awe, and spoke the words as if sheer will and devotion would free the message within.

One lunchtime I followed her to the small supermarket on the high street. At the library, she kept up appearances, but here she was defeated, sad and beautiful. She bought a tub of seafood, noodles, fruit and milk. In the evening, mingled with the spiralling sounds of eastern instruments, the smell wafted up to me like a feast in itself. In the morning I ate grapes and strawberries from her fridge. How I loved her.

25

As I said, it was Zoe who broke the news, scandalized and amazed, her eyes wide with the duty of scandalizing and amazing the rest of us. The details were sketchy, based on gossip that had reached one of Zoe's friends, who worked at the solicitors' office in Sloughgate, and amounted to the fact that the unidentified body of a man had been found by a couple coming back from their holidays. 'You'll never guess who,' she said, turning towards Katya with almost unseemly excitement.

Katya stared back at her. 'Oh my God, the Cooksons . . .'

Zoe bit her lip, her eyes shining with incredulity.

Katya turned to me. 'Should we call them?'

'I think not. Though this might get your sale moving.'

The midday news on Two Counties added nothing, other than to report on the nervous state of Mrs Cookson, forty-six, a pharmacist, who had discovered the decomposing body on the patio of their luxury home on the couple's return from ten days in the Seychelles. The police would not say if they were treating the death as suspicious or how the man had died.

'Surely it must be a burglar,' said Wendy. 'What else would a strange man be doing in their garden?'

'Well, I can't just sit here,' said Katya, standing up instead, and looking out on to the street with her arms folded. 'You know what's going to happen? They're going to blame us for putting our sign up and inviting burglars into their house while they're on holiday. Though, surely, it has to be someone who knew they were away.'

The regional early-evening TV news had a reporter on the scene, or at least on the spot where the police had taped off the lane. They had found out that the house was for sale and had our Heming's sign clearly in shot, with parked police vehicles just visible on the bend, their lights flashing unnecessarily. Eventually a police officer came on and reiterated the bald facts and appealed to anyone who might have seen anything unusual to come forward.

By the next morning it seemed they were looking for the driver of a white 4×4 seen leaving the area the previous week. At the office Josh came rushing in to say that it was his driving instructor who had called in about the white car, and that he had now been interviewed on TV showing the exact spot where he had seen it.

'Who Is Mystery Intruder?' asked the *Sentinel* when it finally caught up with the news on Thursday. Nothing was said about the keys, though their reporter went into some detail about the face of the dead man having been half eaten away by foxes and crows, leading to speculation that in the absence of other information – no anxious friends or relatives had called to report a missing person – he might have to be identified by his dental records. By the time the *Sentinel* came out again a week later, the story had moved on somewhat. 'Intruder Was Owner's Patient' blared the headline. And sure enough, in a twist that I might have expected (because how many top cosmetic dentists are there in a small town?), it turned out that Mr Cookson was himself able to identify Sharp's teeth, having whitened them with laser treatment only a few months previously at a cost estimated by the paper at between £800 and £1,200. 'Plot Thickens' ran a subsidiary headline above a gaudy picture of Sharp taken at one of the events at Warninck's. The caption described him as a local married man and part-time Cambridge professor.

And now, of course, everything changed.

26

BY NOW OUR FOR SALE SIGN was standing outside the Sharps' house as well as the Cooksons' so I could hardly be surprised when a pair of plainclothes policemen turned up at the office with their routine questions. I was able to confirm that I was the owner of the firm and, yes, I had indeed visited the Sharps' property recently (Wendy's note was in the diary) and spoken to Mrs Sharp herself. Mr Sharp had not been present.

'And how did Mrs Sharp seem, sir?'

'Distressed,' I said. 'She had injured her hand.'

'And did she say how she had injured it?'

'In a disagreement with her husband, she said. The evening before. I think she said she threw a cup at him. Perhaps more than one. She had been to the hospital.'

It seemed helpful to tell them what she had told me, which I guessed was what they wanted to hear. Wendy brought coffee, shot a worried look at the two men in what looked like matching suits, one with a tattoo on his hand, and closed my door gently behind her. The younger of the officers made notes and watched as I answered, occasionally coming up with

182

questions of his own. Had I ever met Mr Sharp previously?

'Not that I'm aware of.'

'Do you know a Mr Graham Buxton?'

'I don't think so. Is he on television?'

The officer eyed me for signs of impertinence. 'He works for one of your rivals – Worde & Hulme? He visited the Sharps on the Friday night and said that you were waiting outside, and that he spoke to you.'

'Ah, that would be correct. I didn't know his name. But, yes, it was he who told me the Sharps were in some disagreement.'

'Do you mean a fight?'

'A row, certainly. So I decided to call and suggest that we postpone till the next morning. I left a message on their answering machine. I imagine it's still there if you check with Mrs Sharp.'

The two men looked at each other, as if to conclude their business here, but the senior man had another question. 'I gather you're also handling the sale at number one Eastfield Lane – the Cooksons' house?'

'That's true. Are you in the market, Inspector?'

He smiled thinly. 'It's Sergeant, sir. Detective Sergeant. And I'm afraid it's out of my league. Do you happen to have keys to the property?'

I buzzed Wendy. 'Could you ask Katya to pop in, please?'

Katya arrived.

'Katya, do we have keys to the Cooksons' place?'

She looked uncomfortably at the two men and then at me. 'I'm afraid not, Mr Heming.'

'And can you tell these gentlemen why that is?'

'Because they prefer not to. Some clients don't mind, others do. The Cooksons have resisted so far.'

The two men paused, as if deciding on the trustworthiness of her accent. 'Do you think they're afraid the keys might fall into the wrong hands?' asked the younger officer.

Katya frowned. 'I hope not. You'll have to ask the Cooksons.'

They made to go, and I followed them out into the street. 'Has this case become a murder inquiry?' I asked. 'The papers seem unsure.'

'You can't always rely on the papers,' said the senior man curtly and thanked me for my help. The younger man, less eager to leave, craned his neck to inspect the dusty windows of our unoccupied upper rooms, presumably not so much in the hope of finding an answer there as to give the impression of diligence – omniscience even. Even so, I didn't like it. I joined him in his upward gazing and disguised my unease with a smile.

It was not especially hard to follow the strands of the police investigation. The story had surfaced in some of the national tabloids, which had done some digging on Sharp and soon discovered that he wasn't a Cambridge professor and that he had been eight years younger than his wife.

Meanwhile Katya had begun to deal in earnest with the Cookson sale, which is to say she had been out three times to see Mrs Cookson, who in common with all concerned had been advised not to speak to reporters but had found a sympathetic ear in Katya (a surprise to those of us who had always found Katya's personal warmth a distant second to her efficiency and suspicion of life's touchers and feelers). Mrs Cookson related how she'd had to be sedated on finding the body, but said the biggest shock (which was news to Katya) was that the intruder had had the keys to their house. The police had questioned Mrs Cookson with some intensity – had as much as suggested that she *knew* the intruder, perhaps even intimately. And now the

Sentinel was carrying insinuations that this Sharp had been something of a womanizer as well as a gold-digger. They also mentioned that the white car that had been cited in earlier reports was Sharp's own car, but that it had been repossessed and towed away.

'The Cooksons are divorcing,' Katya said.

'It's probably what they needed,' I said. 'Maybe Mr Sharp did them a favour.'

Katya switched on her doubtful Lithuanian frown and said that Mrs Cookson – whose biggest fear was being unable to sell the house now that someone had been so publicly found dead there – was of the opinion that the man had managed to fall and kill himself in a freak accident. She also suspected her husband's involvement.

'Because how else would the man have got keys to the house?' said Katya. 'Don't forget, your Mr Sharp was one of Mr Cookson's patients. He had money problems. Maybe he couldn't pay his dental bill. Maybe Mr Cookson thought up this plan to rob his wife. She has valuables – gold and jewellery. Mrs Cookson said it was only bad luck that prevented him coming into the house.'

'That seems a little far-fetched,' I said. 'It's not as if Mr Cookson is short of money. And anyway, how do you know Mrs Cookson *wasn't* having an affair with this man? She might have sent him in to rob Mr Cookson of *his* valuables. And, if you don't mind, he's not *my* Mr Sharp. I've never set eyes on the man.'

Zoe, who liked gossip and could be relied upon to enhance any drama in our novelty-starved town, perversely asked for a fortnight's leave. To do some decorating, Wendy told me when I arrived in on the Monday.

'Why now?' I asked.

'She has to take her holiday some time, Mr Heming. And we are fully staffed.'

I myself was back and forth to Mrs Sharp, who wore the same dazed expression she had worn on our first encounter. Katya had visited in the interim but Mrs Sharp – who I thought may have been too distressed to occupy herself with selling a house – had asked for me personally. She kept me busy with small queries about fixtures and fittings, damp-proofing worries and various financial matters. It wasn't a bad idea to revisit. It gave me an opportunity to undertake a slow tour of the house with Mrs Sharp, generously leaving my prints on anything I might have touched in my previous uninvited wanderings. I arranged appointments for prospective buyers to be shown round to further muddy the waters.

Mrs Sharp had received my initial shocked offer of condolence with a long silent look out of the window. Eventually she was forthcoming, though still as tearful, vague, and given to angry outbursts as previously.

'I don't know what he was doing but I can't forgive him. Not yet. And now the police think I had something to do with it!'

I mustered a sympathetic look. She obviously wanted to talk, probably felt alone in this, needed a sounding board. We sat knee to knee in the kitchen drinking coffee while she smoked and expressed indignation about the detectives' hostile questioning and asked me to call her Judith.

'Why would I report him missing? As far as I knew, he'd gone scurrying off to his new girlfriend. I was at my sister's. How the hell could I know he was lying dead in someone's garden on the other side of town?'

'Did you tell them about this woman?'

'I showed them the picture of the two of them together. They said, with all due respect, it could be anybody. Mind you, they took it away with them. It's her they should be looking for.'

I dearly hoped not.

When I got back to the office the two police officers were talking to Katya and Wendy. 'Mr Heming, just in time,' said the senior one.

We went into the back room, where they asked about the day I saw Mrs Sharp on her return from the hospital. I pointed out that, strictly speaking, I couldn't say for certain that Mrs Sharp *had* returned from hospital that morning. After all she was already there when I arrived. The senior man nodded wearily and asked about the state of the house, and I told them that the place was littered with crockery and glass, and that there was blood on the floor.

They glanced at each other.

'And you didn't think to mention this before?'

'I assumed you knew. Did Mrs Sharp not think to mention it?'

The younger officer, who had been perched on the window-sill, now mysteriously closed his notebook. 'Is there anything else you'd like to tell us that you've assumed we already knew, sir?'

'I don't think so. I assume you know about the dog?'

The day after, two uniformed officers arrived and asked that Katya and I give our fingerprints for elimination purposes, using a portable scanner. 'Does this mean it's a murder inquiry?' I asked.

My hands, I realized, were shaking.

'You seem nervous, sir,' said the officer, spreading my fingers.

'This gives me the creeps,' said Katya, whose grandfather –

she had once told Zoe, over Christmas drinks – was a Roman Catholic bishop who had been arrested and tortured by the secret police. 'Why do they now think the man died in Boselle Avenue?'

'It's all part of the inquiry, madam.'

Wherever I went that day I felt that their eyes could be on me. I checked up and down the hill before going into my flat.

Mrs Sharp, when I saw her next, was suffering too, having had what she called the long arm of the law crawling all over the house – a warrant to search which, as far as she could tell, had yielded nothing. 'I mean,' she said, 'why *wouldn't* I have scrubbed the kitchen floor and cleared all the mess up after our fight? And with my hand in a bandage!'

'Indeed, Mrs Sharp.'

'Please – Judith.' She poured more coffee. 'And in any case, I told them, the blood was mine. If they found someone else's blood, I said, it would be poor Barney's. Who of course they insisted on digging up to make sure.' She lit a cigarette. Most upsetting, she said, was being questioned about Barney, whether it had made her feel angry. 'Of course I was angry, I told them. Who wouldn't be? Frankly, I wish I *had* bloody killed him. Douglas, I mean, not the dog.' She shook her head. 'I don't mean that.'

My head throbbed with the effort of processing all that Mrs Sharp knew, or thought she knew – or had told the police – and bedding these things down with the facts as I knew them and what I had told the police. It seemed inevitable that I would be sent sprawling over a sharp protruding detail into the arms of these unforgiving crime fighters.

But, then, weren't the police confusing themselves too? Why, for example, were they obsessed with blood when Sharp had lost no blood?

One revelation was reassuring. For days I had been haunted

by thoughts of the golf club that had been the end of both dog and master. Now it turned out that Mrs Sharp had taken his clubs, along with much else belonging to her husband when he had left, to the dump, or one of the town's many charity shops.

'Because why wouldn't I?' she cried. 'And I was happy to tell the police. I've nothing to hide – here's a man who had sponged off me and cheated and spent God knows how much of my money on having his teeth laser-whitened to flash at other women. And yes, in case we forget, he killed my dog! Of course I'm going to throw his things out. I hate him!'

I had to remain positive. There should have been enough in addition to Mrs Sharp to occupy the police, who according to the *Sentinel* (interest among the national papers seemed to have waned) still hadn't formally managed to get their boots out of the mire of suspicious death and on to the firmer ground of murder, which would doubtless release more funds for scientists and detectives. It suggested that hard evidence was in short supply. It suggested they couldn't be certain yet that Sharp's head injury hadn't been caused by one of the hand-dressed stones bordering the Cooksons' handsome patio. The blizzard of so much baffling circumstantial evidence would, I hoped, continue to blind them to the entire who, where, what and why of this absurd-looking case.

It seemed to me still likely that they would look elsewhere, though it was hard to know exactly what to hope for. I was surprised there had been no mention of the first-year Asian student Sharp had made pregnant. If anyone had a grudge against Sharp it would surely be the family of armed Glaswegian Muslims who had turned up looking for him in Cambridge. Perhaps the police were keeping that to themselves – and if so, what were the repercussions for me? It wasn't beyond reason that already they had a description of the man who walked into Warninck's only a few weeks ago making enquiries about the charming Dr Sharp and had followed the trail to Cambridge.

But would the woman I spoke to have even remembered what I looked like – the busy manager of a busy shop dealing with enquiries all day? Certainly if matters were reversed I doubted I'd be able to describe her with anything remotely close to exactness.

The police continued to circle Mrs Sharp, which inevitably drew me towards the vortex. Again the two detectives arrived at the office. Zoe was back now, batteries recharged, her eyes burning with especial vivacity. 'Can I offer you gentlemen tea or coffee?' she asked, curiosity shimmering off her like a desert mirage. She left the door ajar while she busied herself in our kitchenette, which meant I had to be careful in my choice of words. The officers wanted to know, with more precision than before, the sequence of events. I ran through the story again: that I had been there the night before, left a message on the answerphone, arrived next morning to speak about the sale of the house. 'In fact,' I said, 'Mrs Sharp was on the phone to my secretary here when I knocked on the door. Or rather – in the interests of precision – when I rang the doorbell.'

'And did you see Mr Sharp's car there when you arrived?'

I folded my arms to stop my hands shaking. 'I really couldn't say. As I may have told you, I've never actually seen Mr Sharp. So I'm not familiar with his car.'

'And Mrs Sharp?'

'Her car?'

'Had you met Mrs Sharp before?'

'Not that I know of. Though this is a small town. I can't guarantee I haven't run into her at the supermarket.'

The younger man looked at his notebook. 'A white Audi four-by-four identified as Mr Sharp's was seen by two employees of a repossession company leaving the premises on Boselle Road on the morning of Saturday the fourth. It was later recovered by those employees close to the spot where Mr Sharp was found dead. Someone purporting to be Mr Sharp called the repossession company, advising them where the car could be found. Now why would Mr Sharp drive all the way to the Cooksons' house, ask for his car to be picked up by his creditors, only to wind up dead?'

'It sounds like a case for detectives,' I said with a stiff grin. 'But I have been thinking. Consider this. What if the repossession men simply *followed* Mr Sharp to the Cooksons', waited until he had left the car and then attempted to seize it. Then, if you can imagine . . . a quite furious Mr Sharp comes rushing out, an argument ensues, it turns into a struggle which leaves poor Mr Sharp dead on the ground. What are they to do? They panic. There's no one around, so they carry Mr Sharp's body into the Cooksons' garden, ring their *own* office, pretending to be Mr Sharp, and then the office rings *them* to give them the location of the car. The two men empty Mr Sharp's pockets to make it look like a robbery – or because they can't resist the sight of cash – and clear off with the car. Job done!'

The officers listened patiently (perhaps they had already thought of all this and discounted it, though it seemed to me at least as plausible as Mrs Sharp being the killer), then the senior man asked quietly, 'What makes you think Mr Sharp's wallet was missing?'

The hairs on the back of my neck stood on end. 'Did I read it in the paper?'

Neither of them blinked.

I searched my mind for an answer. 'No, of course,' I said at last. 'It was Mrs Sharp who told me the wallet was missing. Along with other items. I think she mentioned his bags were gone. And his phone?'

'Mrs Sharp.'

'Yes. I'm selling her house.'

The older man looked weary. 'So you are, sir.'

The younger one now asked, with a hint of sarcasm, if there was anything else I might remember about the day in question.

I pondered again. 'I don't think so,' I said. 'I'm pretty sure we have it all covered.'

I breathed out slowly as I watched them leave in their car.

I could barely sleep that night. I closed my eyes and saw the stony faces of the two detectives. My stomach churned. Everything was slipping away – the town, my business, Abigail. I woke up in a sweat.

It was a crazy thing to do, but next morning I walked the short distance to Warninck's. There she was, the woman I'd spoken to a few weeks before, serving at the counter. I recognized her immediately, though, again, I doubt that I'd have been able to place her if she'd walked into my office or if I'd seen her in a bar. And there was no way I could have described her to someone. But isn't that how memory works? Doesn't it all depend on context – recall and recognition not quite being the same thing? That's what I was gambling on. I made one or two passes of the counter, then wandered into her line of vision, lingering as I browsed the 'New This Week' titles and the 'Staff Choices' and the best-sellers on the table. Perhaps it was a risk to speak to her, but my intuition argued otherwise. First, what was the alternative? To sneak around town in fear of discovery? And second, I told myself, how better to avert suspicion than to come right out and, as Mr Mower always advised, look her in the eye and *dare* her to picture me – an affable but not especially memorable man in the tweedy guise of a country-town professional – beating lively, clever, trendy Dr Sharp to death with a golf club?

I frowned and sighed at one book after another until she came over and asked if she could help.

'Holiday reading, I'm afraid. Any ideas for a long flight?'

'Oh, lots. Are you going far?'

'The Seychelles. For the diving.'

'How fabulous,' she said, friendly, but with an undertow of briskness that hinted at other fish waiting to be fried. There was no sense that she detected my true position in relation to water sports or indeed foreign travel (let alone murder), and she simply suggested a couple of beach thrillers. We went back to the counter, where she popped my purchases into an environment-friendly bag and wished me a good day.

There would have been some upset in the shop in the wake of Sharp's death. Brows would have been furrowed when the police arrived trawling for information. Right now, though, this woman had showed no sign that her mind was occupied with anything more than a routine exchange of money for goods. If pressed, she might dimly remember having seen me before, but that was probably true of most of her customers – a good many of whom might have attended one of Sharp's events and afterwards spoken at greater length than I about it. In fact, thinking about it, our conversation on the day in question had been primarily about finding a book, just as this conversation had. She had offered to order it for me and suggested the library might have it, as she probably did every day of the week for someone without necessarily remembering the colour of their eyes, or whether they were bald, for the purposes of an artist's impression or police identikit. True, I had made flattering mention of her literary evenings, but only in passing. It was she who had brought up the name of Dr Sharp; she who had eagerly dug out his card – unreservedly proud of Warninck's association with a Cambridge lecturer – and, holding it at arm's length, had read out his name and position as if welcoming the United States ambassador himself to the London Ritz on the occasion of the British Independent Bookstore Federation's annual black-tie gala dinner and ball.

There was relief here, but needless to say it could not last.

27

IN ALL OTHER MOMENTS my heart was sick for Abigail. She was not to be seen at the library. I imagined her closeted at home in shock, unable or unwilling to declare herself to the police. Twice after dark I drove past her house and saw a light in the upper window. I didn't dare stop. I thought with cold fear of the younger, suspicious detective silently following in an unmarked car, or dogging my footsteps around town.

I yearned for my hard billet in the loft, hemmed in by her mother's old furniture, Abigail below, her warmth and murmurings rising through the house. In my dreams I returned there, my face pressed to the wooden floor, running my finger between the parallel grooves I had cut there until all dissolved and my ghost mingled with hers as she went about her daily business – swabbing the yellow kitchen lino, retuning her quiet radio, inking the milky pages of her notebook with lilac adjectives, emerging towelled and pink from the steamy bathroom. There she was on the bed slowly painting her perfect toenails, a tear on her cheek. Everything I ever wanted was there. It was a perfect summit of wishes, all I had struggled for. The key to her house burned in my hand. I have often had to be patient, learned to take pleasure in the increments of deferred reward. But having tasted this one rare thing – this narcotic distillation of all wants – and then see it snatched away by cruel circumstance? Five days I'd been given and now this! My every impulse strained against caution, fought with good sense. These were hours made bearable only by the vivid conviction that the dawn would break eventually on that elusive sixth day, and that more days would surely follow. My mind floated heavenwards on a fantasy of unending days with Abigail, our spirits entwined, she stirring innocently, I unseen and unseeing, a pulsing life lodged in the fabric of her mother's house in Raistrick Road, inhaling and exhaling behind the walls, beneath the eaves, beneath the floorboards. I was almost numbed by desire, forgetful of the danger that it could all end in an instant, that the whole thing might slide and dislodge and collapse to reveal some fiery hell – or that when the abyss cracked open, I would simply find myself walking towards it.

It was a full month after Sharp's body had been identified that I picked up the phone and heard the voice of a young woman. We had dropped one of our leaflets through her door, she was saying. She had a house she wanted to sell. It was Abigail.

My thoughts were confused – a surge of panic at the sound of her voice and then another at the thought of her selling up and leaving. But here also surely was hope of fresh opportunities. Just to hear her speak seemed to herald brightness and possibility. How could it not?

It was as much as I could do to form the words necessary to arrange a time to call, and within an hour we were sitting opposite each other in her mother's heavy patterned armchairs. Leading me from room to room (though of course I already knew every inch of the place), she looked unwell – her eye sockets dark with worry, her arms folded as she walked, pulling her thin green cardigan around her body like a shroud. Sharp's matching holdalls had disappeared, perhaps hauled to the town dump. I pictured a nervous, disconsolate Abigail there among the hulking battered skips, perhaps climbing the metal steps alongside Mrs Sharp, the two of them ridding themselves of this murdered man's mortal trace, unwitting sisters in wretchedness.

'And would you be looking to buy in the area?' I heard myself ask.

'No,' she said. 'My mother died last year. This was her house. I'll be moving out of town.'

My heart sank. This was about Sharp, of course – her loss, but perhaps too the fear of being implicated in a police investigation. I wondered if she had revised her view of him in the wake of stories that had been circulating – his appetite for spending his wife's money, his suspected involvement with Mrs Cookson, herself now the subject of fresh gossip regarding an affair with one of the GPs in a practice adjoining one of her pharmacies.

I followed Abigail out to the modest back garden. 'It's not much,' she said, 'but there's a lock-up in the street behind.' She unbolted a gate and we exited on to a muddy cul-de-sac, lined on one side with old-fashioned garages with painted doors, each with a number. 'The green one's ours. Mine, rather.' She unlocked it and stood back. It was dark inside. 'You expect it to be damp, but it's not,' she said, walking in and running a hand over the upturned furniture and unwanted household items. 'To tell you the truth, I'd like a quick sale.'

I could have reached out and touched her hair.

'Don't you worry,' I said. 'We'll soon have things rolling.'

She smiled and looked at me for the first time. It was unnerving, after all this time, to be speaking like this. To be this close.

Again, I couldn't sleep that night, but now it was Abigail who was restored to my dreams, pushing out bad thoughts. The next morning I sought her out in the library. She was rearranging a display in the children's area. 'Oh, hello,' I said in my surprised voice.

'We meet again,' she said, straightening up and holding a picture book across her breasts.

'Amazing!' I beamed. 'So . . . do you work here? Of course you do, what am I saying?' I laughed and apologized for wasting her time. 'I just popped in to make sure our ads are in the paper – and the right way up!'

She narrowed her eyes. 'Is that usually a problem?'

'You'd be surprised.' I stood for a moment longer, looking at her. She had freckles along the top of her nose. 'Anyway, I thought I'd say hello.'

'Of course,' she said, smiling. 'And hello to you.'

Later I waited for her in the park, beneath the trees, far from the path. Approaching one of the benches, she dismounted and carefully laid the cycle on its side in the grass. Now she searched her pack, then sat on the bench and began to write in a notebook. I could barely watch.

The next afternoon, I returned to her house to take photographs. We had coffee and went through the paperwork. She was returning to her old flat in London, she told me now. Initially she had been tempted to settle here in town, but things hadn't quite worked out. 'It's not quite me,' she said.

'That's a pity,' I said. 'I imagine London is rather more exciting.'

'I don't know about that,' she said.

She smelled divine.

I asked about fixtures and fittings. She asked if I knew a man with a van for hire. 'I have a houseful of rubbish I need to get rid of – my mother's mainly. I'm told there's a massive charity depot on the way to Wodestringham that recycles and sends stuff to Africa. I don't have a car. I don't actually drive.'

'Why don't you let me help you? We have a van. I have spare time.'

I felt my heart pause mid-beat. This was crazy.

'Is that part of the service?'

'Non-drivers only.'

She laughed. 'I suppose Sunday would be out of the question?'

'What better day for a good deed. Ten o'clock too early?'

'It's a date,' she said.

I wore my Oxfam jacket and casual trousers for the occasion. Zoe was on duty at the office, and I steeled myself against her inevitable comment when I went in for the van keys. 'My goodness, Mr Heming,' she cried. 'Are you in disguise?'

'Just helping a neighbour out with a chore,' I said.

'A female neighbour, by any chance?'

'An elderly neighbour.'

In the end it took three journeys. Abigail already looked more buoyant. She was wearing gardening gloves – said her nails were always breaking. 'Mine too,' I said. She was happy to be amused. She told me about her old job in London at one of the university libraries and her life there. There had been a boyfriend who had baled out (as she described it) when she'd had to come home to look after her mother. 'Probably just as well. I didn't have much time for socializing. But I got in touch with a couple of old friends here after Mum died. Also, I'd taken my part-time job at the library here. So things took off a little.'

We talked about me less, but imagine her surprise when she discovered that one of my favourite recent books was *Suit of Coins* by Barrington Gates. 'I love that book!' she said. 'I have a signed copy!'

'It says a great deal about loneliness,' I said.

'I *so* agree. And exile.'

'You took the words out of my mouth.'

She insisted on buying me lunch in the tea room of a garden centre on the way back. A shadow passed across her face when I expressed sympathy for her bereavement (meaning her mother, though her mind doubtless seized upon Sharp), but she brightened when she learned of my own orphaned years, my suffering at the hands of a cruel aunt. I volunteered, too, the story of my relationship with a local girl that had ended in disappointment and soul-searching when she had simply taken off one day without a word. 'Even though it was some years ago, I've never quite been able to shake it off,' I said, trawling my memory for stray details of my ill-fated liaison with Zoe. 'It occurred to me afterwards that she might have had emotional problems,' I found myself saying, thinking of the antidepressants I had discovered in her bathroom cabinet early in our 'romance' (which, admittedly, I should not have found odd, given Zoe's breezy, sometimes downright excitable, personality). 'I actually discovered her creeping about in my garden late one night. I opened the curtains, and she was actually staring at my window.'

'Oh my God. What did she say?'

'She said she'd been missing me, but hadn't wanted to wake me. Can you believe that?'

Afterwards we strolled down aisles of plants, our hands teasingly close but not touching. She sat on a rustic bench and motioned for me to join her. I noticed one of her nails *was* broken. She told me a joke that I didn't understand about tobogganing. I laughed anyway – perhaps an instant too late because she then laughed even louder, sensing my discomfort. What was happening? There was a silence that allowed us to wonder. Perhaps she was just thinking about her own story – the one she couldn't tell. I found myself not wanting to know. Or rather, wishing I wasn't the only one who already knew.

When I dropped her at home she thanked me again. 'I owe you,' she shouted from the step.

I gave her a salute. Even now, I still feel at least that to be true.

28

And then there was Zoe.

'How would you like to do *me* a favour, Mr Heming?' she said, bringing me a coffee in my office before I'd hardly sat down with the mail. The *me*, I saw straight away, was a continuation of her playful remarks the day before, when she had made light of my casual wear.

'A favour? What did you have in mind?'

'Well.' She closed the door and settled herself in front of me, smiling. 'To be brutal, I have a forsythia, a dead one. Well, practically dead. And it needs shifting.'

She looked at me. I looked at her. Was she speaking in code?

'In fact it needs digging out, uprooting. It's quite a task. And then shifting – to the dump. Organic recycling.'

'It's a tree?'

'You might call it a tree, Mr Heming. I would call it a shrub. The point is, it's a job for a man.'

'I am quite busy. I don't suppose you know any other men?'

'That sounds rather mean, Mr Heming.' She paused. 'I do

have a cousin, Tom, in Northumberland. Perhaps he wouldn't mind popping down the four hundred miles or so to do it.'

'I didn't say I wouldn't, Zoe. Perhaps one evening?'

'I have Wednesday afternoon off. How about then?'

She gave me one of her radiant smiles and skipped off.

It had been a while since I had last set foot in Zoe's flat, a tiny but attractive ground-floor converted terrace less than ten minutes from the high street. Two osteopaths, I remembered, shared a practice upstairs but lived elsewhere. Her narrow, nicely kept garden backed on to the premises of a small auto workshop to the rear, being bordered to the side by a high fence adjacent to an alley, where she parked her car.

If I had one strange story to tell about Zoe it would be the night she found me in her garden. I don't know why she suddenly chose that moment to fling back the curtains (a dazzling cruciform figure against her patio windows), but she seemed oddly unsurprised at my presence, illuminated by two movement-sensitive spotlights that I can only think must have been set off by Zoe herself. She fumbled to open the door. 'Mr Heming, what in God's name . . .' Rather than scream the street down and summon the police, she ushered me in, wearing only a dressing gown. I have to assume she knew it was me out there – had already spotted me lurking. It was possible she had seen me at least two nights previously, hesitating in the alley, lit by the yellow street lamp, not daring to enter.

It wasn't entirely out of the blue. We had had our moment in the office some time before, the two of us working late on something, an accidental brush of bodies, a significant look, a subtle catch of breath, a rise in temperature. It could have happened there and then had I not retreated. Even so. I mumbled something about how I happened to be passing, that I recalled how she'd moved heaven and earth to buy this flat (no drama of Zoe's was safe from the office), that the gate was open . . .

'The gate was *not* open. Did you climb that fence? Are you mad? You could have broken your neck.'

I could smell perfume. Her feet were bare.

She leaned across me to switch off the light and we went through to her bedroom without a word. What can I say? I am only human. There was passion, at least for a time. As I have suggested, the higher its flame burned in Zoe, the more it faltered in me.

All that was a long time ago, and yet I didn't believe for a moment that this invitation to uproot Zoe's shrub was purely a gardening matter. There was too much frivolity and glancing. It was true that the old lightness between us had reappeared in recent weeks. We had visited one or two projects together in my little car. She was as clumsily flirtatious as she had always been and no less reasonably attractive, but – even without the consuming distractions of the Sharp case, not to mention Abigail – my interest in Zoe was no more. Had there been something in my responses that had suggested otherwise?

'I think we'll have to get you out of that jacket,' she said, turning her indulgent smile for the second time in a week on my casual garb. Then, taking my arm, she led me out to the forsythia, which was more like a small tree and didn't look dead to me, judging by the yellow flowers and sprouting greenery, though I am hardly an expert. She handed me a spade. 'I imagine it goes quite deep, but I'm sure you'll be able to get it up,' she said. 'I'll leave you to it. I'm going to run out to the shop for some cold drinks. Won't be long!'

I heard her start her car in the alley and drive off. I shouldn't have been there, and wished I wasn't. Why had she left me on my own? I wondered if it would even surprise her to come back and find me snooping in her private areas. Perhaps it was what she wanted me to do. I felt nothing urging me on. Zoe's novelty had long been faded by familiarity. On the other hand, there was no risk. It was a tiny flat, and if she arrived back too soon, I could simply say I needed to use the bathroom.

I sank the spade into the soil, went back inside, took off my shoes and entered her room. In the light of what I have said, you will forgive my immodesty if I tell you I was expecting at least a shrine to myself, with a photograph surrounded by candles – perhaps an open journal declaring her love on every page. But there was nothing, unless the bed itself – beautifully arranged, with an embroidered coverlet and arrangement of cream pillows – was to be the bait. The curtain was closed, casting the room in a pale, jaundiced shade. There were a few contemporary novels in a pile alongside guides to successful estate agency and basic management techniques. She had the Gates novel and other popular titles I recognized. I wasn't disappointed, but I was puzzled.

I went back to the garden and set to work. The soil, which yielded at first, soon became dense, and the root could have gone anywhere. I had made little progress by the time Zoe returned fifteen or twenty minutes later. 'Come and get it!' she announced, tiptoeing across the patio with a tray containing a jug and glasses with ice. 'Homemade lemonade. Well, homemade by the deli.'

I gulped down a glassful and returned to my impossible task while she sat on a patio chair and chattered.

'Isn't it wonderful that Katya and Evan are getting engaged at last?'

'Evan?' I panted. 'I don't think I know Evan.'

205

She laughed. 'Evan. Her Mister Jones. You're terrible.'

'Am I?'

'What were those policemen asking you about?'

'What do you think? Have they spoken to you?'

'They've spoken to all of us. Even Wendy.'

'Well, there you are, then.'

Her gaiety ebbed somewhat. 'They asked about the Sharps' house coming up for sale. And they wanted to know if I was in the office that Friday, then asked why I wasn't the one to go and speak to them when Wendy took the call.'

'And what did you say?'

'I told them I was busy, and that it was urgent and that I supposed that was why Wendy called you. Are you all right? I do worry—'

'Me?' I carried on working furiously, tugging now at the fibrous trunk of the plant. The sun, out viciously ahead of the summer, was beating down. The sweat was pouring off me.

'You're getting into *quite* a lather, Mr Heming,' she said.

'I don't think I can get it completely loose. I think we need a saw, and then you'll have to poison the root, I think. Isn't that what you have to do?'

She found a saw in her shed, and after more manoeuvring and more panting and pulling I finally had the thing out and on its side.

'Hurray!' cried Zoe, giving me a hug that she didn't quite want to relinquish – a quick yearning in her eyes that was painful to see. 'Well done,' she cried.

She helped drag the plant into the van and we took it to the composting skips near the allotments on the outskirts of town. I could have pointed out that she might have done this part by herself in her own car, perhaps even in a couple of weeks when the foliage had withered down. But I said nothing; just listened to her chattering about this or that day we'd once spent together as we wove through the sluggish afternoon school traffic and muffled noise of children. Clearly she had simply engineered this afternoon of labour and leisure – a project that would providentially throw us together. When eventually we pulled up outside her place, she kissed me on the cheek and held on to my arm. Perhaps she was waiting for me to cut the engine.

'Will you come back in?'

'I think probably not. I need a shower. Best get back.'

'You could have a shower here. We could hang out. The lemonade is still cold. Perhaps something stronger?'

'Probably better I didn't.'

Her teeth were white, her skin smooth, her breath minty fresh. And all for me.

'I think you *should*,' she purred, her gaze like a hypnotist's.

'Maybe next time!' I beamed.

29

ZOE WAS THE DIREST WARNING, and yet she made me hungry for the sweetness of Abigail. I had not envisaged a sexual entanglement with Abigail, or pursued that outcome, or dreamed of it. And yet, soon enough, here it was. Here *she* was, in my office with an inventory of fixtures and fittings that she might more conveniently have emailed. 'It's mainly carpets and curtains,' she was saying, 'but I want to leave the cooker and dishwasher, which are both quite new, plus one or two other items. There're a few gardening tools in the lock-up. I've suggested some prices.' She seemed breathless, as if she'd run here and had only seconds before she had to run again.

'Great,' I said. 'We'll press on with that. And how are things otherwise? The house must seem a lot emptier for—'

'Let me buy you dinner,' she said.

I opened my mouth. 'That would be . . .' I began.

'Tonight,' she said.

'. . . marvellous.'

*

We did go out that night, and again at the weekend. And again in the days following. The deed was duly done. Perhaps there are still those who find it hard to reconcile my unconventional lifestyle to my success with women. It may be explained by a lack of obvious intent on my part. You wouldn't describe me as a predator, not in that way, at least. In Abigail's case it may simply have been a hankering for human warmth in the wake of Sharp's death; and, who is to say that she wouldn't eventually have taken me into her confidence about Sharp, given a little sympathetic coaxing? There was a sense too that I wanted to savour a final frisson of triumph over Sharp – that Sharp was not quite beaten without this phallic coup de grâce. Who knows, perhaps that's what excited me most.

But it had to end. Because for all Abigail's physical beauty, her natural clarity of mind and spoken voice, the intensity of that other *real* intimacy – that breathtaking presence and nearness in which I had invested as an observer and devotee and clandestine attic lodger – began to ebb in the raw moment of our first kiss. I won't say I was simply going through the motions. As I have pleaded earlier, I am only flesh and blood. But I freely confess (without burdening you with excessive detail) that those primal urges were driven as much by thoughts of being secreted aloft in that dim mustard quiet beneath the skylight with an ear to the floor, listening to our muffled tender couplings, as her actual yielding naked presence beneath me. I might further invite you to picture the moment of withdrawal (and I promise this is the last excessive detail), as I jerked out almost rudely at the frantic height of things – not the first time it happened, or the second, but on the third occasion, when the pattern had suggested itself, and when it seemed to Abigail that we knew each other well enough to mention it – when she whispered in the soft lighting of her room, as Zoe had more than once before her, 'You don't have to do that,' and I gave her the same wearied reply I gave Zoe: 'Actually, I do.'

Make of that what you can, if you must. As I said, Zoe was the warning, a perfect illustration of one truth, or at least a truth true for me: that born with the new kicking life of a physical relationship was its grinning death. The foreboding had started. And with it a gnawing sense of waste. Without question, it would come to pass, what I had endeavoured to save myself from, avowed my faith against. Loss of love.

30

WAS IT AROUND THIS TIME that my cousin Isobel turned up? Certainly it was between police visits. Before they asked me to accompany them to the station. I remember walking into the office to find Zoe already chatting away to her. I didn't recognize her at first, not having seen her since Aunt Lillian's funeral. I took her and her daughter, Elizabeth, to a café. I was in a low mood, though polite. Our conversation, as I remember it, was cordial, banal even, the old animosity smoothed to nothing by the passing years. Who would have guessed how much she used to despise me? But this was almost like a social call, as if she had been passing and decided to pop in, though in fact the two of them had travelled in from furthest Norfolk (Elizabeth, sucking pink milkshake through a straw, said they'd come on two trains, and volunteered the names of her primary school and teacher). Isobel had seen the Heming's sign come up on the TV news and had been shocked by the mystery dead man found in someone's garden, though she said no more about him.

She appeared surprised that old Mr Mower had retired (though he would be well into his seventies now) and seemed elated to find me still here and having done so well in business. She watched me intently as I spoke, nodding a great deal as I told her about the town. I am, of course, practised at small talk, and at selling our leafy, bourgeois virtues to outsiders. Her own recent fortunes had been less happy. Her husband had left her – had fled to the Far East with barely a goodbye – and she'd had to sell her mother's house. Now that money was gone. There was a pause in which I offered her money to tide her over, and drew £500 from the bank there and then.

A day or two later she sent me a note saying how lovely it was to see me again and thanking me for the money. Unfortunately, things had taken a turn for the worse. Her beloved old car, it seemed, had come to the end of its life, which was causing all sorts of immediate logistical problems (she listed them), and now it turned out that the roof of her cottage also required urgent attention. And this on the eve of new thoughts about Elizabeth's future. Obviously the village school was fine for now, but could the sleepy local comprehensive match her potential? There was a reputable girls' academy offering a highly manageable fee-paying structure not too far away. Perhaps I could help? She had taken the liberty of enclosing her bank details, and promised to call in a few days.

I felt suddenly fatigued by this intrusion, and helpless to act one way or the other. I found myself wondering if Isobel had actually left town, or whether she was still lurking somewhere. Foolish, I know, but hurrying to see clients or Mrs Sharp (whose house sale had been put on ice during police investigations but who still found compelling reasons to demand my presence), I found myself looking over my shoulder.

As for Mrs Sharp, she was still on leave from work. 'Can I tempt you, Mr Heming?' she would now ask, pouring a glass of white wine, regardless of the time of day. She oughtn't to really, she said. Not with the medication. She smoked almost incessantly. I don't mind it myself (curtains impregnated with the odour of tobacco remind me of my mother), but when it came to selling this house I could see it might be an issue.

The police were still on her back, she said, which further set my nerves jangling. She had given them what seemed to her a plausible account of why her husband – by all accounts short of cash – would have left his valuable wedding ring (a sentimental act, surely, for a man who had been kicked out of his home with only the money in his wallet), and had admitted she had been in the house when the repossession men called on the morning in question. But she had been unable to explain how the card they had dropped through the letterbox (scribbled with the date and time) turned up on the front seat of the vehicle not two hours later, when the same repossession men recovered it from the lane approaching the house where her husband was found dead the following weekend. She was exasperated that the police now doubted her repeated insistence that when her husband had left the house – and she could not say whether it was the Friday night after their fight or the morning following – he had taken with him a matching pair of leather holdalls containing clothing and other essentials.

On top of this, Mrs Sharp had now suffered an unpleasant visit from Mr Sharp's brother Ian. 'I'd never even met him before,' she said. 'He came barging in, telling me the police were harassing him over some phone calls he'd made. Now *he* wanted Douglas's belongings. I pointed out that there was nothing left and that, in any case, as his wife – and certainly in the case of Douglas having died intestate – his estate would probably come to me. Not that he had anything that I hadn't already paid for one way or another.' She blew her nose and said that the man had eventually left, slamming the door behind him and roaring off on a motorcycle. 'He's on the oil rigs in Scotland, he said. But they traced him there and had him in for questioning. He said he hadn't seen Douglas in years. Why would he want to see him now? That's what the police were accusing him of – making enquiries at Douglas's old college in Cambridge trying to trace him, saying his mother was seriously ill.'

'And was she?'

'Of course not – she died years ago! So why would he even be trying to find Douglas? Mind you, I wouldn't put it past him to kill someone. He struck me as the violent type. He was once in the army. Very rough. And the fact that his brother was dead hardly seemed to bother him. No wonder the police suspected him. Anyway, he was hundreds of miles away in the North Sea when it happened, so that was that.'

She left the room and came back with the handkerchief I had lent her that Saturday, laundered and pressed. 'I keep forgetting,' she said, and watched as I tucked it into my pocket.

'When did you lend me that?' she asked.

I looked at her. The question felt like a trick. Did I need to lie? I couldn't work it out. There was always a turning point. A crucial oversight. Something that someone, somewhere, would remember afterwards that would lead to the hangman's noose. I made an excuse and walked back to the office. Again I was exhausted. I couldn't think. I stopped on the corner and sounded her name. 'Abigail . . .'

Once it had been enough to send a shiver of anticipation through my every fibre. Now the sound expired in the air, plunging me into blackness. Across the square, the green-and-white sign that bore my name – two stylized grooves underlining the

H – stirred in the cold wind. Never before had I so keenly felt the weight of error. Gnawing of regret had hollowed me out, promise deserted me, and with it courage. A tear sprang to my eye. I was grieving. Not for something I no longer wanted but for the feeling it had once given me but which had now gone.

31

WHAT FOLLOWS WAS ONE of the most perilous days of my life.

As I may have said before, getting the key to a client's property is relatively easy. Some prefer to be absent when buyers are looking around. They'd rather hand over the keys and let me get on with it. This is ideal. When I'm done, I can copy the keys and return the originals to the owners. Neither the current owners nor the future owners are any the wiser and I have a new house for my collection. In reality, though, most clients are happier to show the buyer round themselves, confident in their own unforced sales manner, their intimacy with the house and its features ('I see you're admiring the cornices – they're authentic Georgian'), their superior local knowledge, their people skills ('Will you have a coffee? My wife's lemon zest medallions are legendary'), and the unique emotional leverage they can bring to a sale, believing that a buyer will be swayed by accounts of how their well-balanced children grew up here (the now unused garden swing providing a poignant reminder of blissful times) before going off to university or drama school. This is no good to me. In cases such as these I will arrange an appointment that is inconvenient for the client – when I know they are out at work or away for the weekend. 'Yes, that *is* difficult,' I hear myself say. 'But why not let me show them round? No, that's no problem at all. My pleasure.' And if there is a shortage of prospective buyers? Well, what is to stop you from just making one up? There's no better time to show a property to an imaginary prospective buyer than when the client is not around to point it out.

The alternative scenario is when the client genuinely can't be at home on the day the buyer – say, a busy out-of-towner with cash in the bank but not much time for house-hunting – has set aside to blitz the area looking for properties. This was the most recent position with Abigail's house. It had been featured in the *Sentinel* the week of our dinner, and there had followed a small flurry of enquiries, two of which had resulted in viewings on Sunday, when Abigail was home. I had attended neither. But this latest involved my picking up the key from Abigail at the library. It wasn't my idea. Zoe had arranged it in my absence, and seeing my name on the client file asked if I wanted her to handle it. It was a moment to retreat entirely. But I took a breath and dived in. Perhaps I thought something might still be retrieved, that somehow I might wipe the error from my head and get back to where we'd been before. I might at least suspend the inevitability of her eventual move out of town and out of my life.

Abigail was businesslike. She'd tied a loop of brown string to the key and a label scribbled with my surname. Her colleagues hovered at the desk, allowing us to exchange no more than a tight-lipped smile.

'I'll have it back to you straight afterwards,' I said.

'Don't worry. Just drop it in the letterbox when you're done.'

I walked across the Common and along the river. The buyer – Mr Peretti, late forties, balding, stocky and tanned – was waiting with a younger man, also tanned but slimmer, along with a tiny older woman, wearing a distinct wig and carrying a dog. I showed them inside. They were chatty and enthusiastic, the younger man rapidly casting an eye over each room in turn and nodding. He folded his arms to parade a small tattoo of an anchor.

'Jason's the creative genius,' Mr Peretti said.

'I can imagine.'

'Oh, look, Paul,' said the woman, who I gathered was Mr Peretti's mother. 'They have a sun lounge, like Maria and Tom!' She was surprisingly light on her feet. She had Mrs Damato's accent.

'That's actually stone-built,' I said.

I emphasized the flexible layout of the rooms. The place was comfortable enough, though some might feel it would benefit from modernization. 'The price takes that into account,' I pointed out.

The men muttered together, with Jason gesturing in a horizontal line with a pinch of his thumb and index finger, as if converting in the mind of his partner the dim downstairs area into a bright open living space that perhaps left the option of a small reading or sewing room. I wondered who of the three would do the cooking, and despite my sombre mood found myself conjuring a sweep of brushed steel and a walk-in larder hanging with strong-smelling sausages and shelves of imported canned fish, pasta, cheese and colourful liqueurs.

We went upstairs, where we found large bedrooms to the front and back, a guest room and the possibility (a necessity) of a second ensuite. 'And then, of course, there's a dusty attic up there. The stairs are boxed in, I'm afraid.'

'So we'll unbox them,' cried Jason. He was already yanking open the door and scampering up like a child. I followed with

Mr Peretti just behind. The heap of furniture remained, but gone were the toys, board games and the standup radio, sold and picked up by a collector a few days before.

'Studio?' said Jason, one eyebrow lifted.

In fact I couldn't help but like them. Weren't they just the sort of unusual household I would normally look forward to visiting in their new home?

I took them outside to the small attractive courtyard garden with its stone terrace and variety of pot plants and trellises. 'It's not much of a garden, I'm afraid,' I said.

'Perfect,' Mr Peretti said. 'We hate gardening but love to sit outside. My mother could do the watering while we drink beer.'

'Oh my son, always joking,' she squealed, holding on to her wig in the breeze. She let the dog loose to sniff among the stones and leaves.

'The owner's moving back to London,' I said. 'It's more than likely she'll leave the plants.' Had Abigail even mentioned them on her list?

I took Mr Peretti out to see the garage but it was locked.

'Don't worry,' he said. 'A garage is a garage, right?'

Standing on the front step, I pointed out the line of trees where the path would take you down to the river, Common and town. 'It's very convenient. And if you have a dog to walk . . .'

'This is Pippo,' Mrs Peretti said.

Hearing its name, the dog looked up at her and then at me.

'Nice to meet you, Pippo.'

Mr Peretti drove them away in a sporty green car. They had other properties to see. I would call him this afternoon or tomorrow unless he called me first. I watched until they were out of sight then I locked up, posted the key, and crossed the road.

Now I stopped and stared again in the direction they had

gone. Something had happened. It was a peculiar sensation. Misery still tugged at me and yet somehow these unknown people – this odd ménage à trois who would, in all likelihood, find something more suitable, perhaps a home with fewer stairs for Mrs Peretti and more natural light for the creative Jason – had usurped Abigail in my thoughts about this house. I had rebuilt it in my head with no room for her, or her mother, or Sharp.

Here was transition as I had always known it. Because didn't everyone come and go? I was the constant. That counted for all the thousand and one places I had put under siege, laid my head, and loved. Beyond the beautiful rumble of approaching and departing removal vans I was there always, behind the walls, beneath the roof, silent and listening, crouching and wondering, leaving my mark.

I walked. The sun broke through the cloud, sharpening the tree shade along the path and putting a sparkle on the water eddying round the reeds in the river where ducks dipped their heads and shook their feathers. Then almost as suddenly the sun went in again, as if it might rain. I was resolved, of course, that I would not speak to Abigail again. She would form her own conclusions, perhaps see the ethical dilemma of a man in my position forming a romantic attachment with a client, not to mention a vulnerable young woman still mourning the death of a parent.

She was an error in the same class as Zoe – or, for that matter, Marrineau: the flaw in face-to-face relations that demeans the mystery, reveals beauty as a sham. It is like a work of art. You walk towards it until all you can see is the paint. And when you back off again, what you had is gone for ever. Nothing is the same. You know too much. And now I knew Abigail too much. I felt the pain of loss, but what would happen when the pain subsided?

Did knowing all this change anything? Or would I forget in time, lower my guard, and repeat the mistake again and again?

Lasting love was not here in one place, but everywhere. The intimacy of serial love – *that* was the key, not this shallow simulation, this spastic avatar of feeling. Just look at this, I thought, picturing the town spread out before me, every house a box of treasure. The town was a whole family of love. To focus, as I had foolishly done with Abigail, was to lose focus. One moved on, up the stony path, round the bend, along a fresh, thrilling precipice.

I increased my step, fuelled by the notion. I thought of the Finches, the first household I had visited with my notebook and camera all those years ago. I wondered how they were doing. They had moved from Holland Road to The Maples. Perhaps I would look them up. Their son, who had been at the grammar school, would be grown up now, perhaps with his own young family. Where was he? I could find out. I could find out now if I wanted to. I could find out about anyone, old or new.

I crossed the little bridge, walking quickly. A funfair had begun to set up on the Common, charging the air with diesel fumes and the hum of generators. The tennis courts, glimpsed between the trees and bushes, were empty. A man was sitting on a bench near the cenotaph, legs crossed, eating a sandwich. A seagull – presumably lost on some migration – stood watching him from a fence pole, folding and unfolding wings, as if uncertain whether to take off. Stay, I thought, you'll love it here. If seagulls had brains, I would say what I want to say every time I sell a house: you've come to the right place. I still believed that.

I reached the edge of the Common and walked up the hill to my flat. My car sat in the courtyard. Approaching the door, I put my hand in my pocket and took out a key. But the key in my hand, with its fibrous twist of brown string and crumpled manila tag, was Abigail's. Had I, could I have – distracted by my thoughts – stupidly posted my own key through her letterbox? But wait, no . . . I had *locked* her door. I searched my pockets quickly, and here it was, my key. And now I froze on the spot. I had locked her door with the key she had given Sharp. It was *his* key – the key I had found in his wallet, the key I had now used myself on numerous occasions – that was now lying on her doormat. The key, with its little red heart-shaped charm, that Abigail had given to her dead lover.

My blood was suddenly thumping so loudly, my mind so noisy with confusion, I didn't hear the car pull into the courtyard as I stood facing the door, puzzling at the two keys, one in each hand, and trying to work it out. It was fine, I realized. I still had her key. It was early closing at the library, but she wouldn't be home until ten past five. And it was now . . . I looked at my watch: 1.28. All I had to do was get back over there, unlock the door, and exchange this key for the other. I was an idiot but all was well. The heat and chaos of thought subsided. I exhaled audibly.

'Mr Heming?'

I turned round. Here were my two police officers, their faces impassive, the younger one squinting slightly in the sunlight. The front door was behind me now. But all I could think, in that moment, as they stood there, unreadably calm, was that they were looking right through me, through the door and through the walls, through to where my keys – my hundreds of keys – hung like links of armour, investing the room with their dim golden light.

'Would you mind if we came in?'

32

'IN?' I ANSWERED, MOVING towards them, away from the door, away from the flat. 'In where?' My heart was hammering.

'This is your flat?'

'Of course not. It's one of the properties we manage.'

'But you were just going in?'

'No, Inspector. I was just coming out. The tenant is away. I have to arrange to get a plumber in for him. I was assessing the cistern.'

'Is it urgent?' the younger man asked.

'I have tied the ballcock up with a piece of string,' I said. 'For now.'

'You're a handyman too?'

'Perhaps you'd like to pop in and check,' I said. I held Abigail's key out to him on its loop of string, the label visible with my name on it. He didn't move.

The senior officer looked impatient. 'I don't think that will be necessary. And it's Sergeant, sir. Detective Sergeant Monks. This is DC Roberts.'

'Of course. Forgive me.'

'It's rather odd that no one at your office seemed to know where you live, Mr Heming,' he said. 'Don't you keep staff records?'

'Of course we do. An oversight, I imagine.'

'And the electoral roll?' DC Roberts chipped in. 'You're a regular man of mystery, Mr Heming.'

'Not at all. They probably spelled my name with two Ms. Or perhaps you did and they didn't. That often happens. Despite all the signs around town for everyone to see.'

Monks blinked at Roberts, who gazed down at his notebook and pursed his lips.

'But in that case,' I said, 'what led you here? Intuition?'

'It seems we were misinformed.'

'So what can I help you with?'

'A few questions. Perhaps at the station?'

'Now?'

'If you wouldn't mind, sir,' said Monks.

I looked at my watch. 'Well, I am rather busy.'

'If you wouldn't mind, sir. This *is* a murder inquiry.'

'Is it? Shall I follow in my car?'

'Probably best if you just accompany us in ours, sir.'

I had never had occasion to go to the police station, though I knew where it was, hidden away behind the shops in a sooty, squat redbrick building. Steps led up to small heavy doors and a small strip-lit anteroom with more beyond. It had the oppressive air of a basement. An officer on the desk logged my arrival without a great deal of interest and pushed a button that allowed further entry. The senior detective held the door while the younger man followed me closely (did they think I was going to make a run for it?) down a corridor with numbered rooms off to the sides, thick windows in the doors.

'Will this take long?' I asked.

'Oh, I shouldn't think so, sir,' said Monks.

He swung open the door to an empty room and seated me at a table. He sat down and asked for my name, age and occupation. I gave as my address the empty designer apartment overlooking the river. Now he summoned a uniformed officer, who stood behind me and said nothing. Monks himself left the room. The minutes ticked by. Clearly he was trying to get me rattled, though knowing that didn't make me less so. Part of me feared that they would soon be busy breaking down the door of the riverside apartment in the hope of finding tweed clothing to match fibres found under the fingernails of the victim (though the tweed clothing in question had long been disposed of), or checking my toothbrush for DNA consistent with droplets of sweat or dried spittle on his clothing. Of course, they would find not so much as a stick of furniture and wonder why.

It was twenty-five minutes before Monks returned, with DC Roberts but with no apology for the delay. He switched on a tape recorder, and said who he was, who I was, the names of Roberts and the other officer, and the date and time.

'Just saves time, sir,' he said. He had a file in front of him.

'Am I a suspect? Or something?'

'Would you prefer a lawyer to be present?'

'No, of course not. Why should I?'

'Why indeed, sir.'

He reassured me that I wasn't under arrest. I was free to go whenever I pleased, though I imagined that could change the second I tried to leave. I crossed my legs and tried to appear relaxed. My big worry at this point was that I could be here, helping the police with their enquiries, for hours. Whatever happened here was unlikely to be worse than Abigail arriving home to find Sharp's copy of her key, knowing that it was I who had left it there.

For obvious reasons Abigail had kept her silence about Sharp. It was why she wanted to leave town – to put this horror behind her and return to her uncomplicated life in London where she had a network of friends and colleagues. She too probably felt her involvement with me was a mistake, an attraction arising from an instinct to be comforted. Finding the key would change all that. Now the horror was on her doormat. Now she would come forward, do the right thing (the thing she probably always imagined she would do as a principled young woman interested in poetry and cycling), declare herself as the other woman, reveal Sharp's missing matching luggage, pour cold water on the absurd theory of his having had an affair with Mrs Cookson and jab the finger of guilt at me, perhaps with a frightened, uncontrollable scream.

'In your own words . . .' Monks was saying, reiterating that this was simply a witness statement. We needed to go through the whole story once more – the moment I had arrived at the Sharps' that day, the state of the house, precisely what Mrs Sharp had said, precisely what had occurred between us and so on.

'Between us?'

'Everything. She was in some distress. Did you try to comfort her?'

'Well, yes, of course, to an extent.'

'Everything,' he said.

I retold the story – the mess, Mrs Sharp's bandaged hand, Sharp's alleged infidelities, the tale of the dog, allegedly killed by Sharp. Should I mention the handkerchief I'd lent her when she was crying?

'Ah yes, the dog . . .'

Every now and then he interrupted to ask about, confirm, clarify or elaborate on something. DC Roberts, his notebook open, watched me, and said nothing. What was his problem? I couldn't believe they had solid evidence of my involvement. All they knew for sure was that I was around on the day, alongside Mrs Sharp. Perhaps they thought she and I were in cahoots. That's what the remark about comforting her was about. Obviously they were just fishing.

By now many more details of the case had trickled out of the press and into the town. Sharp's body had been out for a week in the open in warm weather. Rats, cats and crows had pecked and nibbled at it; foxes had carried off chunks of the poor man. (According to the *Sentinel*, the Cooksons had recently quarrelled with a neighbour who kept chickens over Mrs C's habit of putting out food for foxes in the evening.) What was left of Sharp was badly decomposed. The police hadn't been able to prove their pet theory that the body had been moved – as it would have to have been, for example, if Sharp had died in the fight at home with his wife. Perhaps they were still trying to make a case against Mrs Sharp acting alone – that she had in fact followed her husband to the Cooksons and then hit him with something hard. But there had been two different sorts of injuries: one trauma caused by some unidentified blunt impact, which may or may not have been the patio stones, the other a smack in the head with a weapon that had left a distinct impression, though no one was saying what, or even which blow had killed him. But murder in any event, they had now stated. Perhaps Sharp had stepped backwards, fallen and cracked his head on the patio and then been finished off by Mrs Sharp or persons unknown. This was what was going through the minds of the police and the townsfolk, though none of the various scenarios entirely made sense. However you put together the pieces there were always one or two that seemed to come from a different, missing puzzle.

I reached the end of my statement. We seemed to be winding up. Unbelievably, over two hours had passed since they'd picked me up. The senior man had his hands flat on the file in front of him now, as if he might open it. 'We'll just need to rerun the tape, check that everything's in order, Mr Heming. Technology and all that.'

'Of course.'

DC Roberts left the room. DS Monks asked about the business – whether I was the sole owner, how many staff I employed and so on. What was this now? Had we finished? Was this just small talk?

'Actually, there are one or two other matters. When you were leaving the Sharps' on that day, and you told Mrs Sharp you'd be back later with your sales forms, what happened?'

'What do you mean "happened"?'

'Where did you go?'

'Probably straight to the office. It was a Saturday. Quite busy, I imagine. Probably I got caught up in something.'

'OK, and that's why you didn't return. Not that Saturday, or Sunday, or Monday – or even Tuesday or Wednesday. Mrs Sharp said she had to call your office on Thursday. This tallies with the diary in your office – Mrs Pegg registered the call.'

'Wendy, yes, she's very efficient.'

'But even then, according to Mrs Pegg's record, someone had to attend in your place. Miss Katya Stan-ka . . .'

'Stankaviciene, yes. Soon to be Jones,' I added with a quick smile.

He looked at me.

'She's engaged to a Welshman.'

'So why the delay?'

'Katya?'

'Mrs Sharp. Don't you need the business?'

'To tell you the truth, I did wonder, given the attitude of the husband, whether the Sharps might not be more trouble than they were worth. After all, the man from Worde & Hulme was practically thrown out on to the street by Mr Sharp.'

'True, although now, by this time, of course – the Thursday afterwards, almost a week later – Mr Sharp was lying dead in the garden of your other clients, Mr and Mrs Cookson.'

'Tragically, yes, though I could hardly have known that.'

Monks gazed thoughtfully at me for what must have been a good half-minute while Roberts closed his notebook and waited. Then Monks said, 'Does the name Damato mean anything to you?'

My heart almost stopped dead. But then I immediately realized he was talking about the company I had set up to handle my property and finances. I preferred to keep it private, but it wouldn't have been impossible for a competent investigator to link me, and my agency, with the William R. Heming listed as the sole director of Damato Associates, which owned the riverside apartments and other properties dotted around town. This was not a disaster. If you enquired further – for example, with the tax authorities – you would find that William R. Heming paid what he owed promptly and without argument through a London accountant, who also handled financial transactions and movements of monies on his behalf. None of this was illegal, though I was aware that people who liked their privacy – or secrecy, as Zoe would say – were regarded with suspicion. For someone with an interest in not being noticed, it goes without saying that I didn't want to be suspected.

'Mr Heming?'

'I won't deny that it does.'

'I'm sure this is just tittle-tattle,' he said. 'Someone raking up the past.' From his file he pulled out a photocopy of a newspaper cutting and slid it across the table. 'Ancient news from the Norwich Coroner's Court,' he continued.

When I saw it, my heart started pounding again.

It concerned an inquest into the death of Harold Buckshaw, forty-seven, an unmarried council worker. There was no picture. The headline, over one column, read 'Tragedy of Former Parks Man'.

'This is twenty-seven years ago,' I managed to say.

The lifeless body of Mr Buckshaw, the court heard, had been found by a dog-walker in shallow water following a wintry night. A post-mortem examination found that he had been drinking heavily. The previous August, Mr Buckshaw had been acquitted by Norfolk magistrates in connection with the abduction of two children. Witnesses said that Mr Buckshaw had been depressed when he lost his job with the parks department and was regularly seen drunk in the locality. A police witness said that Mr Buckshaw had previously reported two assaults on his person and criminal damage to a window at his council flat in Lower Eastley. On the evening before Mr Buckshaw's body was found, two young women coming out of the Wherry public house saw him being assaulted by two youths. The cause of death was drowning. The coroner returned a verdict of misadventure.

Someone had circled the reference to the abduction in red and written 'THIS IS HEMING! Ask him about the DAMATOS!'

'So what about the Damatos?'

'I've no idea,' I said. 'The Damatos lived opposite.'

Monks scratched his nose. 'The case notes tell us that your local police spoke to your father, but no action was taken.'

'Well, why would it? I had nothing to do with it. And I was barely older than they were.'

'You were ten. These other children were three.'

I shrugged. 'What can I say?'

'Ah, Memory Lane,' Monks said, opening the file again. 'I don't know what you would make of this letter. It appears to be from the headmaster of your old school to your mother.'

Again, it was a photocopy.

Dear Mrs Heming,

Thank you for your accompanying letter of 12th July and kind donation. I do appreciate your frankness and help in this matter. A Treasure Trove indeed. Though, I trust, not Pandora's Box! As you can imagine, I am as shocked as you are that William has intruded on the privacy and property of the other boys with such disappointing disregard for the acceptable norms of behaviour – or even risk of discovery! That it appears to have gone on for so long is of particular concern. Certainly, had you not withdrawn him from school on account of the other matter, I am afraid William would certainly have been expelled, for technically this is theft, though I appreciate the items stolen – greetings cards, letters, a ball of rubber bands, various personal gewgaws that boys will collect – are of little value in themselves. In the light of the latter observation, I think it best that we do not attempt to return these items to their rightful owners. As far as the school is concerned, we are prepared to put this episode behind us and move forward. I will return the chest, of course.

I accept your point in mitigation that William may have

been affected badly by the death of his father last year, but his behaviour is nevertheless worrying. William's scrapbooks containing information and defamatory comments on other boys are especially disturbing.

You say he has opted not to continue his education but has taken a post with a respectable family firm. In this I wish him well and hope that his experiences have, in some way, taught him good lessons for the future.

Yours sincerely,

E. H. Akers
Headmaster

Again, a postscript had been appended in an angry scrawl of red biro: 'Ask him about his PSYCHIATRIC REPORT'.

'Should I ask you about your psychiatric report?' said Monks.

'Actually, that's my aunt, not my mother—'

'If we could stick to the subject in hand.'

'I really have no idea who you're talking about. This is obviously some kind of mischief-making – and a libel!'

'Who would want to make mischief for you, Mr Heming?'

'My cousin, I imagine. She is deranged, I'm afraid. And resents my success. And, frankly, all this is such a long time ago. It's hard to remember the person I was then, let alone answer for him. Who could? And as you see, the offences were minor. Stealing football programmes and sweets from boys' rooms? OK, you have me!'

'They say old habits die hard, sir.'

'Or sometimes they just die. Have you no youthful indiscretions in your closet, Detective Sergeant Monks? As Mr Akers says here, we must move on.'

'How did your father die, Mr Heming?'

'*What*? He died in a boating accident. In Norfolk.'

'And you were . . .'

'At school. In Yorkshire. I was traumatized. That's why I had to have counselling. I imagine that's what my cousin is raving about.'

Monks pondered, or pretended to ponder, then gave the eye to Roberts, who left the room. I checked the time, fearful that the more I looked at my watch the longer Monks would keep me here, wearing me down, waiting for me to trip myself up with a lie. I sensed something was building. They hadn't finished with me. Abigail would be home in half an hour.

Another ten minutes passed.

I didn't even have my car.

Monks said nothing. He just waited.

If they did break into the riverside apartment (and were they even allowed to do that without arresting me for something?) and find it empty they would then surely return to the other flat, rightly assuming it was mine after all. And then . . .

The door opened and Roberts returned. He was carrying something in a plastic bag. Monks opened it and with exaggerated care laid its contents on the table in front of me.

'Do these look familiar?'

Both men scrutinized me as my hand went to my pocket, and I felt my throat suddenly dry up.

'Opera glasses,' I managed to say.

'Are they yours?' Monks clasped his hands in front of his face and looked over them at me, eyebrows raised.

'What makes you think that?'

'They were recovered from the vehicle owned by Douglas Sharp. The new owner of the car discovered them when he tried to open the tool compartment. Wedged into a crevice, he said. Imagine that.'

Roberts, arms folded, allowed himself the faintest smile. 'Mrs Sharp tells us you were using a small pair of binoculars in her house?'

'It's possible. I use them for checking roofs and gutters, that sort of thing. I suppose you've checked them for fingerprints,' I said.

He gazed at me.

'I'm guessing you didn't find mine.'

Neither of them spoke.

'Otherwise, wouldn't you just clap me in irons right now?'

'Are they your binoculars, Mr Heming?'

'Do you think I might have a glass of water?'

'Please answer the question, Mr Heming. Are these your binoculars?'

'No,' I said. 'Because mine are here.' I took them out of my pocket and laid them alongside the evidence. 'Similar enough, you might say, but not identical. I've had these beauties for years.'

Monks inspected them and handed them to Roberts, who turned them over, as if looking for something that would tell him what to say next.

I looked at my watch. 'If there's nothing else, I am quite busy.'

I ran. I ran as I had never run before. Fine leather-soled English brogues are not running shoes. They pounded the pavement in front of me as if they were separate entities that the rest of me was pursuing. Bemused pedestrians stepped out of my way. I escaped the town centre, down an alley, skirting the backs of the buildings. Abigail would surely be unlocking her bike by now, before heading through the park and on to the river path. From where I was, I calculated, it would be quicker to stick to the main road, the route Abigail herself took when returning from her run, ending with the hill and the crossroads with the baker and the newsagent I had spoken to. I was already out of breath. I had to hope she would be held up – by a colleague, or a flat tyre. I could hear the distant music of the funfair in the park. The park would be full of children. That would delay her. Still I ran. It had to be a mile at least, perhaps two. On I ran, though it was hopeless. I clenched my teeth and ran, past the filling station, past the Wellington, then past the familiar streets and houses above to my left that looked down on the woodland that banked up from the river and the park. Under my breath I named each street in turn until I could run no further. I had to stop. And when I did, and looked back, I saw a bus rounding the bend. I set off running again. I could see the stop, a hundred yards ahead. I sensed the bus rapidly gaining on me and I put out my hand to wave it down. It rumbled past then I saw its indicator slowly flash, before it heaved into the bay.

I clambered aboard.

'Nice day for a bit of exercise,' the driver chirruped.

I could barely speak. 'Fount Hill,' I panted, and offered him a handful of change. 'Thank you. Saved my life.'

But had he? It was twenty past. I looked ahead now, watched the bus eating up the road, readied myself to jump off again. The door hissed and swung open. Now I was loping past the newsagent, across the road in the face of oncoming traffic. I looked for her bike chained to the railings. It wasn't there. I reached the house and leapt up the steps to the blue door, fumbling for the key. And now I saw her, back down the road, a figure in red. There she was, surfacing, steadying her bike, watching the cars to her left, her foot on the pedal. If she looked at this moment, she would see me. I unlocked the door and closed it behind me. Sharp's key was on the mat. I snatched it up and dropped hers to replace it.

There was still time. If I wanted to I could simply open the door and put on a surprised smile – explain that the prospective buyers had arrived later than arranged and had just left. I waited, deciding, my nerves electrified. Two, three weeks before I would have found myself dashing up the two flights of stairs to the attic, curling up in my den of furniture and silently relishing her arrival, eyes closed in anticipation, ears alert for the key, her first movements and murmurs. But that was over. I had dodged a bullet today and anything seemed possible – but not that.

I hated her for it. I hated her for drawing me into this quicksand, away from my life and place and purpose and duty, for giving me something precious and then luring me close and seizing it back.

But of course it was not over. I still breathed. And there would be the Perettis of this world to set my heart beating anew. They flickered in my mind as the time ticked down, as the exquisite heat of imminent discovery rose with the scrape and clatter of bicycle against railing, Abigail's flat tread on the steps. In seconds the key would turn . . .

And then I fled, withholding – deferring – the aching pleasure of the moment, as I had in other houses on other occasions, holding it within myself as a memento of this perilous day, out of the back door, through the garden and breathlessly, thrillingly, into the lane behind and away.

33

THE MASK IS CRITICAL. I bought it from an online hardware super-store, who had it delivered to my office the next day. Zoe signed for it. It is not very attractive. If you opened your eyes and found me leaning over you wearing this mask, you would have a fit. But the instructions say that it will give me fifteen minutes, which will be enough. As promised, the mask was 'Quick and Easy to Don', bright orange in colour, and sure enough a nose clip or mouthpiece was not required. It has not impaired my hearing, though there is not a great deal to listen to at this hour. If I cocked an ear, I might catch the sound of a cat in the yard. If I heard anything else stirring I would start to worry.

I am sorry it has come to this. But it is inevitable. The role of the next victim is ever to clean up after the last. I hope I have drawn a line under things now, and that quiet will follow and torment cease.

34

IF ISOBEL THOUGHT I would not take the trouble to find out where she lived and then get in my car and drive a hundred miles to see it for myself, she didn't know me very well. The colour understandably drained from her face when she opened the door.

'What do you want?' she said, stepping back.

'What do *I* want? Didn't you write telling me of your distressed circumstances? Well, here I am.'

'Elizabeth will be back from school soon.'

'Excellent. How *is* Elizabeth?'

Her eyes flicked to someone or something behind me. A neighbour taking an interest. I smiled at Isobel. After some hesitation, she let me in. The cottage smelled of damp. The furniture – a sofa, an upright piano, a long sideboard and drinks cabinet and a hideous blue stone vase, all recognizable from Aunt Lillian's house – was too big for the lightless front room with its low sloping ceiling and pinched leaded windows. Even on this fine spring day it felt cold.

'It's freezing in winter,' she said, reading my thoughts.

'That's the wind from the Siberian steppe. It sweeps right across the flatness of the terrain.'

'I know,' she snapped.

She didn't offer me tea and biscuits. I sat while she remained standing, her arms folded. I found the resumption of hostilities reassuring. In a way it made things easier. From time to time she peered out of the window, as if the neighbour was still nearby and in sight.

I began by asking what she hoped to achieve by furnishing murder detectives with details of my youthful misdemeanours. 'I was ten, for goodness' sake,' I pointed out. 'I was troubled.'

'You were seventeen when you were expelled from school. You attacked another pupil. He lost an eye. Imagine if the police knew *that*.'

'That's not true. It was nowhere near his eye.'

She shook her head, and gazed out, showing me Aunt Lillian's profile, her disapproving, downturned mouth. 'Anyway the psychiatrist said you were disturbed, not troubled.'

'What psychiatrist?'

'The one my mother made you see after you left school. I do know.'

'I've moved on, like everyone else. I'm a respected estate agent. You could damage my reputation spreading gossip about me. You think because my sign was outside the house where a man was found dead that I had something to do with it? That's madness. At one time or another, my name is on every single street in town. I can see your mother has poisoned your mind against me.'

'I know what I know,' she said. 'And what you *don't* know is how much my mother protected you back then, and more than once. The council would have locked you in a home and your father would have let them.'

'Your mother stole her sister's husband. Her dying sister. Her dying sister who was having a baby.'

Isobel shook her head and gave a snort. 'And what did you do?'

She turned to face the window again. A wave of anger surged through me. I could seize that hideous blue stone vase and stove her head in with it. But now the front door opened and slammed.

A voice called out, 'Hi, it's me.'

I left cousin Isobel's far from happy, but with things settled, or at least with an enforced sort of peace in place. Something had been achieved; something bad had been lanced. It was still light when I set off back. There was no one around, and no traffic for the first mile, which took me from this hamlet she'd had to move to with its down-at-heel cottages, village school and abandoned pub to the A11 and westward to home. I was still angry. Some of the things she had said defied belief, though when pressed for corroborative detail – with Elizabeth in her room, starting her homework with a glass of milk and a biscuit – she'd proved maddeningly persuasive. She'd finally evoked the great name of Marrineau.

'He came here, you know,' she said.

'Marrineau? Here?'

'To my mother's. I was there when he arrived. It was one Sunday. He'd finished at university and had come from Cambridge. He was weird, if you want the truth. He said he had come to forgive but also to be forgiven, or some nonsense like that. He wanted your address, but my mother wouldn't let him have it. He said he understood and respected that. His parents were wrong, he said, to have had you expelled.'

'He said that?'

'He said all sorts of things. He said he'd wanted to be a sportsman but had now found his true vocation, meaning God, as it turned out. He was going to be a priest or a vicar.'

I didn't know what to say.

'He sent a card to my mother, a year or two later, to say where he was. The card came to me eventually.'

'Have you been talking to him? About what happened?'

'What makes you think that?'

'I don't know. Maybe you don't believe in forgiveness.'

But maybe she did. I wondered why she hadn't troubled the police with the story of Marrineau.

She was silent for a time, watching me like a cornered animal. Then, abruptly, she said, 'What do you expect? You're swimming in success with your bloody business and money and we've got nothing. And we took you in. Your father was a mess. And you ate up our energy and time. My mother stuck her neck out for you. And that child . . .' She paused. 'I suffered too, you know. I never saw *my* father at all. I don't even know if he's still alive. And now look at me!'

'Did my father kill himself?'

'I've really no idea. You gave him enough reason to.'

I went for my pocket and she flinched, her eyes defiant.

I smiled at her attempt to provoke me. I told her she could have the money – that I would have given it to her anyway. I unfolded the banker's draft and handed it to her. I said there would be one like it for her every month. Suddenly she was in tears. She wouldn't look at me. Just turned her back and wept. We didn't speak again. Perhaps we never will.

I rang the office from a service area when I got close to town. Wendy assured me that no one had called and no one had left a message. I picked up a takeaway sandwich and coffee and drove on. I arrived back at my flat just after six. The fairground lights were blazing on the Common and music was pumping into the air. I parked the car. Groups of schoolchildren were making their way up the hill, eating candyfloss. I paused on the step to my flat. Call it sixth sense – or just hard-earned intuition – but I knew, even before I'd pushed open the door and ventured in, that someone was already there.

35

'SURPRISE!' ZOE WAS SITTING on the arm of my couch, short skirt, her legs crossed. Her eyes were shining. She was smiling. Was she drunk? One glance told me she had already made herself too much at home to ignore.

'Good God, Zoe, what on earth do you think you're doing?'

'I *love* your keys,' she said. 'I *love* them. I hope you don't still use them all. I know how you do it. I've seen you. I've watched you getting them cut. How do you think *I* got in here? It took me ages to work things out but I've learned from the master.' She beamed at me. 'You're naughty. A naughty magpie. You have my jewelled mirror from Thailand. How did you get it? From my flat, of course. So here I am, getting you back. That's fair.'

Behind her, my collection drawers were safe and locked. But some files were out, along with scattered photographs and rough notes I hadn't written up. My innards were churning.

'Listen, Zoe—'

'No-no-no-no-no-no-no, it's fine, it's fine,' she was saying.

I now saw that she was wearing Sharp's watch.

'Yes – and you have Douglas's watch too!' she said. 'Poor

243

Douglas. But didn't you say to those policemen that you'd never set eyes on him?'

'Douglas?' I said.

She gave me a knowing look. 'Ha . . . Mr Sharp, of course. Don't worry. I won't tell them. It will be our secret.'

'What? Why do you think it's Mr Sharp's watch?'

'Because I bought it for him, of course! I wish I hadn't. He was bad news, though I shouldn't speak ill of the dead.' She looked round in sudden puzzlement. 'This is weird. Why don't you have a bed?'

'You bought it for him? You knew him?'

'Ah, I can see what you're doing. You're being all, what is it . . . chivalrous. Oh, Mr Heming, you were right *there* – in the office when we came in. He kissed me right in front of the window. You saw us.'

'Who? When?'

'Ages ago. Last year. And then you followed us to the bowling alley. Did you think I didn't see you? You're so sweet, but aren't you in big trouble? What happened, Mr Heming? No, let me tell you.'

Clearly she was raving. Except . . . except that it was true. I *had* followed her once. Maybe once or twice, with a man. Certainly no more than three times. Back to her place. Last year, maybe the year before. That was Sharp? Could it have been?

'Wait,' Zoe said. She was at the table and turning my laptop towards me. 'You can try to deny it, but look – it's right here on your memory stick. You filmed it at Warninck's on one of their authors' nights. Here's Douglas, here's me. And some of our book group. And here's his wife, who he'd forgotten to mention he hadn't left after all. And a bit later on is some other poor woman he leapt on the minute I'd dumped him, who was no doubt soon at it with him in the back of that huge car he has, in the woods. Oh he loves that. In the car. They were together in the restaurant. Did you really think I cared about him? Is that what you were thinking when you sat us right across the room from him and that poor mousy woman from the library, the two lovebirds sitting there like a couple of teenagers? Were you trying to rub my nose into it? I forgive you, of course. I know you were trying to avenge me. Or you thought I loved him. Or something. Seriously, if you were jealous of him, no need. He made a fool of me. He was despicable. But I never loved him. It was always, always you.'

She seemed almost delighted with herself. I was dazed by it. It was dreamlike. I remembered what Mrs Sharp had said about the anonymous note she had received. 'Was it you who sent his wife the photograph of Sharp in an embrace with the other woman—'

'In an embrace!' She laughed. 'You are funny. But, oh God. I truly wish I hadn't done that. That's what set it all off. That's why she went for him. When I heard, I was sick with guilt. I couldn't tell anyone. Do you remember? I had to take time off. I had to ask the doctor for some soothers. You know what your trouble is?' she asked suddenly.

My mind was trying to think how it would end. I couldn't be – I *refused* to be – seen like this. I wanted her to stop talking, but I was afraid of what might happen when she did.

'You're too nice,' she continued. 'Wanting to help everyone. I can see you walking right into the middle of the Sharps' fight, or rather when she'd already hit him with something. A baseball bat. Or, no, wait . . . it was next morning, wasn't it? OK, obviously it must have all flared up again, and Mrs Sharp was in a state when you arrived, and you could see it was an accident, or that she hadn't meant to hit him so hard. You *always* see the best in people! And you thought, what about the Cooksons' place? Because obviously she couldn't move him on her own. But why didn't you think what might happen next?' She shook her head. Oh boy. 'And you really oughtn't have gone to see her *quite* so often afterwards. No wonder the police want to talk to you every five minutes.'

She stopped to take a sip from a glass that seemed to materialize from nowhere and I saw now that there was a bottle on the floor, three-quarters gone.

'What's happening here, Zoe? What are we doing exactly?'

She stood up now and came over to me. She was wearing scent. She looked into my eyes and kissed me full on the lips.

'We are sorting you out, of course,' she said.

We had dinner and champagne at the Two Swans, which wasn't my idea of a relaxing evening. As usual, Zoe did most of the talking and drinking. I can't remember what we ate. She said nothing of what she had seen at my flat, which was unnerving. I do remember she had sweet ideas of how she could help more at the agency. How she could take on more of my workload. I was too good to my staff; there must be some cost savings to be made or more tricks to maximize profits.

'And yet,' I said at one point, 'we are the most successful agency in the district. We must be doing something right.'

Exactly, she told me. Imagine how much more successful it could be if we really pulled together!

Despite myself, I was touched by her concern. The truth was, of course – and she wasn't to know this – I already had more money than I needed, and I already had the business running in the friendly, ungrasping way that tended to get me where I wanted to be.

Yet in every way she wanted to 'help'.

'The problem is, we give far too much away,' she was saying in the taxi back to her flat.

'You're right of course,' I said. 'I must think about that.'

'You're *too* nice.'

'Indeed I am.'

'Oh, William . . .'

Things progressed, though progress was not the word.

Together we would make a great team, she insisted as we snuggled beneath her duvet after a bout of self-consciously energetic sex. And if the police continued to cause a fuss with regard to my whereabouts on the morning in question, she said, the plan now was that I would simply confess our secret relationship. For her part, Zoe would back me up, since she hadn't been in the office that morning anyway. It was simple: I had gone back to her place. We had made love. Yes, I would admit that I should have gone back to the office, but I just couldn't keep my hands off Zoe for five minutes. That's how crazy we were for each other, though obviously it had to be kept from the rest of the team until such time as we made it official, so to speak.

'Official?'

She nuzzled into my shoulder. 'Just kidding,' she said, though of course she wasn't.

At the office she brushed her fingers against mine when our paths crossed, just as she had during our earlier, ill-advised romance. At one point she brought a single chocolate heart from the upmarket gift store in the precinct and laid it on my desk beside my coffee.

For now I had to stay focused. I spent the next two nights with Zoe. I told her I wouldn't be around at the weekend, explaining that I had to drive out to Norfolk to speak to my cousin about an aspect of family finance. Zoe made a glum face.

'You know what they say about absence,' I said.

She consoled herself by stroking my hair while asking long searching questions about my family. I replied with equally long mendacious answers. I did have one question for her, of course.

'Zoe, do you think I might borrow your binoculars tomorrow? I seem to have lost mine somewhere.'

'Actually, come to think of it, so have I,' she said. 'In fact I don't think I've seen them in ages.'

On Friday, while she was busy at the office, gaily plotting a hike in our rates or cuts to our benefit packages for first-time buyers, I drove to her flat and let myself in. I made use of her laptop. I thought about the tiny dimensions of her two rooms. I opened and closed doors. I had brought my tool roll and a bag of dusters. At the risk of impugning the weaker sex in a single sweeping observation, I do think women living on their own can often take their eye off the ball when it comes to the greasier end of essential household maintenance. Zoe's broom cupboard, for example, contained a particularly ancient Dreadnought floor-standing boiler. Judging by its patina of grime I doubted it had been serviced in years, if ever. I unwrapped my tools and got to work adjusting the burner pressures. The Mark II in particular had proved reliable down the years for accidentally asphyxiating homeowners while they watched TV. If the flame turned yellow, carbon would block up the heat exchanger, eventually releasing enough carbon monoxide to down an elephant. The appliance notably lacked a fresh-air inlet, which meant it needed to take oxygen from the room. Which meant that, first, I had to go round checking all the ventilators, removing the plastic covers and folding a fresh new duster into each. Finally I swept my work areas for stray screws and debris and packed away my tools. If there was any pleasure in this, it was merely that of a job well done, if that's not too perverse.

In the evening we bought an Indian takeaway and settled in front of a martial arts film drinking wine until I made excuses about having to hit the road early in the morning. Which was not wholly a lie.

'Drive safely,' she said, yawning already.

I fully expected her to be dead by Monday.

36

I SUPPOSE IT HARDLY matters that I lied to Zoe. I took the train, first south to London and then north from King's Cross. In Leeds I hired a car and continued west through the small former textile towns and semi-rural communities on the edge of the Dales. I killed an hour sitting in a tea room with a pleasing panorama of the Aire valley before eventually rolling into the parish of Wollesworth some time after lunch.

I dropped my bags at the nearest B&B – a village pub – and set out to explore. A lane bordered on one side by a housing estate and on the other by a field of indolent cows led after a mile of strung-out cottages to a decent-sized square and a busy open-air market where shoppers – mainly women loaded with carrier bags, their necks craned, looking for bargains – made their way from stall to stall, sometimes trailing one or two small children, or trying to manoeuvre a pushchair through the narrow thoroughfares. At one side of the square the guildhall was still used for some formal purpose, but the corn exchange had long been converted to an indoor shopping precinct emblazoned with 1970s lettering, while neighbouring buildings – once no doubt the pride of solid traders and merchants – housed discount stores, betting shops and cheap cafés. A group of boys in sportswear sat beneath an ancient stone cross smoking cigarettes and passing two large brown bottles between them. Occasionally one or the other of them would spit on the worn grey pavement. Much of their language – you could hear it from twenty yards away – was unsuitable for a public place on a Saturday afternoon. Outside a fast-food outlet was a lone busker – a yellow-eyed man of probably no more than thirty, balding, thin and grizzled – who sang and played an acoustic guitar with two of its strings missing. I threw a pound coin into his Tupperware box and was rewarded with his desperate rictus.

Could this really be the place?

I heard the peal of bells, working up to chiming the hour, and I followed the sound, out of the square. I walked for a minute and, reaching a bend in the road, saw the mass of a medieval church some way ahead, set back from the traffic and surrounded by a wall and railings. I entered through a black iron gate and mounted three brickwork steps into the churchyard, assailed by the smell of the grass, freshly mowed between uneven stumps of gravestones, some sunken with age but many bright with pots of flowers. Above, a steeple rose black against the pale sky, marred by a giant red-and-white barometer showing how the fund for repairs was coming along. Which was not well.

I carried on, skirting the church, past a building in its own grounds – identified by a disfiguring sign as St Alban-in-the-Dale Church Hall and Community Centre, but probably the original rectory – and out at the other side. Here, in its own cul-de-sac, was a featureless 1970s brick-built detached house. A dusty path lay to the side of a large rear garden partly obscured by a short stretch of untrimmed privet. I was aware of a tapping sound and a dog barked once as I approached. I couldn't see the dog but, as I passed, the figure of a man rose abruptly and faced me across the gate. His hair, a pale nest of straw, was as unkempt as his privet and he wore a baggy sweatshirt and jeans. He squinted at me in a peculiar way for a moment, a smear of grease on his chin. He was holding a can of something, and I saw now the frame of an old motorcycle standing nearby, its chrome parts laid out on sheets of newspaper, where he had evidently been crouched when I came along.

'Hullo!' he said.

I responded with a smile. 'Repairs?'

'Just cleaning her up a little.'

I nodded and hurried on, uncertainly, wondering if this had been a mistake. The path narrowed and sloped downwards into the trees.

Behind me his voice called out again. 'Hi there, hullo!'

I turned. He was hurrying after me. He was a burly man and faintly bowlegged, but moved with surprising ease.

'I'm afraid you won't get across the stream at the bottom there. The ford's up two feet.'

'Oh. Right. Perhaps I'll . . .'

He squinted at me. He was wearing a smile, which now widened slightly. 'I know you.'

'Yes, I think you probably do.'

'Heming?'

'The Reverend Marrineau, I presume.'

'Well, well,' he said simply. He appraised me with his good eye, the other staring cold as marble beyond me into the bushes. What did he know?

We shook hands and marvelled at our meeting as we walked back to his gate, where the dog stood in the garden, wagging its tail.

'Here's Toby,' he said.

'Not Fido, then?'

'Aha!' He chuckled. 'I see your little joke there. Very clever.'

He must have guessed I wasn't here by accident, but only asked if I'd come far and commented on the heavier than usual traffic on account of the Shepping Fair. He had urgent business there himself, he said, this afternoon, and when I told him I was staying nearby he looked at his watch and suggested we go out there together now. 'Give me five minutes,' he said.

I waited on an uncared-for wooden bench in the yard under the querying eye of Toby. The garden enclosed an apron of hard, flattened dirt and a raised area with an expanse of scrub lawn, untamed brambles and ivy, a shed and a rusting swing and slide set. An array of T-shirts and underwear hung motionless on a rotary washing line. It would be the work of twenty seconds to cut through the brake pipe on his bike, should anyone find they had an axe to grind. Or a heavy candlestick to the head. This town was probably full of violent drunks with no money, and vicars were a soft touch.

Marrineau re-emerged in a baggy cream suit with clerical dog collar and a dramatic black eye-patch. 'Forgive the fancy dress,' he said.

We drove to the fair in his old car. This was his day off, he said, but he had agreed to referee the children's touch rugby and later award prizes for chutneys, sausages and pies. When we arrived, a succession of people greeted him or pulled him to one side to speak to him, their eyes eager and expectant. They called him David. I wandered off. A brass band played, sheepdogs ran an obstacle course, a woodsman turned a lathe fashioned from ropes and tree branches. Then, there he was, bulkier but graceful as ever, moving among the boys in his absurd cream suit and eye-patch – and I suddenly recalled that this was exactly what he was doing the last time I'd seen him twenty years ago, dashing among the Minors at school with a borrowed teacher's whistle on a cord and a bandage across half his face.

At Preserves and Pies, he made a humorous speech and my heart went out to him again – the golden boy who had wounded me with his cool disregard and cruelty, remade into this man of God, loved by all again but also now bestowing love in return. The applause for the winners of best jam and chutney was charged with admiration for him.

'My own two boys are usually here,' he said as we drove back. 'But my sister and her husband have taken them to Florida for the week. Sarah and I can't compete with that,' he said, laughing. He dropped me outside my B&B. 'I have a couple of calls to make. But please join us for supper tonight. Unless you have a better offer. I feel we have lots to talk about. Shall we say eight?'

He hadn't mentioned the wife and I hadn't seen her. I wondered if – I worried that – Sarah might be *the* Sarah. The birthday girl at the party. It turned out that it wasn't. But whoever his wife was wasn't there in any case. 'No,' he explained as he manoeuvred a dish out of a hot oven, 'it's just me and Toby now. Sarah left a couple of years ago. Three, actually. Frankly, I didn't blame her,' he said, cutting into the steaming crust of one of the prize pies from the afternoon and serving it up with chips and peas. He licked his fingertip. 'She put up with me for fifteen years before she made her escape. But I still see her almost every day, and the children often. They're not far away. We divorced so that she could remarry. Nice chap. She met him on a retreat, believe it or not. A man who could give her a little more comfort. She still feels terribly guilty, I can tell, though she needn't. Penury was our undoing, as I'm afraid it is for many in the ministry. It's the modern way.'

He paused and closed his eyes – suddenly overcome, I thought, with a moment of regret; but no, he was just hollowing out a silence in which to say grace. 'Thank you, God, for this splendid pie – and for bringing my old friend William to share it with me.' He looked up. 'Do tuck in.'

It was odd to hear my Christian name being spoken so often in recent days.

I brought up the subject of his visit to my aunt long ago, but he dismissed it. 'I was rather overzealous, I think,' he said, slowly loading his fork and then quickly unloading it into his mouth. 'I felt I had been saved and was eager to try out my new skills.'

'Saved from what?'

'Myself, of course. And Sarah was the girl who saved me. We were at Cambridge together. Sarah was reading divinity, I fell for her wisdom and good looks, and she persuaded me to change from geography. The rest was history,' he added with a laugh. He raised his knife high like a cross brandished against evil. 'I had been lost and now was found, as the song goes – was blind and now could see. Or half see. That was the problem, needless to say. My sporting career was over. I could put on the brave face, but I was being slowly poisoned by despair. I had the idea that nothing was more important than cricket. I couldn't imagine being somewhere else entirely.' He ate as if he hadn't eaten all day. 'I hope you don't feel bad about the eye. I can say now that you did me a favour. Taught me a lesson. Made me think. And look at me now.' He laughed again. 'You changed me. You.'

'I'm afraid I didn't know about the eye.'

He waved away what he took to be my concern. 'Of course. It was a gradual loss, starting with nerve damage, an infection that spread and refused to clear up, then aggravations. It was compounded, hastened, by a rugby injury. But, as I say, here I am.'

I nodded agreeably. Marrineau had forged something useful out of the past. He wasn't dwelling on it. He mentioned the old school – not twenty miles from here – and old Mr Stamp, who he said had died recently. But we didn't return to the act of violence that had had me expelled. If there was a moment I might have stabbed Marrineau to death with one of his own unmatching table knives, it had passed.

'This pie *is* excellent,' I said.

'You arrived on the right day. Yesterday was sausages with a jar of curry sauce. And yoghurt to finish off with. Today we have apple cake!'

He was delighted to find that I had survived my expulsion from school and prospered with my own business.

'We are both small-town people,' he said, turning his one soft grey eye on me. 'We each have our flock.'

I was so struck by this remark I could barely swallow. It was as if he saw in a moment through to who I was, to my own sense of mission. My own love for people. It seemed like a parable when, later, he told me about a man, a former parishioner, whom he regularly saw on his visits to a secure psychiatric hospital. The man, a farmer, had shot three men and a woman with his shotgun, killing the woman. 'They had been intruders,' he said. 'He believed that they had plotted against him and his wife. There was no evidence for it, of course. They were innocent ramblers, out walking, rucksacks, boots. They weren't even on his land. Who knows what evil he saw in them. He couldn't elaborate. He just knew it to be true. He felt it in his heart and in desperation pursued them and gave them both barrels, so to speak. Perhaps twice. I know nothing about guns. Of course it was a terrible crime, but this man cannot even now be separated from that belief. He is insane, of course – officially it comes under the umbrella of schizophrenia. He had been sectioned more than once before. But at the extreme it is also an example of blind faith.'

'Isn't that your bread and butter?'

'We have the Gospels,' he said. 'Witness statements. But in the end we're either compelled in our hearts to believe or we are not. That's why it's so hard. The only difference between the sane and the insane is how many people you can get to agree with you. The story of Jesus and his miracles and the Lord revealed – the very spreading of the Gospels – is the story of our moving from one state to the other. Two thousand or so years ago they'd have thrown me in jail for my madness. Or worse, of course.'

By now Marrineau had opened a bottle of Napoleon brandy he'd won in his own Christmas raffle. 'I'm afraid I didn't have the strength to put it back in. Sin provides too. Which is why it's so appealing.'

I have no taste for drink but I joined him in saluting its quality. He drank without inhibition. He was full of joy. He told me that he was not lonely; on the contrary, he chose to be alone. 'Believe it or not, I've had no shortage of offers since Sarah left. But my life now is more focused. My parameters have been redrawn to best carry out the labours I promised God I would devote my earthly life to. And it works. No one gets hurt, by which I mean by my negligence, by which I mean Sarah.'

He had not once enquired into my own religious beliefs (I have none), but urged me nevertheless to come to his 10.30 service in the morning. 'There'll be baptisms, so don't sit too near the front, followed by my sermon, which is not to be missed. This week, temptation. It's actually a diatribe against credit cards, which is one of my bêtes noires. Debt is so destructive. I try not to be too judgemental but Jesus and I would have been in full agreement on how much violence you might legitimately inflict on moneychangers.' He grinned, squinting at me. 'I'm joking. But tomorrow I won't be.'

He talked me into staying. 'The spare room is always ready for guests,' he said. 'Plus, I've heard that your B&B has a serious bedbug problem. Or was it rodents? I'm sorry, that's not true. I must stop saying the first thing that comes into my head. But please, do stay.'

I lay in the dark, aware of the faint ticking of the clock in the hall. The old Marrineau would have taken an eye for that eye. I wondered how Zoe was getting on. I fell asleep to the sound of snoring from the next room, transformed in a dream – in which I was unable to apply brakes on a heavy vehicle rolling slowly backwards – to a distant road drill. When I awoke he was gone. There was a note in the kitchen: 'Two (non curry) sausages in the fridge are yours. Have an egg. Cornflakes in pantry – M'.

I went back upstairs. Marrineau's bedroom was untidy. And dusty. There was a pile of laundry next to the basket. The drawers, yanked open, their contents in a jumble, suggested a frantic search for some arcane item of clerical garb – collar studs, I imagined. There was a garish plaster crucifix on the wall above his bed of the sort available in Italian souvenir shops and a tattered paperback copy of the Bible on the side table. Opposite the bed was a colourful tapestry, doubtless woven by Marrineau's female devotees, that read simply JESUS IS OUR LORD.

I was disappointed to find no traces of the old Marrineau. The wardrobe rattled with empty hangers as I looked in vain for his rawhide jacket with its leather fringes; his boyhood sporting trophies were nowhere to be seen. In the bathroom his enviable crocodile-skin gift set of razor and brush had been replaced by an electric shaver. A single toothbrush stood in a mug, above it a clouded mirror that I imagined Marrineau standing before every morning, tugging a comb through his tangle of hair, adjusting his eye-patch and feeling blessed.

The dog appeared in the doorway and came to be patted, sniffed at my leg, woofed and padded off again. I searched through a concertina file of old papers in the hope of finding a letter from my aunt or Isobel, or even a copy of my damning boyhood psychiatric report. Weighed down by a snowy Nativity paperweight was a pile of more recent correspondence – messages of thanks, a note from the family of someone who had died, a postcard from a couple on honeymoon. As I leafed through, I came upon a photograph I had seen before, and with it a letter. It was headed St Mary Hospice, Meldringham, and was dated some months previously and written in ink by an unsteady hand.

Dear Marrineau,

   You should have this. You may even remember the day
I took it. Perhaps you wondered why. But you were young,
of course, and not given to questioning masters. You were
hurrying with your gym class across the Middle lawn. I called
you back, asked you to give me a smile for my camera. I'm
afraid I had planned it in advance. It was foolish of me.

   I took photographs of other boys too, but this is the only one
I kept. I am deeply ashamed and yet at the same time I cannot
regret it. I have lived at the wrong time – though not for very
much longer.

   My confession, such as it is, ends there. I have never
touched a boy. I am guilty only of loving from afar. I am

grateful for your visits and prayers (no doubt I shall need them where I am going), but I would rather you didn't come again. I am sure you will understand.

I am sorry for the distress this will perhaps cause you.

Yours sincerely,

Geoffrey Stamp

I hadn't the heart or stomach to eat Marrineau's last two sausages. Instead I walked back to my B&B, showered and had breakfast there. Then I drove the hire car back to St Alban-in-the-Dale in time to see the congregation coming out. Marrineau was at the door in his robes and black eye-patch, shaking hands and laughing. Ladies of the parish, rejoicing in their eccentric, charismatic pastor, queued up to praise him, some calling him 'Father', some 'David'. As the crowd drifted away he spent ten minutes in particular with one side-whiskered and florid gentleman who could only be a farmer. Wholeheartedly roaring about something together, they looked like a comedy double act. I lingered until the man had rumbled away in a muddy Range Rover before approaching Marrineau.

'I missed your sermon. And now, alas, I must take my leave.'

'That's a pity. Not tempted to stay for our homeless Sunday lunch? It's free if you take part in doling it out.' He didn't wait for my answer but pointed down the road. 'I've just talked that man with the whiskers into a large donation.'

'Good news for your church spire.'

'Ha, let me tell you a little secret. As much of the cash as I dare skim off goes to keeping my groups going – youth support, mother-and-baby, my drop-in centre for the unwashed, unwanted, the unemployable, the lonely, the inadequate, the unappealing, the plain needy. People would rather give money to buildings. Sometimes I think, bugger the spire. Until it's actually falling down, I suppose.'

I promised, as he'd hoped, to have my bank send him a cheque.

We shook hands and I drove off. Why had I come? I'd wanted to get out of town. And what better alibi, should I need one, than to have spent the weekend with a clergyman in Yorkshire – an old friend from a good family and a good school. But curiosity was behind it too; even a sense of unfinished business. Who knew? He had felt it too. Maybe he wasn't too disappointed to find that I hadn't needed 'saving', as he put it. I hadn't apologized, or asked for or offered forgiveness. We had engaged in an unexpected way – though it wasn't as friendly as we were each determined to make it look. It occurred to me that, for Marrineau, doing the Lord's work wasn't about making friends but gathering donors, tin-rattlers, volunteers, disciples, listeners – a clientele of the faith. He could have been selling a house. Perhaps we just glimpsed a little of ourselves in each other, enough to spark one evening into a beatific glow, two flints shaken together in a box.

I thought about Isobel and the girl, how I had done right by her. Maybe even changed her opinion of me. The point was, it was time to move on and, Marrineau's God willing, continue with my own good work. And if that sounds a little self-congratulatory, just imagine what our town would be like without me.

37

I GAVE IT ALL DAY MONDAY. I thought it might take time to track down Sharp's golf club – or, rather, set of clubs – but I'll be damned if they weren't in the first charity shop I walked into. I almost immediately recognized the bulbous green-striped head of the club protruding from the bag. I had feared – hoped now – that the pattern on its metal striking surface (parallel lines pleasingly not unlike my own sign) might be matched to an imprint left in the skin, flesh and bone of Sharp's right-side temple. I made a circuit of the shop, inspecting unwanted jigsaws, knick-knacks and worn clothes. I was reluctant to buy the whole set of clubs and risk jogging the memory (during the renewed surge of investigation that would surely follow) of the elderly lady who ran the shop. It seemed to me less risky simply to wait until she was in the back room sorting the contents of the bin liners that one saw piling up in the doorways of all such shops over the weekend, then slip the club out of the bag and walk out with it to my waiting car.

At the office, Wendy was flustered with news that Zoe had not turned up this morning to meet buyers at the Curries' place and that it was Katya's day off. 'We can hardly send Josh on his own.'

'Don't worry, I'll deal with them.'

'I called her but she's not answering.'

'I'll try her later. She's probably having one of her down-turns.'

'Downturns?'

'Yes, she won't want people calling her every five minutes.'

Late in the day, I rang Detective Sergeant Monks.

'Just a thought,' I said. 'And this is probably nothing. But having made a few enquiries, one of my staff *does* seem to have mislaid her binoculars. And I'm absolutely sure it *is* nothing but . . .'

'But?'

'Well, that's the point. This is rather delicate.'

'And yet, Mr Heming, I sense you want to tell me about it.'

'It's perfectly innocent – well, sort of. The fact is that Zoe – who is, I should say, an excellent young woman and a valued member of staff. Well, when I told her about the binoculars you'd found . . .'

'You told her?'

'Yes, and something rang a bell with her, I could tell. And then, sure enough, later she stepped into my office and told me she'd once had a brief relationship with Mr Sharp – Douglas, as she called him. Which, as she explained, was why she didn't want to deal with the sale of his house when it came in. If the binoculars found in the car *are* hers – and she thinks they probably are – that's how they would have got there.'

'In the boot?'

'Well, quite, that's what I said to her.'

'And what did she say?'

263

'She became cross and said, "Use your imagination, Mr Heming."'

'Ah.'

'The trouble is, I'm not certain that she really wants to tell you, though I'm sure it's just a matter of eliminating her binoculars from your inquiry. Understandably she doesn't want to get involved—'

'Is Zoe in the office now?'

'No. She hasn't been in all day. I think she might be off sick. She does suffer from depression from time to time.'

'Address?'

'Ah. I'm going to have to get back to you on that. Wendy has now left for the day and I'm afraid she has the keys to everything. Would first thing in the morning be all right?'

There was a pause in which Monks sighed. 'If you could do that.'

I had to think hard about Sharp's handsome matching leather holdalls – the advantage of having them versus the danger of Abigail finding them missing and wondering if she ought to do anything about it. I had an idea where she had put them. I'd thought it odd that the key to her lock-up garage had been missing when I'd shown the Perettis round, and it made sense to assume that that's where the bags were now – Abigail would have moved them into her lock-up garage after she and I had cleared it of her mother's rubbish. But the other reason the spare lock-up key was missing, I now realized – or reasoned with some confidence – was that I already had it, that it was the key with the green wooden fob I'd taken from her backpack on that hazardous day in the library.

First I needed to be sure Abigail would be safely at work. I knew the times of her shifts, but she was nowhere to be seen at the library. I stood outside for some minutes trying to spot her, before driving to Raistrick Road. Here I called her landline. No answer. I rang at the door. I went round the back of the terrace to the garage. The green of the fob was a perfect match for the wooden door, and sure enough the key turned in the lock. But the bags weren't there. The garage was empty of everything but a few gardening tools.

I relocked it and looked up at the bedroom windows. Something wasn't right. I went round to the front door and let myself in. The echo that rose through the house said it all. I tried the front room, the living room, the sun room, the kitchen. I dashed upstairs. The house had been almost entirely emptied, almost certainly by one of the clearance firms that advertised in the paper. The curtains and carpets remained, along with a small assortment of items – a lamp or two, a wicker chair, a rug – that she evidently intended to come back for. The two holdalls were among them. I called the library and asked for Abigail.

'I'm sorry, she left two days ago. Can anyone else help?'

I called Abigail's mobile but couldn't get through.

I tried again. I didn't know what I wanted to say. Perhaps I just needed to know it was over.

Eventually I went through to the back of the house. The key was in the door. I opened it and took the two holdalls out to my car, returning with a tyre lever. Then I locked the door from the outside, wedged the lever into the door crack and leaned hard on it. The wood, rotten round the lock, creaked and splintered, and the door burst open. I slotted the key back in on the other side in the locked position and left the door ajar.

I was almost home when the phone rang. It was her.

She started with a long breath. 'Look, I'm sorry, I've been

meaning to call. The truth is . . . well, I've moved back to London. I just felt the whole thing was getting on top of me. And I'm sorry I took the coward's way out. It was an impulse thing. The truth is I'm really not fit to be in a relationship right now. Also, I've decided I can't face the hassle of selling the house at the moment. I don't know why . . . it's just too difficult, I'm sorry. I know it seemed that we—'

'No, no, that's fine,' I interrupted at last. 'No problem. Bad timing. Please don't even think about it. I'll take the house off our books. And obviously you're free to take up with another agent – or anyone, really.'

I tried not to sound too cheerful when after a few moments more we exchanged awkward goodbyes. That was what my unbending devotion to Abigail had come to. And yet how could it ever have ended otherwise?

38

I'M AFRAID THIS IS where the real story ends, at the dead of night in a small but 'gorgeous' garden flat, a well-managed Victorian conversion with access to the high street and the usual facilities. 'And with two osteopaths on the premises!' as Zoe had joked when she'd signed the contract and come skipping back from the solicitors brimming with life. The property had been distressingly out of her reach and yet she had somehow pulled it off, miraculously talked them down by an unbelievable margin.

'Maybe they just liked me,' she said.

I cannot say her triumph that day had nothing to do with me, or at least Damato Associates, who have money to burn – more money than one man of frugal habits can reasonably cast to the flames – when the occasion calls for it. That was out of the goodness of my heart, long before my ill-advised romantic dalliance with Zoe. Before all of this.

I stand over her in my absurd mask. My fear was that I would find her lying on the sofa with the TV still blaring, or worse, in some macabre position – on all fours perhaps, in the way of a Pompeian greengrocer or barber – overcome in a surprising, terrible need for air. But here she is, gone in her sleep, her face radiating a discernible, vivid pinkness in the light of the radio dial. Her killer is still here, of course – unseen and unsmelled – even now seeping into the pores of the room, redoubling and purifying its evil with every minute.

I unroll my toolwrap, position my torch, and set about removing the gags I'd stuffed behind the plastic vents. In the sitting room the congealed leavings and debris from our Indian takeaway on Friday cover the coffee table. Here are our two wine goblets, dark-streaked in the flitting beam. She had opened a second bottle of red after I'd left, and drunk most of it. I take one of the glasses – the one on the right as I faced the TV – and some of the foil containers and packaging and push the whole lot deep into a carrier bag.

It could have been a last supper. The balm of alcohol. She has taken paracetamol, too, in the kitchen. Perhaps she awoke with a headache, thinking she had flu, and then went back to bed. In the bathroom, a half-used blister pack of Prozac sits on the lip of the white basin with another glass to the side, almost full of water. I return to the bedroom. I think of her lying there throughout the night and day, brightness coming and going at the edges of the curtains, and the visiting sounds of local traffic and neighbours. Her face is tilted towards the window as if in some final tragic appeal. It occurs to me, seeing her here now like this, that she has always looked the part.

If I were Marrineau, I would pray for her, commend her to a higher power. But I am stronger than Marrineau. For me, there is no higher power. For me, the buck stops here.

39

YOU MAY REMEMBER THE small service I performed for the elderly Mrs Wade some time ago. She is still alive and kicking. She still drives her small cherry-red car to church and to the Thursday market and occasional hospital appointments. More and more often now, she takes the train to visit her daughter Rachel in Ely, stays overnight and returns the next day. I am happy to 'house sit' during these times. Today I have never needed it more. The day has yet to dawn, with its rosy promise of trouble. I lie with my knees slightly bent on Mrs Wade's cottage sofa, with its polished wooden arms and ornate, quilted throw, and close my eyes.

Think of it if you will as decompression, a process of returning from a distressing height or depth, though you might equally think of a gentle, power-giving rejuvenation – envisage an advanced alien being, lowering himself at the end of a hard day into a bath of nurturing chemicals or a pulsing cocoon rich with energy waves. That is me.

My mind returns to Abigail, not with yearning but regret. An error every bit as prominent as Zoe, but what have I learned? That I lost love, and the sublime feelings that held me in its grip, by allowing myself to be sucked into something less real (or more real, I suppose, conventionally speaking). Marrineau was right when he talked about redrawing his parameters, choosing aloneness – or at least the solitary path – as the one way to serve. I too have all I desire within bounds I have myself established – my chosen space with its proximity to life, its sharp, measured rules and control and low, confining ceiling. I already know what works. Stay there, I tell myself. Just stay.

I have to smile when newspapers – so predictable in their attempt to explain the behaviour of those transgressing social norms or the workings of the deviant mind – speak of 'the double life' led by this furtive criminal or that. In fact the reverse is true. It is normal people who have a 'double life'. On the outside is your everyday life of going out to work and going on holiday. Then there is the life you wish you had – the life that keeps you awake at night with hope, ambition, plans, frustration, resentment, envy, regret. This is a more seething life of wants, driven by thoughts of possibility and potential. It is the life you can never have. Always changing, it is always out of reach. Would you like more money? Here, have more! An attractive sexual partner? No problem. Higher status? More intelligence? Whiter teeth? You are obsessed with what is just out of reach. It is the itch you cannot scratch. Tortured by the principle that the more you can't have something the more you desire it, you are never happy.

There is no twoness about me. My life is seamless. I have all my wants in one basket and the daily wherewithal to pursue and enjoy them. I brook no frustration. (Indeed, what could better define frustration than a locked door? And what simpler remedy than a key?) My parameters may seem narrow but the world within them is bounded only by the imagination itself. I am as complicated and susceptible to error as all humans, but in the ways that matter I am as happy and indifferent as the beast in Abigail's poem under that dark sky of hers.

My cocoon, rich with energy waves, releases the spore of a distant memory. I think of my father, who died of misadventure – of drowning, like the man in the cemetery, though in deeper water. Was this also what my aunt had protected me from? I had felt nothing, in any case, except a release from a sense of his disappointment. Perhaps, like Mr Stamp, he loved from afar. I refuse to have been shaped by him or her. Whoever I was and still am is all my own work, the result of knowing from an early age that I would have to hollow out a place for myself, the width of myself, and keep myself there. In this I have succeeded. I rarely think of him. My aunt, who never seemed especially happy with my father – as though she had simply inherited him on her sister's death – always said he was 'bad with his nerves'. Sleep then, sleep, I urge.

In sleep I feel my father's hard middle knuckle between my shoulder blades. He prods and loudly barks at me to answer his questions but my lips are sealed. It is days since I fled from Mrs Damato's house, that fine uproar filling my ears. Now my father, his mind in a frenzy of suspicion, has found a small perfectly white sock jammed between the water pipes in my room. A souvenir, nothing more, though that explanation would hardly soothe this exploding man. My aunt bundles him from the room before things turn to a raging flurry of smacks. But now she grips my shoulders and makes me look into her own wild eyes. Things are going to change around here, she says.

Our street has become a place of sadness and whispered voices.

At night, beneath the dissolving layers of memory, I spy

little Angela again for a worrying instant – lost and tearful, grimy and barefoot, stepping from the green of the railed-off park into the sudden shade of the cul-de-sac before her. Here she pauses, her face distorted by distress. The street is narrow, cobbled and mossy, its length darkened by overarching trees that stand like Grimm's hideous giants with reaching arms and spindly fingers, fungi protruding from their damp recesses. And now she sees me drop from the sooty wall at the foot of the Damatos' sloping garden, the kind older boy who showed her the coloured matches. Hope is kindled in her eyes. But I take one look at her and flee. Her concerns are no longer mine. Does she follow in slow pursuit? Perhaps she is herself being pursued. With uncertain shoeless gait she begins the gauntlet of this frightening street towards the gauzy sunlight some endless-seeming distance ahead, her wailing ignored by the unfriendly terrace dwellings along here, their backs turned to her, displaying only high, blackened outhouses.

An ice-cream van sends out a familiar peal of bells, urging her on. Someone will save her. Is that what she thinks? I cannot know how she sees the world. I cannot know how many minutes it takes her to reach the end of the trees – only that the street ends as suddenly as it began, but this time with a road of moderately busy traffic, where little Angela is tossed into the air by a vehicle racing down the hill and struck again by a second racing up.

Her bunny-rabbit is never found, and is henceforth a mystery.

40

I AM OUT OF SURPRISES. There are no twists to come. What follows is a sort of epilogue, though I don't especially wish to dwell on the fallout surrounding poor Zoe, who died exactly two years ago today (marked by a notice placed by her parents in this week's *Sentinel*). There is one thing. In an almost comical turn of events, she came *this* close to taking DC Roberts with her – he being first on the scene and a man who will heroically take it upon himself to burst into a girl's flat after banging on the door and front window, which according to neighbours had been curtained for two, three or even four days. He was on his knees almost as soon as he set foot in the place, or so the story went. If the uniformed officer accompanying him had not been so quick off the mark – having seen the danger for what it was (she had been a firefighter in the forces) and managed to drag him out – he would have been a goner himself, according to the paramedics who screeched in only minutes later. True to form, the *Sentinel* missed that particular nugget, preferring to direct its unerring powers of misinterpretation on lurid revelation – Zoe's 'loneliness', her 'dependency' on prescription drugs and alcohol, the discovery of her cat, dead in the hall (I can promise you she had no cat), its claw marks 'allegedly' visible on the inside of the front door.

Towards the end of that morning, DS Monks (he is now an inspector) arrived at the office to bring the grave news about Zoe, offering the footnote about Roberts with a proper lack of drama, as if gas poisoning were all part of the job. He was tight-lipped on everything else. I doubted then that he was entirely convinced by my helpful trail of breadcrumbs from Zoe to Sharp; perhaps it was his superiors who later found it as irresistible as it need be and instructed him to wind things up. Whatever their misgivings about Zoe's involvement, it was enough to be able to announce that they were not looking for anyone else in connection with Sharp's death. It took the national papers – the Sunday tabloids in particular returned in force – to spell out Zoe's link with Sharp (if not quite with his death), describing her alternately as 'spurned' and 'jealous' or 'smitten' and 'tragic', between them pre-empting the coroner's eventual open verdict on the question of whether Zoe had taken her own life (by the unusual method of asphyxiation by faulty boiler) while suffering from depression following the death of Sharp. This theory was partly predicated on the website history of Zoe's laptop, which revealed recent research into the dangers of faulty heating appliances. Was it not possible, her father asked DS Monk (Zoe's father made an admirable inquisitor) – indeed more than likely – that she was worried her faulty boiler *was* faulty but didn't get further than looking up symptoms on the internet? Monks conceded that it was at least more than possible. One of Zoe's book-group girlfriends came forward to confirm that there had been a passionate affair between Zoe and Sharp but that she had broken it off when she found out he had lied about having left his wife. Had Zoe gone back to him in recent times? She could not say. I myself was able to give evidence that Zoe had displayed erratic behaviour that seemed to me consistent with a therapist's report confirming that Zoe had been receiving treatment for a mild depressive disorder for some years, but the coroner, often to be seen adjusting her glasses, seemed unswayed one way or the other. Mrs Sharp, with negligible consideration for the feelings of the deceased's parents, gave curt evidence to the effect that Zoe was just the latest in a string of her husband's infidelities and was probably the woman in a photograph that she had given to the police, who had done *nothing* with it, though she admitted, on further questioning, that only her husband had been clearly identifiable in the picture. The coroner shared Monks's reasonable doubt that the prospect of a visit from the police to discuss the binoculars found in the back of Sharp's car would have been enough to trigger thoughts of suicide, since there could be a more innocent explanation for the binoculars being there (and indeed DC Roberts had turned up an old police caution for Sharp, who some years previously had been caught engaging in a 'sex act' in the back of his car). At no point did the court allow itself to consider fear of prosecution or profound feelings of guilt as possible factors in Zoe's death (since no authority had proved her culpable or blameworthy), though the newspapers had given ample space to evidence suggesting that she may have been present at his death or shortly afterwards. After all, Sharp's watch and wallet were found in Zoe's underwear drawers (oddly, his phone was never found – a pity, because who knew what deleted directory and call details might have been retrieved by police computer experts?). A golf club was discovered under her bed, though the police could not say with certainty that it was the murder weapon – and who could blame a girl living alone for keeping a golf club under her bed? Sharp's leather holdalls were piled neatly, one upon the other, in the box room, but what did that mean? Nothing, conclusively.

The coroner stuck to the facts, leaving the town to its whispering. And what whispering! Had Sharp simply gone back to his old flame Zoe when his wife kicked him out, and then the next morning pursued some unknown urgent business at the Cooksons' empty house, where he had met his death at the hands of some unknown assailant? Perhaps he had told Zoe he was going for a run – after all, he had been wearing a tracksuit – but then taken his car! Could Zoe have suspected some sort of double dealing? Had she heard of his affair with Mrs Cookson (I'm afraid this was fast gaining currency as hard fact), followed him and then angrily laid about the scheming bastard on the Cooksons' patio with a golf club? Or perhaps Mrs Sharp had exchanged further harsh words with her husband that Saturday morning (he might well have returned home to talk some sense into her), followed him to the Cooksons, assumed the worst of Mrs Cookson – perhaps even rightly, and as far as the town was concerned, there seemed no reason not to – and continued their fight from the previous night, though this time perhaps Mrs Sharp had reached for a gardening hoe or similar deadly implement (a golf club seemed an unlikely thing to find in a garden). Some preferred to picture Zoe as the 'spurned' and 'jealous' woman in an alternative version of the above scenario – following the man who had refused to leave his wife for her and then killing him in a furious spasm of rage as he took his matching luggage out of the car with a view to lying low at this *new* lover's house (i.e. Mrs Cookson, who in anticipation of Sharp being thrown out by his wife could have furnished him with a key) while she and her husband were away.

I could go on. It was quite a puzzle. But the point now was that, the focus having shifted to Zoe's inquest, the only people who doubted that Sharp had driven himself to the Cooksons and then been killed there were those who still doubted that it was a murder at all. Hadn't even the police first thought the man was a drifter who had come to grief by falling down drunk over patio stones?

I went to both funerals (must they always come along in twos?). Zoe's was loyally attended despite the attempts of police, court and newspapers to stain her character. Sharp's attracted an inordinate number of young female students, who sat to the rear of the crematorium along with three or four dishevelled grown-ups with unshined shoes whom I assumed to be Sharp's work colleagues. Abigail was thankfully nowhere to be seen; nor was Sharp's brother. Mrs Sharp and her sister seemed to have turned up merely to demonstrate a determination to remain tearless.

Mrs Sharp had asked if I would go, though we had little to say afterwards. The one thing that surprised me (though perhaps it shouldn't have) was how my antipathy towards Sharp had disappeared as rapidly as my 'love' for Abigail. That dawning reality was like waking from a frightening illness of the mind, a sort of madness. It wasn't difficult to recognize the same illness in Zoe, whose infatuation for me had escalated into a willingness to cross lines. What sort of girl lures a man to dig up a forsythia with the cold plan to rob him of his house key? She said she wanted to help me. But what would have happened when she awoke from her madness?

*

277

Last Sunday morning, to mark the second anniversary of their daughter's death, Zoe's parents, family and friends gathered for a short memorial service at St Benedict's chapel and laid flowers. Her younger sister, Emma, spoke of the nature of sisterhood and the human capacity for renewal. She is a teacher, married with a toddler, and is very different from Zoe. I wondered if she lived in town and on what street. I said that we all still missed Zoe terribly, and she said Zoe used to mention me often. Everyone from the agency was there except our new girl – another eastern European whose name is shortened to Tuni from something much longer. She is sweet and irresistible but ferociously competitive, which has made Josh raise his game. The bad news is that Katya is pregnant and may be leaving, notwithstanding the firm's generous maternity provision. Her new husband, Evan, seems not to like me very much. I find that some men in particular are like dogs. I am a smell they can't put their finger on, if I might be excused the unsavoury metaphor.

I can't say I haven't had one or two anxious thoughts about Isobel (speaking of people who don't like me very much), who might well have surfaced to harass the police with the 'coincidence' of two young estate agents from the same firm dying in their own flats only seventeen years apart. But she kept her distance. She has responded to my recent enquiries after her health and the progress of young Elizabeth at her expensive new school with an unexplained picture postcard from the Lake District. This may be as cordial as things will be between us.

I'm sorry if this is beginning to sound like a family newsletter. Perhaps I just want to emphasize my feeling, in common with most people, that progress isn't necessarily about change but about things turning out as we want them to. To this end I should report that the house on Raistrick Road is now owned by Damato Associates (snapped up for the asking price via Worde & Hulme) and, like its neighbours, has now been converted to student flats. Katya shifted the Cooksons' place at the edge of town with surprising speed, given its notorious new history. And, almost finally, a lovely Asian family has moved into 4 Boselle Avenue. I haven't been to visit yet, but it is something to look forward to.

After the memorial service broke up on Sunday I spent a couple of hours at the Perettis'. They finally settled on a Victorian terrace not unlike Abigail's place, but bigger and sunnier and featuring a modern annexe for Mrs P that looks down on the park from the other side of the river. From Jason's 'studio' in the loft, with a decent pair of binoculars, you can see straight into Abigail's old attic (though, as I have said, I have never sought pleasure in that sort of thing). It's an ideal situation for us all. Mrs P has access from the rear to the living spaces of the main house, while the upstairs belongs to the boys. Today the pair of them were in London for a football match. They are season ticket holders and never miss a home game. Mrs Peretti was downstairs, cooking ahead for the evening meal. I love the way she chatters to herself and to the dog. There is never any danger of her coming up and Pippo – yapping excitedly round the kitchen – is too small to climb the steps. It does not quite deliver the thrill of full immersion (which I have yet to attempt after Abigail), but what more pleasant way to help pass an otherwise sober Sunday? I found a bag of toffee eclairs hidden in Mr Peretti's desk, and sat down with a file of impenetrable letters from his solicitor, before sifting through a set of dramatic photographs of Jason taking part in some kind of live art exhibition. I still haven't got to the bottom of what

Jason does (his studio is equipped mainly for working out and lying down). But there's plenty of time. They are good people leading lives as interesting to me as to themselves.

Afterwards I walked back to my riverside apartment (reluctantly I have adopted the prudent habit of keeping up two dwellings, this one with a bed and recognizable furniture) following a circuitous route via the leafy streets of the north side. The afternoon still had plenty of warmth in it. Early summer is my favourite time, with its smells of creosote and mower fuel, the buzz and bang of carpenters, the clang of scaffolding going up and skips being filled. These people are the town's engine, its living parts. Dressed in spattered clothing and trainers, they come and go to the DIY warehouses and construction wholesalers, arm themselves with hammers and drills. Occasionally I will see a face I know from somewhere but does not know me, fixed in its intention, its eyes set on some achievable future. What hopes, I wonder, charge their imaginations? Where do they think they are going? Where will they fertilize their eggs? Where will they die?

In my lair beside the Common, among my stacks of files and pictures and observations, I have a stupendous sticker chart showing where everyone has been, where they have settled and moved on to – each house-move a line drawn from here to there in coloured pencil, a criss-crossing of desires and dreams, one upon another, across town, out of town and back (newcomers and leavers have little arrows to indicate direction of travel), weaving this way and that until they are indistinguishable from one another, making a great tapestry of wishes, a vast life of plans. I will sit for hours poring over it, cross-referring among my keys and maps and family profiles and holiday snapshots, a god at play.

And why not? This is who I am, guardian of the plans, though I have no plans of my own, of course. I am happy on the fringes, listening and watching, excitedly awaiting your next move. I dissolve into the surroundings and breathe your air. I come in peace. I bring my love.

Acknowledgements

Big thanks to Chris Riddell, Jon Linstead and Tim Adams, without whom I would still be at the thinking stage; to Neil Smith and Jonathan Wilson for unflinching man support; to all at the Fellow in whose precincts this book was brought to the boil. Highest regards to Veronique Baxter and Susanna Wadeson for their guidance and good sense. And love to my wife, Sue, for the usual countless personal reasons.

William Heming – in his doubletalk about the double life – read at least the prologue of Adam Phillips's excellent book *Missing Out: In Praise of the Unlived Life*. Any errors arising are his rather than mine, or indeed Adam Phillips's.

ABOUT THE AUTHOR

Phil Hogan was born in a small northern mill town, and now lives in a small southern commuter town. He is married with four children and has been a journalist for twenty-five years. He is also the author of three previous novels and a book of collected columns about family life.

The Inspiration for *A PLEASURE AND A CALLING*

It's hard to pin down the moment that William Heming sprang into being. You could say he coalesced rather than sprang, though there must have been a point in the thinking process when he started to seem knowable; a point where you might predict what he would do next. Like most fictional characters, Heming is a product as much of accident as design, knocked and pulled together by other elements of a book in its endless early making and unmaking – its still-shaky structure, unsettled foundations, and other unformed characters all bumping about trying to get noticed.

One of the illusions of having completed your book is to per-suade yourself that the characters you created were there all along; that you just had to make them talk and maybe kill or have sex with one another. The truth is that for much of the time you're closing your eyes and ears and hoping for the best. Unless that's just me. I won't pretend that a lot of the process didn't involve spiking the drinks of my friends, dragging them to a dark cell (or corner of a pub) and forcing them to help me out of some inescapable narrative hole I had dug for myself.

My wife once told me about a cousin or aunt or sister-in-law who'd had a ceramic artwork stolen from her house. The house had been up for sale and the culprit, it turned out much later, was a man showing buyers around the place on behalf of the estate agent. It turned out too (perhaps he had appeared in court – I don't know) that the man was a retired policeman. Apparently, it is not uncommon for agents to retain trusted, personable individuals to open up properties on an ad hoc basis.

Our man seemed interesting. The ceramic artwork had not been worth much – but then perhaps nothing he had stolen was worth much (I assumed the thieving had become a habit). I started to wonder what deep-lying psychological impulse was behind his behaviour. Maybe he had been drummed out of the force unfairly and wanted some sort of twisted revenge – certainly that was a way into a novel. Perhaps he had it in his mind to commit crimes, and then – yes! – solve them, to the astonishment of his slow-witted former colleagues, perhaps with the finger of blame left pointing at some real corrupt officer of the law.

I really didn't want to write about a policeman, though. I wanted to write about someone ordinary, or rather someone who looked ordinary but wasn't. And, given that, wouldn't it be simpler, I thought, just to make a thief out of an estate agent himself – a person who had access to other people's houses all the time? Thievery was not enough though. Other acts of mischief came to mind. I dwelt for some time on that notion of revenge – or, more attractive, that spirit of the citizen vigilante whereby one man might utterly destroy another man's morale and life as punishment for crimes against good manners. (Some of that spirit remains, of course.)

For a long time, too, I envisaged Heming as a conventionally weird villain, but this unhelpfully kept suggesting a focus on the detective trying to track him down – the dogged pursuer finally kicking down the door of Heming's secret lair to reveal his gleaming, obsessive secrets. Eventually I realized the boot was on the wrong foot. It was Heming who needed to tell the story. It was he who needed to do the revealing. And the questions would be more fundamental. What was his story? Where had he come from? What was his problem? And – what consistency could I bring to his character as a result of finding out these things?

Anyway, that was the beginning. That's when Heming moved in, hollowing out a space in my head – the dusty attic of my idling thoughts – creating doubt and havoc, fiddling with the lights, making a nonsense of my great ideas when I was asleep or making me forget things at the supermarket. That was him as he turned out: insidious, discreet – and so quiet, of course, you wouldn't have known he was there at all.

Phil Hogan, July 2013

Some Questions for Readers

Do you think that this novel is particularly unsettling because the crimes and trickery take place in a domestic setting, rather than an unfamiliar location?

How important was the location to the story? How powerful was the author's description of the landscape/community?

What events in the story stand out for you as memorable?

Which of the secondary characters stood out for you?

What was more important, the characters or the plot?

Did you ever sympathise with Mr Heming? Were his actions justified revenge or just vindictive and malicious? Why?

Do you think *A Pleasure and A Calling* is a fitting title for the content of this novel?

Critics have said that *A Pleasure and A Calling* is reminiscent of Highsmith's Mr Ripley, do you agree?

What do you think about the female characters in this novel? Were they portrayed in a positive way?

The author used the structural device of flashbacks; how did this affect the story and your appreciation of the book?